Praise for THE FIX

**IPPY Awards, Gold Medalist in the YA Category, 2016
USA Best Books Awards Finalist, 2015**

"First shot out of the gate, Sinel bravely addresses tough topics, demonstrating that the weight of secrets can pull us under—and their release can save us from drowning.

—Holly Schindler, critically acclaimed author of
A Blue So Dark and *Feral*

"A bewitching, beautiful, and brave debut. Readers will marvel at Macy's resilience. Natasha Sinel's writing devastates and uplifts, by turns. An important story of one girl's journey to rewrite the blueprint of her own life by facing the truth inside herself."

—Carrie Mesrobian, award-winning author of
Sex & Violence and *Perfectly Good White Boy*

"In her YA debut, Natasha Sinel paints a riveting picture of a teenager haunted by her past and struggling with her present. Macy's world is richly drawn, heartbreakingly real, and difficult to put down. The Fix shines."

—I. W. Gregorio, author of *None of the Above*

"In this masterful debut, Natasha Sinel explores how a shocking act of betrayal can be overlooked within an otherwise loving family. A vivid storyteller, Sinel tackles an emotional topic, portraying the pain and repercussions of Macy's experience with an honest sensitivity. I was hooked from the opening pages of The Fix."

—Yvonne Ventresca, award-winning author of *Pandemic*

The FIX

NATASHA SINEL

Sky Pony Press
New York

Sky Pony Press books may be purchased in bulk at special discounts for sales promotion, corporate gifts, fund-raising, or educational purposes. Special editions can also be created to specifications. For details, contact the Special Sales Department, Sky Pony Press, 307 West 36th Street, 11th Floor, New York, NY 10018 or info@skyhorsepublishing.com.

Sky Pony® is a registered trademark of Skyhorse Publishing, Inc.®, a Delaware corporation.
Visit our website at www.skyponypress.com.

10 9 8 7 6 5 4 3 2 1

Library of Congress Cataloging-in-Publication Data is available on file.

ISBN: 978-1-5107-3119-6
Ebook ISBN: 978-1-5107-0028-4

Cover design by Sarah Brody
Cover image by Trevillion Images/Elisabeth Ansley

Printed in the United States of America

For Mom and Dad

The FIX

CHAPTER ONE

Sebastian Ruiz got me thinking about things I'd wanted to forget forever. And then he disappeared.

Rumors were flying in the junior hallway. Even though Sebastian was a loner, his name suddenly took on celebrity status. He'd tried to kill himself. He'd OD'd. He'd been shipped off to military school. He'd been kidnapped. If it had been anyone else, I would have thrown an alien abduction theory into the mix.

But it wasn't someone else.

It was Sebastian Ruiz—who only a few days earlier had come to Rebecca's party and had shaken me up like a long-forgotten snow globe and then walked away, leaving me to the impossible task of catching all the fluttering bits of false snow.

I hadn't even wanted to go to Rebecca's party. Hours before, I'd been sitting under the oak tree, flipping through my well-worn copy of UC Berkeley's architecture program brochure. I stared at my favorite photo—six students enraptured by a professor with wild white hair and bushy eyebrows. If I squinted, the girl on the left with blondish-brown hair could be me.

Then Rebecca called.

"Don't bail on me," she said immediately.

I hesitated, trying to think of a good reason why I couldn't go to her party. Every other Saturday, Rebecca's mom worked the double-shift at the radio station. And that's when we'd break out the sex, drugs, and good ol' rock 'n' roll. But that night, I just wasn't in the mood.

Apparently, I'd hesitated too long, because Rebecca jumped on the silence.

"Listen, I can hear you wracking your brain for an excuse. You don't have one. This is bullshit."

"I'm—"

"Seriously," she said. "Jasmine can't come, and there's another guy coming, so it would be me and like seven guys."

"What guy?" I asked. Fresh blood was rare. It was always the same group of eight to ten of us. The drama club stoners and me.

"He's not a drama guy. Chris ran into him at the diner this morning and invited him."

Chris—my best friend with benefits, boyfriend, whatever.

"Name?"

"Sebastian," she said. "Tall, skinny, glasses. Kinda cute. You know who I'm talking about?"

"Yeah," I said, making sure my voice sounded normal. "He's in my English class."

I didn't tell Rebecca that for the last few weeks during class, I'd been making eye contact with Sebastian more frequently and longer than was probably acceptable for someone with a boyfriend. I didn't know what it meant. Nothing, probably. Just that we were both bored and happened to be looking up at the same moment. Or maybe not.

"So?" Rebecca said. "I need you to come."

Mom poked her head out between the sliding doors, her face flushed from yet another marathon on the treadmill.

"Are you having dinner here?" Mom shouted across the yard.

"No," I yelled back. "I'm going to Rebecca's."

She closed the door quickly, lest any air-conditioning escape.

"Oh, thank god for small miracles," Rebecca said. "Come over soon."

"Okay." I rolled up the Berkeley catalog and went around the house to the garage so I wouldn't have to see Mom.

Hours later, I was on Rebecca's porch with the regulars. Ryan and Tyler sat on the floor, their backs against the railing. They hooked up occasionally, and lately Tyler wanted more, but Ryan insisted he wasn't gay. Tyler was holding back tears.

"That doesn't even make sense," he said. I knew what would happen next. Ryan would feel bad for hurting Tyler, he'd put his arm around him, and take him somewhere to "talk."

Cody, Rebecca, and Salim sat on folding chairs at the small table in the corner, playing Never Have I Ever with shots of vodka. Matt straddled the beer cooler, drumming it with his hands to the beat of the music—something by some Broadway diva they were all obsessed with who'd recently gone solo.

Chris sat on the porch swing next to me, his arm stretched over my shoulders. He held a can of beer; I nursed a vodka cranberry. He waved a gnat away from us. Because I'd known Chris since birth, we didn't have to talk much.

"Never have I ever been in a threesome!" Rebecca called out. Cody raised his hand proudly and took a shot of vodka.

"Really?" Rebecca frowned at him. Cody was her ice cream, her spaghetti and meatballs, her wish upon a star. And every now and then, Cody would decide that she was his too.

Rebecca came over to the porch swing and squished herself between Chris and me. She put her hands in Chris's thick blond hair and kissed him loudly on the cheek and turned to me and licked the side of my face.

"Gross!" I yelled.

"My two best friends. Together. Include me, please," she said. "Come on—Cody's done it. Let's do it."

Chris choked on his beer.

"You're wasted," I said, wiping my cheek.

"But I *love* you guys," she whined.

"And we love you," I said as she stretched her body across us, her head in my lap and her legs on Chris's.

She yawned, which made me yawn. It seemed like Sebastian wasn't coming, and I didn't want to admit to myself that I was waiting for him, so I began preparing an excuse to leave.

But right then Sebastian turned the corner onto Rebecca's street, his hands deep in his jeans pockets.

The way his shoulders slouched reminded me of the first time I ever saw him, a few days before the start of fourth grade. I'd been fighting with my mom, and I needed to get out of the house, which felt toxic with our screams. I ran toward my oak tree, making my way past the pool to the back of our property. But there was a boy sitting in my spot.

A skinny boy with glasses and big feet. I felt anger burning up inside me. Who the hell was this kid, and what was he doing under *my* oak tree?

I stomped right up to him.

"Who are you?" I demanded.

The boy quickly closed his book. It was thick with glossy pictures of planets and stars on the front—wispy rings circling one of the planets. Sunlight reflected off his wire-rimmed glasses, and when he squinted, he revealed white teeth that contrasted with his light brown skin. He put his hand up to shade his eyes, which were dark brown and fringed with the longest black eyelashes I'd ever seen. A smooth, white scar cut through his left eyebrow, making a gap where the hair didn't grow.

"I'm Sebastian," he said.

"What are you doing here?"

"Uh, my stepfather is here." He pointed at the house. "He meets with your father. He builds a room maybe." English was definitely not his first language.

Dad was thinking of doing an addition on the family room—making a sunroom.

I was annoyed. This boy was in my space. But he wasn't taking the hint to get up, so finally, I sat next to him. He showed me his book about the solar system.

"It's a new book," he said, pointing at the shiny binding, "but it is already out of date."

"What do you mean?" I asked.

"The International Astronomical Union is changing what means planet. And Pluto becomes a dwarf planet instead of a planet."

"So, they can just do that?" I asked. "Change what's always been just because a few old guys say so?"

Sebastian shrugged. "A planet clears the area of its orbital path. A dwarf planet does not do this. Pluto does not, so it is a dwarf planet."

"Whatever that means," I said.

"It means that it *appears* the same, but it does not *do* the same, so it is different."

For a second, my mind swam with planets and dwarf planets, the way things look versus the way things are. I tried to digest the meaning of what he'd said, and perhaps even a deeper meaning, when my sixteen-year-old cousin Scott jumped out from the other side of the tree, scaring the hell out of me.

"Who's he?" Scott asked.

"Sebastian," I said, when I could breathe again. Sebastian nodded at him.

"What'cha reading?" Scott asked.

"Nothing," I said.

"I'm going in the pool," he said. "Let's hang out after he leaves."

Scott walked over to the pool and dove in, making a loud splash.

"Want to swim?" I asked Sebastian, even though Scott had implied that he was not invited.

"I don't know how."

I looked at him like he was crazy. "Then what do you do in the summer?"

"I read," he said. "I study."

"Well, if you're gonna live here, you need to swim. Nobody studies in the summer."

We watched Scott swimming laps, his strokes perfect. I felt the pull to go to the pool, the pathetic need to do what Scott wanted, like I always did.

"Well, I'd better go," I said.

Sebastian picked up his book and walked toward the driveway where his stepfather's truck was parked. He turned around and waved, and I felt a sudden pang of loneliness. I went inside to put on my bathing suit—the orange one that made me feel brave like a lifeguard.

Dad didn't ever build that sunroom.

I didn't see Sebastian again until ninth grade when all the area schools combined into one high school. And even then, he wasn't on my radar.

Until now.

Sebastian still had the same features he had at nine years old—light brown skin, dark brown hair buzzed short, impossibly long eyelashes behind wire-rimmed glasses, and a long, straight nose. But now he was tall. Really tall.

Chris called out to Sebastian. "Hey, you showed! Nice."

Sebastian pulled his earbuds out and stuffed them in his pocket.

"Hey," he said, taking the porch steps two at a time.

A couple of the guys reached out to him for a dude handshake-bump thing. Rebecca got up and gave him a Euro double kiss—one on each cheek. Then he turned to me.

"Hey, Macy," he said, his voice quiet and deep.

"Hi." I hoped he wasn't expecting me to do the double-kiss thing. While Rebecca could pull something like that off, I definitely couldn't.

After Chris handed him a beer from the cooler, Sebastian appeared to be listening to him and the other guys speculate about who else in the junior class might have had a threesome. I stayed on the porch swing with Rebecca. She analyzed major celebrities who'd gotten their start on Disney TV shows, and I tried not to be aware of Sebastian standing just a few feet away from me.

A little while later, Sebastian headed upstairs with everyone to get high. He looked at me like he was waiting for me to come too, but I didn't.

The second time everyone went in, Sebastian stayed behind with me, and for a split second, I felt uneasy. If his dark eyes made me feel the way they did in a classroom full of people, what would happen when we were alone, the moths flitting in and out of the dim porch light our only witnesses? He perched on the railing in front of me and cracked another beer.

"That looks comfortable," he said. He no longer had even a hint of an accent.

"Sure is," I said, plumping up the flowered pillow behind my back.

He stood up to his full, lanky six-foot-many-inches.

"Room for me?" he asked as he walked toward me.

I nodded.

The old rusty chains creaked as he sat next to me. We pushed our feet against the peeling gray porch floor, swaying back and forth. I wondered if Sebastian could feel the wisps of hair that had escaped from my yellow bandana and were dancing in the spring breeze toward his face.

I stared at his giant sneakers—orange, unlaced high-tops. Graffiti covered the sides of the soles. There were pictures of eyes—some with huge teardrops—lips, trees, a bird.

"That's cool," I said, pointing at one of the eyes on his left shoe. He held it up so I could see better.

"That's my 'eye of the world' eye," he said. "It watches over everything." He pointed two fingers at his eyes and then at mine, back and forth—the *I've got my eye on you* gesture. Then, with exaggerated seriousness, he locked his gaze on mine. My pulse raced.

We both laughed uncomfortably.

We looked at the street and continued swinging back and forth, back and forth. My heart finally slowed to its normal rhythm.

"I got you with that one, right?" he said. "I'm kind of a ladies' man."

I raised my eyebrows at him.

"I'm serious! Check this out!" He held up his thin but solid arm, pushed the sleeve of his T-shirt to his shoulder, and pretended to flex his bicep; he frowned when nothing happened.

"Ha, ha," I said.

"I don't have a BMW, or any car, actually, but I do have a sweet BMX." He paused. "If you're nice, I'll take you for a ride—you can sit on the handlebars while I pedal. You're impressed, right?"

"I didn't know you were trying to impress me." I smiled, vaguely aware that the classroom eye contact had moved to flirting and my boyfriend was just inside the house.

"Well, you know," he said. "It's always worth a try."

And then his face got serious. "I'm sorry I stared at you the other day. In the hallway."

"Huh?"

"Oh, never mind," he said. "I thought you caught me looking."

I wanted to say, "Don't we catch each other looking all the time lately?" But of course, I didn't. Instead I said, "When?"

"You were outside the art room. I'd never seen you there before. You were looking at your phone and you had this sad expression for a second. I felt like I was looking in your window with the shades up or something."

His honesty was both scary and refreshing. I remembered that day. Sometimes when I felt like being alone, I hung out near the art room. I liked the smell of the paint and clay.

"So, what was up? What made you so sad?" he asked.

"It was no big deal, really. I applied for a summer internship, so that was just the inevitable 'thanks but no thanks' e-mail."

I cleared my throat, wishing the sound could be like an eraser. I hadn't told anyone that I'd written to a small architecture firm in town about the possibility of working there in August. Not even Rebecca or Chris.

"Doesn't sound like no big deal," he said.

"I thought it might help with college applications, but whatever, I'll find something else."

"Where do you want to go?"

"Berkeley," I said.

"In California?"

I nodded.

"Why so far?" he asked.

"Because it's so far." I laughed awkwardly. And also Berkeley had one of the best undergraduate architecture programs in the country. "Where do you want to go?"

Sebastian shrugged. "So then, what are you doing this summer, now that you don't have the internship?" he asked.

"In July we're going to Nantucket. I always work at a T-shirt store while I'm there. What about you?"

"Babysitting my half-sister, I guess. My mom's a nurse with a crazy schedule, and my stepfather's got his own building company, so it's looking like Sofia will get to go to Camp Sebastian."

I wasn't one of those girls who got all gushy about guys being good with kids, but I couldn't help smiling.

I noticed a design on the top of his shoe, between where the laces ended and his big toe.

"What about that one?" I asked. It was so swirly and intricate; I could barely make out its shape. "Is it a key?"

He looked surprised. "I didn't think it was that obvious."

"It's not," I said. "I can just sort of tell. It is, right?"

He nodded slowly. "To lock things up."

"Like what things?"

"You know," he said. "Stuff that should be locked up. Dirty magazines, money, bad guys, secrets."

I stared at the key on his shoe—the blue swirls and whirls. I couldn't see where they began or ended. I squinted to see the details in the dim light.

"What kind of secrets?" I asked.

"Any secrets. Most embarrassing secret. Go."

"Oh, no," I said. "I'm not playing this game."

"I'll show you mine if you show me yours."

"Very funny. . . . Fine," I said. "Here's one. When I was eleven, I was dying to have this Barbie ski chalet—it seemed so cozy on the commercial. It had a pretend fireplace with logs and everything. But I was too old for Barbies, so I ordered it in secret with my mom's credit card. When it came, I hid the box under my bed. After I finally put it together, my cousin caught me, and I never heard the end of it."

Sebastian looked at me. "That's the best you can do?"

"Yup. What about you?"

He shrugged. "I had a Ken."

"Huh?"

"I had a Ken, and all he had was a cardboard box for a house. I could have brought him over to your place."

"Liar," I said, punching him lightly on the arm.

"You too," he said.

"I wasn't lying!"

"Maybe, but the Barbie ski house is not your biggest secret. I know you're hiding big stuff."

"I'm hiding big stuff? You got that from talking to me for less than ten minutes?"

"Lucky guess," he said. The way he looked at me—like he had my number—was impossibly frustrating and attractive at the same time.

"I didn't say you were right," I said. "What are you, clairvoyant or something? Telling everyone what's lurking underneath the surface?"

He took my hand and turned my palm up.

"Ah, yes." He traced a line along my palm. He furrowed his brow. "Many secrets, a tall, dark man, and a long life with some struggle but much happiness."

He let go of my hand. I hoped he couldn't see my cheeks burning red.

"So, what is it that makes me so completely transparent to a hack seer such as yourself?"

"Hack? Me? My skills are unparalleled. I am the most experienced observer in town. That's what you learn to do when you come here from Spain in the middle of third grade and you don't speak English. And the Latinos call you *conquistador* and want nothing to do with you. You keep quiet and you learn."

"Well, you sure aren't keeping quiet now," I said.

"I know, right? I'm pissing you off. I didn't mean to do that."

His eyes met mine and didn't stray. Finally, I needed to breathe again, so I looked down at my knees.

"So . . ." I said. "What about me made you think I have some big secret?"

I couldn't help it. I had to know.

He hesitated.

"What? Go ahead. I can take it."

"Nothing," he said. "I just see there's something else in there, besides all this—school, the parties, the drama shtick. But no one sees it because you hide it."

What the hell? I had an urge to just get up and walk away, never talk to him again, but my body stayed where it was, unmoving.

"I hide it. How exactly do I do that?"

"Well, A) all your friends are in the drama club. You hang out with people who need the spotlight all the time so you don't have to have it shining on you. And B) your expressionless face."

"What are you talking about?" I said, my voice bitter.

"You kind of keep your face at a low hum," he said.

"Oh my god, now you're freaking me out."

"See?" he said. "Like that. You didn't raise your voice or change your facial expression when you said that, and I know you're at least a little pissed, so you're covering it up. You're very good at it. That's how I know you have a secret."

What was happening? It was just a regular Saturday night in May.

Time to change the subject.

"You never told me where you're applying," I said.

"Don't know yet. Don't you get high? You didn't go inside."

He was just as skilled at changing the subject as I was.

"Me?" I said. "I'm the gullible dumbshit who believes those inane urban legends. You know, like the guy who hallucinated his face was an orange and peeled it off. You're into it?"

He looked away from me, took a sip of beer.

"Maybe," he said.

"Like in a bad way?" I asked.

"Is there a good way?"

"I don't know. I guess not. But everyone here seems to have a good time."

"Why do you hang out with these guys if you don't get high?" he asked.

"Rebecca's my best friend. She loves to party. And Chris. And the rest of them—the drama club guys—well, they *are* entertainers after all, so they're very entertaining, especially when they're high as hot-air balloons. And they don't care that I don't partake, if that's what you mean."

Sebastian looked at me as though he wanted more.

"And to keep the spotlight away from me, right?" I added, elbowing him gently in the side. He smiled and elbowed me back.

"Yeah," he said. "Somehow I don't really see you hanging with the cheerleaders."

"No?" I tilted my head and batted my eyelashes. "No rah-rah for me?"

"No rah-rah for you."

"Why are *you* hanging out with these guys?" I asked. Sebastian hadn't said much more than monosyllables to them—acknowledgements of "killer weed" or an occasional movie review.

"Well, your friend Chris invited me," he said. I cringed at the mention of Chris and the way he emphasized the word *friend*. "And they've got good weed."

"For such good weed, you don't seem high," I said.

"You should see me when I'm not high. I'm very, very sober when I'm not high," he said, pulling his mouth down in a frown.

He looked at his watch.

"Am I keeping you?" I asked.

"I promised I'd babysit tonight. My mom's got the night shift and my stepfather's out of town."

"How old's your sister?"

"Four."

He downed the rest of his beer.

"And you're okay to take care of her like this?" I held my drink up, indicating the beer, the weed, whatever else they had in there. "Isn't that somewhat irresponsible?"

"I can handle my substances," he said, and then his voice was suddenly gruff, almost angry. "I'm not like them—your friends and your boyfriend. I'm nothing like them. I don't even know what I'm doing here."

I felt the heat from his breath on my cheek, slightly cooler than a fire-breathing dragon. He stood up quickly, making the chains on the swing bounce, and went to the edge of the porch. His body was rigid, his fists clenched.

He leaned his forearms on the porch railing, looking out onto the street. I wanted to tell him that it was okay. That I knew whatever had made him angry wasn't directed toward me. That I was angry too. But I wouldn't even know where to begin.

He straightened and gripped the railing with both hands. Then he opened his hands, gripped, opened again. He did this a few times.

"I'm sorry for that—whatever that was," he said quietly, "I shouldn't have said that about them. Your friends are cool. I'm the ass."

"It's okay. I understand," I said.

He came back to the swing and sat so close to me that if I moved my knee just a millimeter, we'd be touching.

"I think too much," he said. "I can't stop. Even getting high. It numbs me, tones things down a little, but not enough."

He put his hands on his head and rubbed the fuzz there. He looked at me, and I tried to read what his eyes were saying. But I found it difficult to concentrate when he was this close to me, when his skin radiated heat toward me.

"Why am I telling you this?" He was looking for something from me, like he needed me—me specifically—but I was paralyzed.

He kneaded his hands together in his lap and placed them on his knees like he was trying to keep them still.

"Do you think too much?" he asked quietly, so quietly I barely heard him.

"I try not to. Thinking makes everything worse."

"Like what?" he said. "What's so bad?"

His eyes made me want to tell him something. I had to stop that from happening.

"Nothing," I said and looked away.

"Got it," he said, softly.

"Maybe you're too smart." I wanted to get the conversation back onto him. "That's why you think so much."

"Oh yes," he said, his lip curling up on one side. "Way too brilliant for my own good, right? It's a nice theory, but unfortunately I'm not all that smart. I just study a lot."

We were both quiet for a few seconds.

"Do you remember that summer when we were kids?" he asked abruptly. "When I was at your house with my stepfather?"

I nodded.

"You told me I had to learn to swim, so I did." His voice got quiet. "Maybe we could swim sometime."

Sebastian and me. Bathing suits. My pool. Together. That would never, ever happen. Suddenly, I felt such a deep loss, I had to blink quickly a few times to make it go away.

"I don't swim anymore," I said.

"Really? I remember you telling me it was the only thing to do."

"Well, I guess it's not."

He looked at me then like he knew me, like no one had looked at me before. Not Chris, not Rebecca, not anyone in my family. It was freaking me out. It was making my heart stutter. It felt good—it felt horrible. I was in a strange, marvelous, frightening dream. I could hear the voices inside the house and the bass of the music, but it was just background.

"Macy, I—" And in the same second he said my name, I heard Rebecca yelling it, "Macy!" and then she was at my side.

"Oh goddammit, I have to talk to you!" she said, slurring her words. No doubt Rebecca was having a Cody crisis.

I stared at Sebastian, willing the dream to stay, and yet relieved that I could pull my veil back down.

"Hey," Rebecca said to Sebastian, and then, giving me a quick, curious look, "sorry, gotta borrow my girl."

"Gimme a minute," I said to her.

"Hurry!"

She went back into the house.

"What were you going to say?" I asked Sebastian, but he wouldn't meet my eyes.

"Just that I've gotta go," he said.

I stared at him.

"My sister," he said. "Remember?"

He walked down the steps.

I jumped up from the porch swing and leaned over the railing. He was already on the sidewalk, pulling the earbuds out of his pocket.

"Do you want me to drive you there?" I called out to him.

"Isn't that somewhat irresponsible?" He laughed. "I'll see ya."

I watched his body disappear down the sidewalk and into the darkness.

And then I was alone with this thing—whatever it was—that he'd unleashed, after years of being locked away.

And that was it. No one saw or heard from him. Nothing.

CHAPTER TWO

I couldn't stop thinking about Sebastian, but by the twelfth day, his disappearance was old news. Everyone else moved on. But I had to know where he'd gone, what happened to him. I'd asked around some, but no one knew anything, and I didn't want my friends to know I was looking that hard. As far as they knew, I'd never even talked to Sebastian until Rebecca's party.

I replayed our conversation in my head, dreamed about him, about his eyes—eyes that seemed to invite me to tell him everything, eyes that seemed to know me better than I knew myself.

And then, on the thirteenth day, as I was driving to the last day of junior year, my phone buzzed.

REBECCA: Just got the real 411 on Sebastian. He's @ NWH psych ward. Tried to off hmslf.

I pulled over to the side of the road, my hands shaking so much that I kept missing the right letters and had to start my text over.

ME: How do u know?

REBECCA: His stepdad's buildng mom's boss house. Mom just asked if I know him!

I swallowed hard.

REBECCA: Pills? Slit wrists? 4 me bathtub/hairdryer thng. Quick, no pukng. What wud u do?

I couldn't respond.

REBECCA: U there?

I couldn't blame her for making jokes about the news— she didn't know that it wasn't just gossip to me. I'd never told her how much his disappearance had been plaguing me. If we'd been talking about anyone else, I would've answered her: *No way. Jump off mntn. Fly. B free!*

REBECCA: Macy???

Even though I *had* thought of the possibility that he was dead, I'd dismissed it. I mean, who dies without anyone knowing? I'd thought about his eyes, which had seemed sad, but also so open. Maybe if I hadn't been so busy thinking about how quickly he'd seemed to figure me out, I would have paid more attention to what *he* was feeling. Maybe if I'd listened a little better, I would have known that he was so unhappy. Sebastian read me like an open book that night, so why couldn't I have done the same for him? I twirled a chunk of hair with my finger, a habit I'd started way back when I gave up thumb sucking. I barely knew Sebastian, but I had to know what had happened.

And then, some other crazier version of me took over. I turned around and drove straight to Northern Westchester Hospital.

My car idled in the parking lot. I couldn't cut the engine. Not yet. Then I'd have to go in and that would mean I knew what the hell I was doing there.

I put my hands on the steering wheel, willing it to give me a sign.

REBECCA: Where the H r u? Ur skipping last day of school?!

I took a deep breath, powered off my phone, and then cut the engine.

I got out of my ugly-but-all-mine silver Civic and stepped onto the sidewalk leading to the main door. Birds sang their songs. My heart beat the bass line for them.

The automatic door slid open. Inside, the lights were fluorescent, buzzing. The industrial gray carpet seemed softer, more luxurious than it should have been. There were semicomfortable looking chairs and a piano in the lobby, which struck me as ironic—the Hospital Hotel. But despite its appearance, the smell was undeniably hospital—a mix of citrusy sterilizer and cafeteria hot meals.

I approached the elevator and looked at the sign next to it, which showed the departments and their floors. I couldn't find anything remotely like Psych Ward or Psychology. I even looked at the Ms for Mental Health. I was about to give up and go back to my car, relieved in a way, when I heard someone say, "Can I help you find something?"

A girl with an official-looking name badge stood next to me.

I cleared my throat.

"Is there a psych ward here?" I asked.

"Behavioral Health." She pointed at the words on the sign. "Fourth floor. Just see the receptionist when you get up there." She pressed the elevator button for me and then backed up, but I could tell she was looking at me. She probably wondered whether I was checking myself in.

"Thanks," I said as the doors opened and I got on. I listened to the beeps as the elevator rose and then I got off on the fourth floor.

The woman behind the reception desk was giant—a linebacker with bright red lipstick and auburn shoulder-length curly hair. When she smiled, I could see red smudges of lipstick on her whitened teeth.

"I'm here to see Sebastian Ruiz," I said. Suddenly, I hoped she'd say he wasn't there. Maybe it was just another rumor.

She looked at her computer screen, click-clacked her fingernails on the keyboard.

"And your name?" she asked.

"Macy Lyons."

"I don't see you on his list."

"No, I'm not on it," I said.

"I'm sorry, love." She looked up, her eyes sympathetic. "You have to be on his approved visitors list to see him. I hope you didn't come a long distance."

"No," I said. "It's okay."

My sanity was returning. I'd had one conversation with Sebastian—*one*. Unless you counted the one about planets when we were nine. Showing up at the psych ward was enough to put *me* in the psych ward.

"You can write him a letter," she said. "Or you can ask his parents to arrange a visit."

"How long will he be here?" I asked. What I really wanted to ask her was, *What happened? Did he really try to kill himself? How? Why?*

"I don't know, sweetheart," she said, as though she knew she was answering all of my questions.

After lunch, I met up with Chris at his locker. Chris—my set-building, blond, blue-eyed neighbor and friend since before kindergarten. Chris—my boyfriend of six months.

"Hey," Chris said, playing with the string of my hoodie. "Kinda weird, you know? Last day of junior year. Next year's gonna be so different."

"The dreaded application process," I said. Berkeley was going to be impossible now that I didn't have the internship at the architecture firm. I had zero experience in anything architecture-related, other than obsessive hours on home-building apps and websites. What would I say in my application? I like seeing how the details of houses make them into homes, and I can picture myself making them someday? I felt my skin prickle with impending failure.

"Come over after school," Chris said, touching my neck. I shivered.

"You cold?" He leaned in and kissed me.

I shoved his chest. "Come on," I said.

His face fell and I immediately felt horrible.

"You know I hate PDA. It's cruel," I said. "Some poor freshman innocently walks by and gets an uncontrollable hard-on. He's got his tent-pole pants and everyone makes fun of him and the next thing you know he goes all Columbine on the school."

"Why can't it be a girl wanting *me*?" he said.

"You, huh?"

"Yeah, me," he said, smiling. Chris was undeniably cute. Until sophomore year, he'd been thirty pounds heavier and there were many times when I had to defend him from the dirtbags who teased him or the girls who giggled at their own fat jokes. It made me so mad that he wouldn't stand up for himself and let me do his fighting for him. But when puberty hit late and in his favor, he thinned out, his acne cleared up, he got his braces off, and he turned into a *bona fide* hot guy.

"Fine," I said. "A sweet sophomore girl holding a burning torch for you, doodling your name in every notebook—and then gets her eye on *this?*" I gestured my hand back and forth between our chests. "Can you imagine the devastation? A trauma like that could send her straight to the nunnery, for god's sake. I can't be responsible for that, Chris. Can *you?*"

"I can't," he said. "Though nearly impossible, I will refrain for her sake. And for tent-pole-pants-guy. Let's meet up here after last period."

And he went off to class.

But Chris hadn't been enough of a distraction. I couldn't shake the image of Sebastian's eyes that night on Rebecca's porch. He'd been about to say something important. I flip-flopped between desperately wanting to see him and never wanting to see him again, especially since he'd been the one to stir up stuff I didn't want to think about.

I took my seat in English, Sebastian's absence next to me so strong, it felt more like a presence in itself. I let the din of phones turning to vibrate mode, textbooks opening, gum snapping wash over me. There was a millisecond of calm and then a sudden epiphany: Because of Sebastian, for the first time in my life, I wanted to know someone else's deepest darkest thoughts. And I wanted someone to know mine.

CHAPTER THREE

That night when Dad called, I was sitting at the kitchen counter reading blogs on dreadlocks.

Ever since Sebastian had said that I was hiding, covering something up, memories and doubts were seeping into my thoughts all day every day—while I brushed my teeth, hung out with Rebecca or Chris . . . and forget about sleep. I'd started questioning everything.

Now I was like Pluto, the non-planet. I appeared the same, but I wasn't the same. Not anymore. Not on the inside. And I didn't want to look the same anymore either. Dreadlocks were a huge change, not fleeting like dying your hair or piercing your eyebrow. I was going to be the dreadlocked Pluto. I'd bought the hair products, watched the video instructions, gotten Rebecca on board to help, but I didn't have the courage yet.

While I was watching the video on how to back-comb properly for the twentieth time, the phone rang and Mom picked up.

"Really?" she said. "Another night? You know what tomorrow is, don't you?"

It only took me a second to realize that it was Dad on the phone, and he was spending yet another night away, which meant no first-day-of-vacation breakfast with him tomorrow.

No matter how busy he was or what state he was in, on our first day of summer vacation, Dad was *always* home to celebrate with my brother Gavin and me, and Scott before he'd moved to the city. Dad made us chocolate chip waffles with whipped cream and strawberries, played catch or badminton with us, and then headed off to work or to the airport. He'd never missed vacation breakfast before.

I loosened some hair from my ponytail and twirled it around my finger.

Then Mom spoke into the phone in her fake cheerful voice, "Okay, honey. Sounds like you've had a long day. You should take an Ambien. Make sure you get some good sleep."

She hung up and turned to me.

"Dad just got back to the office from San Diego, but he has a client dinner tonight and an early morning meeting, so he's just going to stay in the city," she said.

I nodded, not sure how she wanted me to react. Was I supposed to get angry so we could rag on him together? Or did she want me to be all sympathetic that Dad was working so hard? Mom and I didn't speak the same language. And since Dad was our translator, I was flipping through the Bitch-to-English dictionary as fast as I could in my head. But it was coming up blank.

"What do you want for dinner?" Mom asked.

I shrugged, twirling my hair tighter.

"You know, Macy, would it kill you to just answer a simple question once in a while?" She opened the refrigerator, stood with her back to me, slammed the door shut, and walked out of the kitchen.

A few minutes later, I heard the squeak-squeak of the treadmill in the home gym above the garage. Mom had asked Dad to fix the squeak, but he hadn't gotten around to it.

It was an unspoken rule in our house that mornings worked best if we all avoided one other. But the next morning, on our first day of summer vacation, Mom broke the rule. And she didn't just break it—she took out a hammer and bashed it, crumbling its bones into little bits, and then wrung its neck for good measure.

"Guys, I need to tell you about a change in our summer plans," she announced to Gavin and me, pouring her second cup of coffee. "We can't go to Nantucket next week."

My bagel popped up from the toaster. I scorched my finger trying to grab it.

"What?" Gavin said, his mouth open wide in shock.

Poor Gavin had enough to worry about—his skinny geeky self was heading for the big leagues next fall—high school. This kind of "change of plan" was not something Gavin could deal with well. We *always* rented a house on Nantucket for a month after school ended. Every single summer, every single year of our lives.

Plus, Gavin's heart had already been broken this morning once he realized that Dad really wasn't coming home for first-day-of-vacation breakfast.

"You can't just cancel our trip," I said, trying to stay calm.

"Scotty has to make up a couple of classes for his degree. We can go when he finishes. Maybe in August," Mom said. Even though Scott was our cousin, Mom and Dad had been taking care of him since he was a baby, way before I was born. Aunt

Judy would drop off Scott with Mom for "just a few hours" and then pick him up three or four days later as though it were nothing. Mom and Dad became his legal guardians when Judy went to live with a freaky cult in Montana.

Maybe because he was abandoned or something, Mom and Dad always gave Scott whatever he wanted. Boarding school when he got kicked out of public school. Backpacking around Europe all summer after boarding school. Dad used connections to get him into Columbia, and now Scott wasn't even going to graduate with all his credits. And, of course, Mom was making sure the entire universe revolved around him yet again.

"That's fair?" I yelled. "You're changing the plans of the entire family because Scott partied too hard to finish his degree?"

"His thesis advisor left midyear," Mom said. "And he's been incredibly busy running the nightclub."

"Mom, he's like a three percent owner. He's not running anything."

"That's not very supportive, Macy," she said, shaking her head.

I glared at her. Supportive, my ass. He had all the support he needed from Mom and Dad.

Gavin sank down in his chair at the table and slowly ate his cereal.

"Steven and Tucker won't be on Nantucket in August," Gavin said quietly. He hadn't found his soul mates here like he had there. The summers on Nantucket were Gavin's time to shine.

I didn't want to let on to Mom that I was upset too. I'd have to call the T-shirt store on Nantucket to tell them I wasn't coming at the last minute and then I'd never get a job there again. Why hadn't Dad warned me about the change of plans? I felt a tug at my heart, like he had betrayed me.

"Come on," I said to Gavin. "I'm going to Rebecca's. I'll drop you off somewhere."

I ran upstairs to get my dreadlock products.

Gavin and I sat in silence as I drove the few miles to Mount Kisco center.

"We'll figure something out, Gav," I said. "Maybe you can go stay with Tucker for a week or something. I bet Mom'll be cool with that."

He shrugged. "Yeah, maybe."

I dropped Gavin and his laptop off at Starbucks and then, fuming at Mom, Scott, and even Dad, I headed to Rebecca's, hoping she'd be able to entertain me into forgetting.

When I pulled up to her house, she was on the porch, picking up beer bottles.

"You gonna just sit there? Get your butt over here and help!" Rebecca yelled to me.

I started up the porch steps.

"What happened to you last night? You left before Chris," she said as she dumped a plastic cup full of cigarette butts into the garbage can. Rebecca had hosted the entire junior class for the last day of school blowout the night before. It was the best party of the year, but I'd left early, unable to play fake while images of Sebastian in the psych ward were crowding my brain.

I picked up a bottle, dumped the beer out into the bushes, and then chucked it into the blue bin. While we may not drink responsibly, we do recycle responsibly.

"I was tired," I said.

She looked at me.

"What?" I asked.

"Something's going on with you. You've been acting all weird lately. You're not screwing things up with Chris, are you?"

"No. Chris is fine."

"You'd better be good to him," she said. "You still owe him for setting us up."

I hadn't planned on adding another drama freak to my list of friends. Chris and his set-building was plenty of drama for me, but in ninth grade, Chris introduced me to Rebecca, a card-carrying actress, complete with the booming voice, in-depth knowledge of all things Broadway, and the desire to get up on stage. And she was irresistible. We effortlessly turned into the Rebecca-Macy show, and Chris was demoted to understudy. But even though he'd convinced me to make him leading man six months ago, the Rebecca-Macy show would never end its run.

I pulled the bag of dreadlock products out of my bag.

"Can we do it today?" I asked.

"Really? You're ready?"

"I think so. I know it's gonna hurt like hell, but I really want them."

"Okay," she said. "Let's do it! We'll finish cleaning up later."

"I'll do the front, you do the back," I said.

We went to the TV room, set up the products, rubber bands, comb, and brush on the coffee table.

"We should get a towel or something," I said. "It could stain."

"Look at this couch. Like anyone would notice."

The couch in their TV room was a brown fuzzy material that had seen too many years of sitting butts. In fact, with Rebecca and her three older brothers, I didn't even want to know what had happened on it.

"It's still your mom's couch," I said.

"Oh, fine." She left the room and returned with a thin unraveling Spider-Man towel.

Rebecca spread the towel on the couch, and we got to work sectioning, back-combing, and twisting my hair. We'd been studying it for two weeks already and now it was happening. Mom would freak.

"We're not going to Nantucket until August now," I told Rebecca. "Maybe not at all."

She looked up. "Seriously? Since when?"

"Since this morning when my mom announced it. It's because of Scott. I don't want to get into it." Rebecca was one of the few people who saw through Scott's charms. It bugged me when she'd go off on one of her rants about him, though. I had that *I can complain about my family, but you can't* syndrome. But today, I didn't have any weapons to defend him with.

"Well, I'm delighted you'll be here," she said.

"Did you just say 'delighted'?"

"I wanted to try it out. See if it could be a new word."

"No," I said. "It can't."

"Bummer. It sounded so lovely in the script I read last week."

"Not 'lovely' either," I said, touching the back of my head. Rebecca whacked my hand away.

"What're you gonna do here?" she asked.

"I guess I'll find a job. I'm kind of late to the game."

"I *just* got an e-mail from Darren at Marwood. One of the counselors dropped out last minute. He's desperate."

Rebecca stopped pulling on my hair and looked at me cautiously. She knew my love/hate feelings for Marwood Club. Scott, Gavin, and I were basically raised there. Mom dropped me off at the nursery when I was a baby, sent me there for preschool, camp, swim lessons, everything. It was convenient for her while she worked out, played tennis, got facials, and ate lunch with her girlfriends. Even though I'd grown up there, it was never *my* place. Marwood Club was Mom's territory.

"Um, no thanks."

"Don't be an idiot," she said. "It's a great job. It pays well and it's only eight thirty to twelve."

"I don't even like kids." I tried to ignore the stabs of pain brought on by Rebecca's rough twisting technique.

"How do you know? Have you ever talked to one?"

"Do they talk? I thought they just cried and shat and snarfed boogers everywhere," I said.

"We're going there and you will tell Darren you want the job."

I rolled my eyes at her but I didn't say no. At least it would be something to get my mind off my mother and suicidal Sebastian.

"Ouch!" I screamed as she yanked a tangle from the back of my head.

"Sorry."

I wiped a tear. She tugged the same spot again.

"Ow! Go easy back there, it's sensitive!" I said. "I need a break. My scalp's on fire."

"Okay." She stood and surveyed our progress. "Looking good. We're almost done."

I went into the bathroom and looked in the mirror. The front was done—small, tight, twisty, blond dreadlocks that framed my face. They were short right now, but they'd grow.

"It's good," I said to my reflection.

Rebecca had already gone outside to finish cleaning up.

"Oh nasty!" Rebecca screamed. I went out to the porch. She pointed at a bush that was splattered with bits of yellowish puke. I gagged and backed my way toward the front door.

"Animals! No respect," she yelled as she pulled the hose out from the side of the house. She looked up and pointed at me.

I froze, one foot inside the house, one on the porch.

"Come back here, you traitor! Can't even stand the sight of a little puke? Come on down here and help me."

I shook my head no, but I was fighting laughter. I was over the puke already, but now it was just fun to get Rebecca all riled up.

"You get down here or I'm telling everyone that you still sleep with Fozzie Bear."

She dropped the hose and pulled out her phone.

"Let's see," she said, scrolling. "Who has the biggest mouth? Jasmine?"

"Don't," I said, trying to stop myself from laughing.

"Do you think Jasmine would find it amusing that badass too-cool-for-school Macy Lyons has to drive ten minutes home to get her Fozzie Bear before spending the night at my house? What do you think, Mace?" She held out her hands like a balance. "Cleaning up puke versus letting out your biggest secret to the world?"

My biggest secret. If only sleeping with Fozzie Bear was my biggest secret. Some things were too big even to share with your best friend.

I gave her the finger, trudged down the steps, grabbed the hose from her, and started spraying the bush. It wouldn't be my fault if I accidentally soaked her too.

CHAPTER FOUR

I slept at Rebecca's and the next day, after deliberating the emptiness of the summer that stretched ahead, I drove to Marwood Club with her to find out about the camp counselor position.

"*Please* will you come with me to Juice Paradise on Monday? Pretty please?" Rebecca gave me her puppy eyes and the pouty lips.

"Fine. But you're crazy."

Despite her unquestionable hotness, Rebecca was always on a diet. She had an old-school movie star face with perfectly smooth pinkish skin and huge turquoise-blue eyes that looked fluorescent in certain lights. Her naturally white-blond hair was cut short, framing her high cheekbones and strong chin. And she was curvy in all the right places. Even though she knew her body was sexy, she was certain her curves would prevent her from getting the lead roles in romantic comedies or in musicals on Broadway. Rebecca had *plans*. So, despite my unheard pleas and protests, I was always checking out diets with her. Juice Paradise was one of those places that claimed if you bought their disgusting green concoctions, you'd lose belly fat fast.

When we pulled into the parking lot of Marwood Club, I saw Mom's black Porsche Cayenne in front. I parked in the back where there was less chance of running into her.

We entered the Club, the familiar smell of sweat and hand sanitizer hitting me. Not much had changed since I'd last been here—maybe some fresh paint, some new chairs.

"Hey, Macy, haven't seen you in a while!" Rose, the woman behind the desk, said. "You looking for your mom? I think she's on Court 5."

"Nope, just came to talk to Darren," I said, pointing at the camp director's office.

Darren was on the phone in his windowless office. Piles of dog-eared camp forms and bags of Goldfish cluttered the floor. He held up a finger to let us know he'd be one more minute and gestured for us to sit in the two chairs across from him.

Darren was starting to look his age now—gray at the temples, reading glasses, some pudge under his chin. But back when I was at camp, he'd been the hottest gay man in town. All the Marwood women swooned over his Superman good looks. They competed for him—who could be seen with him the most. Mom had been one of those women, taking him to plays, going out drinking with him and his friends late into the night. But now that Darren had a husband and two kids, those nights didn't happen anymore.

He hung up the phone.

"Macy," he said. "What a sight!" I wondered if he was remembering my last stint at tennis camp, when I'd "acciden-tally" sent a sharp low backhand to Hilary Clement's stom-ach. She deserved it, telling everyone I'd never learned how to smile.

"I *love* your hair," Darren said. I had my dreads held back with a long beaded scarf.

"Thanks," I said. "New look. All good here?"

"You know. Same stuff, different year."

Rebecca got right to the point. "Macy wants the open counselor job."

"Seriously? Here?" Darren said, like he'd just heard a suicide bomber was outside the building.

"I know it's late. I had a job lined up but it fell through at the last minute," I said.

He nodded and cleared his throat.

"Macy will be awesome at it," Rebecca said. "She's really good with kids, and I'll teach her everything she needs to know."

"Macy, really? I never thought you ... liked it here much," Darren said.

He wasn't wrong, though my issue wasn't with the place itself. I'd really just wanted some privacy and there wasn't any. I'd tried to tell Mom that once when I was around seven. I'd promised her that if she'd just let me stay home that one summer, I'd read and be quiet and I wouldn't bother her. That idea didn't fly.

But even with my history with Marwood, I did want the job. Money would get me some freedom from Mom.

"You know what they say," I said. "Shake hands with the past and all?"

"Sure, well, just be sure to use Purell after," he said, chuckling at his own joke. "Alright. A trial week. Let's start with that. Be here at eight on Monday. Rebecca, you'll get Macy caught up on the schedule."

Rebecca clapped her hands.

"Thanks, Darren," I said. "I really appreciate it."

Rebecca was already out the door.

"Macy," Darren said as I was halfway out. "I know you'll do great."

Something about that—his confidence in me—made my heart flutter a little.

"Thanks. I won't let you down."

Later in the afternoon, Rebecca and I shared a large tomato and mushroom pizza at Marcella's. Rebecca justified the pizza when we ordered it—"at least we're not getting pepperoni and sausage."

"I'm assuming you didn't tell your mom about the job?" Rebecca asked.

I looked at her like she was crazy.

"What about your dad?"

I shook my head.

"Why not?"

"He's on his way to Chicago or somewhere."

I'd written Dad an e-mail about the job at Marwood, but he hadn't replied yet.

"Do you think your dad's having an affair?" she asked. My soda went down the wrong pipe and I coughed up a mushroom. Rebecca was never afraid to put things out there.

"No, do you? Maybe that's why Mom's such a bitch all the time. No. I don't think so. Gross. The idea of my parents having sex with each other or anyone else is revolting."

I was sure that Dad wasn't having an affair. Or at least I thought I was sure. Would it make any difference?

"At least I don't have to think about that," Rebecca said. "My mom is definitely not having sex. I don't think she's had a date since Vampire Tom."

We cracked up laughing. Tom had these weird fangy teeth and always drank red Gatorade. One time we teased her mom about Vampire Tom taking a nice juicy taste of her neck. She laughed and told us to shut up, but a few minutes later we caught her checking out a hickey on her neck in the mirror. The relationship was over by the end of the week.

After I dropped Rebecca off, I felt this need for quiet, for peace, so I kept the music off. I thought about writing Sebastian a letter, like the receptionist at the hospital suggested, but I had no idea what I would write.

When I got home, Mom was standing in her usual spot at the kitchen counter eating fat-free plain Greek yogurt.

"Who's Sebastian?" Mom said the second I walked in the door.

"Huh?" Was Mom a mind reader now? Had I said his name aloud?

"There's a message on our voice mail from Sebastian's mother. Who is he?"

I tried to swallow. Why was Sebastian's mother calling me? Was she angry that I'd tried to visit him and meddled in their family business?

I ran to the phone and punched in the codes.

Mom watched me. I turned my back to her.

"Hello, I'm looking for Macy Lyons," the woman's voice said in a thick Spanish accent. "This is Maria Ruiz, Sebastian's mother. I have a letter for you from Sebastian. I have to go to work now, so I will leave the letter at my front door, okay? The address is 433 Pine Street."

Sebastian wrote me a letter. I hung up the phone and turned around.

Mom was right in my face. Her hand was up, and she was about to touch me.

"I just . . ." she said. She put her hand on my head and held one of my dreadlocks between her fingers. "Hmmm. I like it."

"Um, thanks," I said. *That* was not what I was expecting. "I need to go."

I ran for the door.

"Wait!" Mom said. "Who is he?"

"Just someone from school," I said. "He's sick. I was thinking about visiting him in the hospital." It wasn't a lie.

"Oh, that's terrible. Why haven't I heard of him before? What's wrong with him?"

"They don't know yet."

"Well," she said. "Maybe you shouldn't see him in case it's something contagious."

Yeah. Suicidal bacterial infection.

"It's not."

"Hold on a minute." She took her bag from the hook in the mudroom, rummaged for a second, and pulled out some antibacterial gel. "Use it. A lot."

I took it and grabbed the doorknob.

"Oh, I forgot to tell you," she said when I was half out the door. "Scott and Yoli are coming for dinner next Tuesday. Whatever your plans are, you need to be home by six."

I got in my car and slammed the door, but I could still hear Mom as I started the engine.

"Did you hear me, Macy?" she shouted. "Put it in your calendar. Next Tuesday night. Home by six!"

"We'll be home by six!" Mom shouted. She was taking Gavin to speech therapy.

I was seven.

"What'cha reading?" Scott asked after we heard the car leave the driveway. He was fourteen.

"Um, Superfudge," I said.

Scott turned on the TV.

"Okay, Macy, enough reading, this is going to be our secret," he said.

A secret. Hmmmm. I slid a bookmark in my place and put the book down.

"What?" I asked, hoping for something good. Maybe Scott had some of those Hostess pink snowballs. Mom never let me eat junk food. Sometimes Dad would buy me Hostess pink snowballs when he took me to Manhattan. He would let me eat both of them, even though we knew that I'd have a tummy ache for the rest of the day. The pink snowballs were our secret. I never told Mom about the snowballs. I was good at keeping secrets.

"I'm going to teach you about football," Scott said. My face must have looked disappointed because he said, "Hey, football is awesome. You'll be able to impress your boyfriend."

"I don't have a boyfriend." Why would I want a boyfriend? Even though Chris was my friend and he was a boy, I never wanted a boyfriend.

But I was excited about the football lesson. Scott was so cool. He was fourteen. He had tons of friends and was always so busy doing things with them, but when Mom asked him to babysit, he said yes. He said hanging out with me was fun.

I watched the men in helmets and all their giant pads on the screen.

"Am I rooting for the green guys or the red guys?" I asked.

"The green guys. They're the Jets. They're our team."

"Okay," I said.

He started to explain touchdowns and field goals, offense and defense. When he got to downs and yardage, I started yawning.

"Come here," he said.

I drove down Main Street and turned left onto Pine. Number 433 was two blocks down on the right. Sebastian lived right in the center of Mount Kisco, where there were sidewalks, and the houses were small and close together. That's why he'd been able to walk to Rebecca's that night, I realized—he was only a few blocks away from her house. And only a few miles away, on the border of Mount Kisco and Bedford—my neighborhood, if you could call it that—was the opposite with long gated driveways, giant houses with pools, and acres and acres of manicured lawn against wild forests. Even though we were less than an hour away from Manhattan, the historical white houses, wide open spaces, horse farms, and occasional quaint dirt roads made it seem like the city may as well be on another continent.

Sebastian's house was just a house, nothing remarkable about it, but it seemed like a house lived in by people who were good. Small, white, a front porch with two rocking chairs on it. Some neat landscaping and tulips and other colorful flowers coming up, and a flagstone walkway. An envelope was taped to the red door.

I took the porch steps two at a time, the urge to read Sebastian's letter propelling me.

Just as I grabbed the envelope with *Macy Lyons* written across the front in boy handwriting, Sebastian's mom opened the door. Her black hair was short and styled. She was beautiful, even wearing baggy green hospital scrubs.

"Hello, Macy," she said, and I froze, feeling like I'd been caught with my hand in the cookie jar.

"Oh, hi," I said. By the tightness in her lips, I wasn't exactly sure how welcome I was here, even though she'd been the one to ask me to come. I decided to just come clean.

"I'm sorry I went to the hospital. I guess I wasn't really thinking of your family's privacy or anything. I shouldn't have done that," I said without taking a breath. I started twirling a dread and then stopped.

She smiled at me, still tight-lipped, but a smile nonetheless.

"Please sit down," she said, gesturing inside the house. It was bright, and the afternoon sun made the un-air-conditioned living room stifling hot. I picked a green plaid chair that had an afghan draped over it, and Mrs. Ruiz sat on the cream-yellow couch across from me. I could see a clear bin filled with pink toys in the corner of the room—princesses, My Little Ponies, Polly Pocket. Sebastian's sister's toys.

"Okay so, I am going to speak very honest with you," she said. Her Spanish accent was so thick, I knew I'd have to pay close attention to understand everything she said. My hands were clammy. I waited for the lecture to come, for her to tell me to stay the hell out of their business.

"Sebastian will not be happy with me, but it's for his own good," she said.

She stared at the wall for a second, as if she were reconsidering.

"I work so many hours—I don't know who are his friends in school. I know he goes to the parties—and now I know why, because he could find alcohol and drugs—but who knows him, who are his friends, you understand?"

I nodded, but I didn't really understand. I was barely keeping up with deciphering her accent, let alone what she was really trying to say.

"You are his friend?" she asked, staring at me with dark brown eyes not unlike Sebastian's.

I hesitated for a second.

"I guess so," I said. "I don't know."

She seemed to consider this for a minute.

"Then, if not his friend, why did you go to the hospital?"

I felt my face get prickly hot with embarrassment. I took a deep breath.

"Um, when I heard he'd tried to, um, that he was in the hospital, I was upset. I saw him the weekend before. And I felt like . . . was there something he said that I should have noticed? I don't know."

She looked at me, and her eyes were warmer now.

"Oh, no, there was nothing you could do." She paused for a minute. "Macy, I need to know something of you."

"What?" I asked.

"Do you do drugs?"

Now I was really sweating. I wiped my upper lip.

"No," I said. It wasn't *exactly* a lie. I had *tried* some, but there was no reason for her to know that, right?

"Let me explain," she said. "Sebastian is not talking so much in the hospital. He knows you visited, and now he talks more. He is happier, says the doctor. He wrote you a letter." She gestured at the unopened letter clutched in my hand. "I think maybe if you visit him in the hospital, it would help. We visit, but if he has a friend, that might be good."

"Oh," I said, trying to digest. I looked down and started fiddling with the tassels on the afghan, wishing I had a glass of water. My throat felt like it was closing up.

"If you go, I need to make sure that you do not do drugs. Sebastian needs only friends who do not do drugs."

I shook my head, still worried my voice wouldn't work.

"I'm making you uncomfortable," she said.

"No. It's okay."

She looked down at her hands, resting in her lap. She twisted her wedding ring around her finger a few times.

"Everything is uncomfortable. My boy is in the hospital, and I don't know how to help him." Her voice cracked, and her face twisted in sadness. But she immediately pulled herself back together into tough no-nonsense nurse mode.

She looked at her watch.

"I will be late for work," she said. "Please think about visiting him. But you should not feel the pressure."

She stood up, and I immediately stood too, feeling the rush to my head. I put my hand on the arm of the chair to steady myself. Luckily, she was already looking for her bag, getting ready to leave, so she didn't notice. When I felt okay again, I caught up to her at the door. We walked out together.

"I hope you can understand," she said. "I just want to make my son better."

I nodded.

She fished in her bag and handed me a business card. MARIA RUIZ, RN.

"Call me anytime," she said. "I can talk to your mother too, if she has a question."

I nodded, but why would I tell my mother any of this? And then I realized that maybe other people *would* tell their mothers this kind of thing. Chris probably would. Maybe even Rebecca.

She got into her car and drove away. And I was left standing on the porch, Sebastian's unopened letter in one hand, his mother's phone number in the other.

I sat down hard in one of the red rocking chairs and leaned forward, putting my head between my knees. The dizziness still hadn't gone away completely.

I stared at the floorboards of the porch and noticed the little bits of wood that stuck up, waiting to shove splinters in some poor little girl's unsuspecting foot. Then I remembered those agonizing moments when Dad would hold my foot tight and do his tweezer surgery on splinters. I'd scream and carry on even though it didn't hurt that much. It just felt so good to have a real reason to scream and cry. And then the relief when it was over and the comforting hugs and ice cream I'd get afterward.

I sat up slowly, allowing the blood to distribute evenly again. I rocked the chair a few times. Why was I nervous? I *did* want to see Sebastian. Especially now that his mom said I could help him. That should have completely freaked me out and scared me off, but it didn't. The only thing scaring me was that his letter might say the opposite—that he *didn't* want to see me. I turned the envelope over. I felt exposed there on his porch in the middle of town, so I got up and ran to my car. Once I was in and the door was closed, I ripped open the envelope and unfolded three pieces of lined notebook paper inside.

Dear Macy,

I'm in the Psychiatric Ward (they call it Behavioral Health here). I guess you knew that, because I got a message that you came here. I tried to figure out why you came. But then, I really only care that you did. So, now I'm dying to know what you would have said.

I'm sure you want to know why I'm here. No, I didn't try to kill myself. That's probably what people are saying, if they're saying anything. My mom read my journal, and I wrote some pretty bad shit in there. She thought I was suicidal, so she sent me here. The truth is, I don't think I was suicidal, but I am addicted to painkillers, and pretty much anything else I can get. I thought I had it under control, but they've made me admit that I didn't. Before I got here, I'd wake up every morning and say I wouldn't take the pills anymore. And every day I did anyway. And that made me depressed and angry and hate myself for being so weak. And it made me not want to wake up in the morning to have that hopeful feeling again. I disappointed myself fresh every day. So I guess the whole "not wanting to wake up in the morning" thing made my mom think I didn't want to live anymore, which is sort of true if you think about it, but it's not like I had any plans to do anything about it.

This place is exactly how you'd picture it. Some of the people here are really messed up. We're not allowed to have anything, not even combs, because one girl tried to slit her wrists with one. The first few days here without my pills were hell. Anything you can imagine about hell, it was worse. But they're giving me lots of meds to help with that. My roommate is really messed up. He sees things. He'll probably never get out of here. Not everyone is like that, though. Some kids are just going through something they can't really handle on their own.

One thing, though, when I get home, I'll have a collection of pretty funny stories. The other day, this guy Ralph tried to escape. He stripped naked, covered himself with Vaseline, and started running for the door. The staff couldn't catch him because he was so slippery. Finally, someone threw a blanket over him and got him back to his room. The whole scene was pretty hilarious, even the staff guys chasing after him were laughing.

It made me miss home, though, watching Ralph try so hard to get away. I miss my little sister. She thinks I'm at engineering "sleep-away" school.

I think about that night at Rebecca's all the time. I wish I'd stayed and talked with you more. I didn't realize it until I got here. And hearing that you came here made me happier than anything in a long time. I'll probably regret writing that.

You can write me back if you want. They'll open the letter to make sure there are no pills or blades or anything in there, but you can still write whatever you want. I swear they definitely don't do ~~that whole crossing out thing so you can't read what the other person wrote~~. It's not like that at all. ☺

We get phone privileges if we're good, and I've been good. So maybe we can talk at some point.

Sebastian

P.S. Here's a little psych ward humor one of the guys found online. He convinced the staff to let us hang it up in the common room because it's "healthy to laugh at ourselves a little."

PSYCHIATRIC HOSPITAL PHONE MENU

Please select from the following options:

If you are obsessive-compulsive, press 1 repeatedly.

If you are co-dependent, please ask someone to press 2 for you.

If you have multiple personalities, press 3, 4, 5, and 6.

If you are paranoid, we know who you are and what you want, stay on the line so we can trace your call.

If you are schizophrenic, listen carefully and a little voice will tell you which number to press.

P.P.S. Here's that eye you liked—the one that's always watching over you. And also a picture of my giant muscles to protect you when you're in danger.

I stared at the eye—the same one I'd seen doodled on his shoe. Below it was a cartoonish drawing of a giant bicep sticking straight up from a ridiculously skinny arm. Next to that he'd written, *I've been working out.* I smiled, surprised at his ability to keep his sense of humor in there. I took a deep breath, trying to process it all. I folded the letter carefully.

I grabbed my math notebook that was still on the floor of the car, ripped out a piece of graph paper, and started writing.

Sebastian,

I'm glad killing yourself wasn't on your agenda, but it sucks that you're there (understatement? I have no idea what to say here). I'm sorry I stormed over to hospital. When I heard you were there, I kind of freaked out. I couldn't stop thinking about that night either. I wish you'd stayed to talk more, too. What were you going to say before you left?

I realized I'd been holding my breath. I let it out; knowing I was insane and completely lacking impulse control, I just kept writing.

We don't really know each other, but I'm here for you if you need me. Really.

Macy

P.S. Your mom said that if you wanted me to visit, she could put me on your list. Do you want me to come?

I folded the paper sloppily, stuffed it in the envelope, crossed out *Macy Lyons* and wrote *Sebastian Ruiz* on it. I ran back up to the porch and slipped it through their mail slot, my heart pounding, my brain swimming. Exposed.

CHAPTER FIVE

My stomach wouldn't shut up as I drove to the hospital. I was so nervous, I couldn't even look at the scrambled eggs and fruit salad Mom had made, let alone eat.

When Mom asked me where I was going, I'd quickly said the library with some overdue books, so then I ran back upstairs to grab a stack of books which were, in fact, overdue. One of the novels had a picture of Earth on the front and it reminded me of the solar system book Sebastian had with him that day under my oak tree. I'd asked Mom to get it for me after that day and I'd read it cover to cover, remembering what he'd said about things looking one way but acting another. All of the solar system books we owned were in Gavin's room due to his short-lived obsession with Mercury in middle school, so I ran in and found the book on his bottom shelf. I flipped through it, ripped out the poster stapled inside, and ran to my car.

So here I was again, sitting in my car in the hospital parking lot. And this time I knew that I was actually going to see Sebastian. I had no idea what to say to him. Now the poster seemed like a stupid idea, but if nothing else it would give us something to talk about.

I went through the automatic doors, straight to the elevators, and pushed the button for the fourth floor. I pressed my hand to the cold mirror on the elevator wall, took my hand away, and watched as my fingerprint slowly disappeared.

The doors opened and I walked up to the desk where the same receptionist from the other day sat.

"May I help you?" she asked.

"I'm here to visit Sebastian Ruiz. I have permission this time."

She looked at me closely.

"I was here the other day. I wasn't on his visitor list, but now I am." I said this matter-of-factly, to convince myself as much as her.

"Oh, okay," she said, nodding. "What's your name?"

"Macy Lyons."

"Yes," she said. "Here we go. And your code?"

I'd tried to memorize the code that Sebastian's mom gave me so I could prove I was me. But of course I'd forgotten it. I took out my phone and found her most recent text with instructions and read off the code.

The receptionist picked up the phone, told someone I was here, and repeated my code to them. Then she hung up.

"You can have a seat," she said. "A nurse will come to get you soon."

"Thanks."

I sat down, staring at my chipped fingernails, trying not to pull at my dreads. The second hand on the school-style clock hanging above me tick-ticked quietly. I heard some muffled voices through the doors—laughter, some carts being wheeled, doors closing.

Suddenly my phone rang. Loud. The receptionist raised her eyebrow at me. It was Rebecca. I quickly tried to press the DECLINE button, but I accidentally hit ANSWER.

"Damn," I said.

"Nice to hear your voice too," Rebecca said.

"I can't talk," I whispered into the phone.

"Where are you?" she whispered back, mimicking me.

"I'll tell you later."

"Tell me now," she said.

The double doors that led to the actual psych ward swung open, and a petite black woman, a little younger than Mom, strode through like she meant business. She looked around, and her eyes settled on me.

"Later," I whispered into the phone, pressed END and turned the ringer off.

"Are you Macy?" the woman asked.

I nodded.

"Alright," she said, plopping herself on the chair next to me. She sighed, like it was the first time she'd sat all day. She was wearing one of those doctorly white jackets over jeans and a blue shirt. "I'm Rashanna. It's good you came, but I don't want any monkey business. You understand?"

Holy tough-ass. Wait. Monkey business? What?

"No smuggling anything in here, no touching inappropriately, etcetera, etcetera. Did you bring him anything?" she asked, a little more gently.

"Just this," I said, showing her the poster. "It's—it's just a—I don't have to give it to him. It was just a last-minute thing."

She smiled. "No, that's fine. That's nice."

"And, um," I said. "Sebastian and I are just friends, so there won't be any . . . you know."

She laughed. "Good enough."

Even though her voice was tough, her eyes weren't—they were light and sweet, like honey. I immediately felt more comfortable.

"Put your things in here," she said, opening a small locker. I shoved my bag into the locker.

"Phone too," she said. Then she closed the locker and pocketed the key. I felt naked without my stuff.

"Come on," she said quietly. "Let's go see Sebastian."

She took my wrist in her hand, which was dry and cracked, probably from washing it a thousand times a day.

She let go then and walked toward the double doors. She flicked her badge in front of the sensor and pushed the doors open.

I followed her, watching the white jacket swish back and forth as she walked. She led me past some offices with closed doors, a room labeled ACTIVITIES ROOM, an open nurses station, a small staff kitchen, and a room called the COMMUNITY ROOM where I could see kids sitting through the glass door.

The room was big, with a TV, a couple of orange and green couches that looked like relics from the eighties, and some folding chairs. A pale girl, who must have weighed about eighty-three pounds with long stringy reddish hair, and her opposite—a huge guy in denim overalls—played checkers at a small folding table. A short, blond guy sat on the large window ledge writing in a journal. Another guy and girl watched a game show. Other than the super skinny girl, they all looked pretty normal, like regular bored kids. I'd pictured goth-looking creatures with piercings and cuts all up and down their arms, straitjackets, around-the-clock group therapy, and cell-like rooms. I hadn't thought of them playing games, watching TV, just hanging out.

"Here we are," she said, as she gestured to a small room next to the community room. "The visitor meeting room."

I stood outside the doorway. Sebastian sat inside the room on a wooden chair with nubby lime-green upholstery, staring out the window. He was wearing all gray—gray sweatpants, a gray T-shirt. His skin looked gray too. Like he'd been stained to match his clothes. If possible, he looked skinnier, his wrists bonier, his arms longer. His hair had grown out since I'd seen him at Rebecca's. Instead of his usual buzz cut, there was an inch or so of fuzz.

Sebastian looked up then and saw me. For a second, he looked at me the same way he had on Rebecca's porch. Intensely.

"Look what the cat dragged in," Rashanna said, walking over to him. I followed, my heart in my throat.

Sebastian smiled at me, but his eyes had dulled.

"Hi," he said.

"Hi," I said.

Rashanna gestured for me to sit across from him. Other than a small square table, there were two chairs—one was all wood and one had a sun-bleached red vinyl-looking seat. I chose the all-wood chair.

"I'll be back in fifteen minutes," she said. Then she fake-glared at Sebastian. "I expect you to open that mouth of yours and make words come out."

She walked away and, through the window to the hall, I could see her stop briefly to talk to the emaciated girl who'd come out of the community room.

"That's Jodi. She's anorexic," Sebastian said.

"Yeah, I figured." I leaned my elbows on the table.

"They have to write down everything she eats." He looked out the window.

"Which one is your roommate?" I asked, beginning to regret coming. He didn't seem to want me here.

"Short blond kid," he said. "Probably writing in his notebook."

Finally he looked at me again. Now his eyes were hollow, worn-out, and there was no shine to them. It was like he'd used up all his energy in that first look he'd given me.

"So, how are you?" he asked.

"Me?"

"Yeah, you. How are you?"

I laughed awkwardly. "I'm doing fine. How are you?"

"Great, really great. An all-inclusive vacation. I ring a bell and get everything I could ever hope for—a glass of water, a thousand pills, some prying into my head. Sometimes I even get an extra cookie at lunch."

I didn't know how to react to his sarcasm.

"It sucks," he said. "I can't do anything but sit around and think."

"And that's exactly what you *hate* doing, right?"

He smiled. "You remember."

"I remember everything about that night," I said, and then I realized how that sounded—like I was obsessed. "I mean, I keep thinking about if things could have been different."

"What do you mean, different?"

"Like, if I could have done something," I said.

He shook his head. "No, no way. I hate the idea that you would feel any responsibility."

I stared at his fingers, which seemed impossibly long. I noticed a few scars on the knuckles of his right hand, and I wondered what they were from.

He shook his head and looked down at his fingers, too, flexing them.

"It's okay," I said. "As long as you say I'm responsibility-free, then we're good."

"Oh, see that girl?" he whispered loudly. I turned and looked out the glass door. A disheveled girl with greasy brown hair and too-tight sweatpants walked by with a watering can.

"That's Lindsay. She's our resident green thumb. She waters the plants every day," he said.

"That's nice," I said, wondering why he was telling me this.

"All the plants are plastic," he said, and smiled, so I did too.

"Does she know?"

"If she does, she won't admit it. I think the job makes her feel important. But it's kind of funny to see Rashanna scooping the water out of those plastic plants every day when she's not looking."

"That *is* pretty funny," I said, and I liked that Rashanna let her keep doing it.

"Sometimes," Sebastian said quietly, "I think about that night, and I wish I'd gotten a ride with you instead of leaving like I did. I think maybe then we could have kept talking and I wouldn't have felt so alone. Then I wouldn't have written that stupid shit I wrote in my journal that made me more depressed and I wouldn't have taken that extra pill that made me crash before I had the chance to put my journal away so that when my mom came in the morning to wake me up, she wouldn't have seen my journal all open on the bed and then she wouldn't have read it . . . and then I wouldn't be here."

"Wow," I said. "That's a lot of thinking."

He laughed a little. Even though he looked like hell, when he laughed, his cuteness came all the way through. His dark brown eyes lit up, and his eyelashes cast a shadow underneath. His mouth stretched wide. And with his light brown skin and the glasses and the fuzzy hair and the tall thin body, it was all good.

He caught me looking.

"Something's different," he said, staring at me.

"The dreadlocks," I said, suddenly self-conscious.

I had a scarf wrapped around like a headband, so you could only see the dreads coming out the back. I pulled a few out to show him.

"Cool," he said, and then he looked out the window, like he couldn't focus anymore. I swallowed my hurt pride at his lack of interest in my dreads, which I pretty much attributed to our talk that night.

"Tell me what's going on out there. Tell me about the last week of school. What did I miss? Don't leave anything out."

He looked at me anxiously. I hadn't thought of Sebastian as someone who'd be hungry for gossip, but a starving man would eat dog food without a second thought. I'd give him whatever I could.

"Okay," I said. "So . . . okay, the biggest thing, other than of course the rumors about you and where you were—"

"There were rumors about me?" He seemed curious, not mad.

"Oh yeah. Of course. Everyone knew you were gone, but no one knew where you went. Seriously, why didn't anyone know? That was weird."

"I keep to myself mostly," he said.

"But I figured *someone* would know. I asked around. No one really knew."

He smiled flirtatiously. "You asked around about me?"

"Just a concerned citizen," I said, unable to contain my own flirtatious smile.

"Okay," he said. "So, other than the kid trying to off himself—which, by the way, I didn't—what was the big news?"

Sebastian was smiling. His eyes were shining. I was helping.

"Okay," I said. "So, you know Mrs. Levin?"

"The guidance counselor? I do. I have been known to need some guidance every now and again."

I laughed and continued. "So, this sophomore kid, Clay Bennington—do you know him?"

Sebastian shook his head.

"Me neither. But anyway, he drove off campus totally without signing out or anything and went to Starbucks, and while he was parking, he saw Mrs. Levin sitting in her car. He was afraid he'd get caught, so he scrunched down in his car and kept waiting for her to leave, so he could get his coffee or whatever. But suddenly, Mrs. Kamitzky drives up and parks—"

"The bio teacher?" Sebastian asked.

"Yeah, the bio teacher. She walks up to Mrs. Levin's car, gets in, and they start making out."

"No!" Sebastian said, exaggerated astonishment on his face.

"I swear." I laughed. "Like full-on groping and all. And so Clay Benington hightails it out of there and goes running through the halls like a maniac telling everyone."

Sebastian laughed. And then he stopped and suddenly his face had a greenish tint to it, and he looked like he was in pain.

"Are you okay?" I asked.

He got up and ran to the trash can and started throwing up. Huge, loud heaves.

"Oh my god," I said. "Are you okay?"

I went to him and put my hand on his back. He was still throwing up, and I could feel his back convulsing with every heave. I willed myself not to throw up with him.

"Hold on," I said. "I'll get the nurse."

I ran to the door.

"Rashanna? Hello? Anyone?" My voice sounded small and mousy in the hallway.

Rashanna came immediately. Her face looked concerned when she saw me.

"What is it?" she said.

"Sebastian's sick. He's throwing up."

When Rashanna got to the room, Sebastian still had his hands on the trash can, but he seemed to be finished vomiting.

"Come on, let's get you lying down," she said, her voice quiet and soothing. "Back to your room now."

Sebastian started to walk, with Rashanna's hand firmly on the small of his back. He towered over her, but she was clearly the one in charge. I followed them.

Rashanna looked back at me, like she'd just remembered I was there. "Sebastian needs to rest now."

"Is it okay if she comes to the room?" he asked.

"Next time. I want you to rest some now," she said.

He looked at me and shrugged. "Thanks for coming."

"Oh," I said. "I forgot to give you this." I shoved the poster at him. He unfolded it, turned it around. I could see the crease marks and the little holes from the staples where it had been fastened in the book.

"It's—"

"The solar system," he said. "I remember. The book I was reading that summer."

"Yeah." I looked down at my hands. He was studying the planets on the poster. "I ended up buying the book and it came with this, so . . . it makes sense you should have it."

He smiled now. A real, full smile with deep dimples in each cheek. A smile that took my breath away.

Rashanna stood back and stared at him.

"Whoa. You be careful where you point that smile, my boy," she said. "That's powerful. You know, that's the first time I've seen that thing?" She looked at me now, and her honey-brown eyes could've lit up a small town.

"Sebastian, go freshen up and then head to your room. I'll walk you out, Macy," Rashanna said, her bossy self again.

"Bye," I said to Sebastian.

"Bye."

Sebastian ducked into the men's room and I walked with Rashanna down the corridor. The whole time she was shaking her head and clucking her tongue.

She used her badge to open the doors to reception.

"You should come back if you can," she said. "He wasn't really feeling great today. I wanted to tell his mom another day would've been better, but he was insistent."

"I'll come back if he wants me to," I said.

She nodded as she opened the locker and gave me my bag.

"Tell him I hope he feels better," I said, and then realized how dumb that sounded. "I mean his stomach. Whatever. You don't have to tell him anything."

She smiled. "I'll tell him."

She turned, and the doors closed behind her. I pushed the elevator button and waited, listening to the click of the receptionist's nails typing on her keyboard.

When I got outside, I breathed in the air and blew out the stale hospital smell that seemed like it was stuck in my nostrils.

I sat in my car and pulled out my phone. Another call from Rebecca. One from Chris. A text from Jasmine, one of the drama club girls, asking if I had a red scarf she could borrow for an audition. And a text from Mom asking if I would please pick up her dry cleaning while I was in town. And one from Scott.

SCOTT: Hey. Sorry bout Nantucket, kid. Heard ur way bummed. I'm such a fuck-up, huh? At least I must make you look good, tho!

I dropped my forehead onto the steering wheel and tried to massage out an ache that seemed like it would never go away.

CHAPTER SIX

At seven thirty on Monday morning, I grabbed a handful of M&Ms from the antique Chinese urn in the living room, which happened to be Mom's secret chocolate-fix stash. Gavin was still asleep. He'd sleep until ten. I thought Mom had already gone to her spinning or Zumba or whatever brand of torture she'd chosen for the morning, but she was still in the garage when I got to my car. She was decked out in a ridiculously expensive black and pink gym outfit—black sneakers, her hair in a perfect blond ponytail.

"Where are you off to so early?" she asked, eying my very short cut-offs, flip-flops, loosely held-back dreadlocks, and the breakfast M&Ms halfway up to my mouth. Damn, I hated being caught in the act.

"I got a job," I said. We both got in our cars, so now we were talking through the windows. Ridiculous.

"Really?" she asked.

"Yeah, Mom, really."

"No need to give me attitude, Macy. Can't we ever have one simple, easy conversation?"

"Sure," I said. "When? Now?"

"That would be nice. Where will you be working?"

"I will be working as a camp counselor at Marwood Club," I said with the fakest polite smile I could manage.

"Really?" I couldn't read what was in the "really"—pleasant surprise that I got a job there or skeptical surprise that I could get a job there?

"Well, how did you get it? Did you talk to Darren?"

"Of course I talked to Darren. He gave me the job." Mom had the look of a woman betrayed. It's not like she and Darren still hung out. But apparently, women like Mom get extra territorial over their gay male friends.

"I didn't know you were interested in working with children, particularly at Marwood," she said softly.

"Well, since you cancelled Nantucket, I figured I should have *something* to do."

"That's great, Macy. I'm proud of you for taking initiative. What time do you finish up? Do you want to meet up at the café after?"

How to play this? She was being nice. I could try to be nice too.

"Sorry, Mom, I can't. I promised Rebecca I'd check out Juice Paradise with her."

"Oh, Rebecca and her diets," she said.

"Yeah. I'll see you there, I guess," I said. Mom started backing out at the same time as me. We both stopped at the same time. We both laughed, awkwardly.

"You go first," she said.

"Okay." Was she just being polite or did she want to judge my driving? I did a perfect backward three-point turn and waited for the automatic gate at the end of the driveway to open. I waved in my rearview mirror as she came up behind me.

She honked then and got out of her car. Now what? She trotted over to me and leaned into my window.

"Did Scotty get in touch with you?" she asked. "He felt so bad about our trip getting cancelled, and he wanted to talk to you about it."

"Yeah, he texted me."

I should have known she'd put him up to that text.

"Don't forget he and Yoli are coming for dinner tomorrow night," Mom said. Yoli was a big shot gallery owner in Chelsea. She was exotic, model-gorgeous, brilliant, a Harvard grad, blah blah blah. Even *I* could have fallen in love with her.

"Mom, I can't. I have plans," I lied.

"Six o'clock," she said.

I smacked the steering wheel hard and started driving. She got back in her car and followed me the whole way to the Club. As an employee, I had to park way down the road and walk. She waved and tooted her horn as she drove past me toward a primo spot in the front of the Club. When I knew she couldn't see me, I gave her the finger.

"I can't believe you're here. I really can't believe it," Rebecca said as she struggled to put socks on a little boy's wet feet. We were at the kiddie pool, finishing up free swim. Most of the kids couldn't really dress themselves, so we were getting them ready to go to story time. I was helping Darren's daughter, Avery, pull on her shorts. She grabbed me around my head as I pulled them up.

"Macy?" Avery said, touching my dreads. "Your hair is so beautiful." I thought of Sebastian. Did he think my dreads were beautiful? He'd noticed them, but barely.

"Thanks, Avery," I said. At drop-off in the morning, Avery had clung to Darren, crying, so I'd promised to take extra special care of her. I was surprised by how much I liked her. I had no idea that four-year-olds said such funny shit all the time. Like this little boy Gabe said, "Guess what? Yesterday night my mom farted in the bathtub and it made gigantic bubbles." They're just like these miniature people who think they know everything, which sounds annoying but is actually pretty cute when coming from a squeaky-voiced mini-human.

When all the kids were dressed, they put on their backpacks and marched to the giant shady tree for story time. Once they were settled on the grass, eating their goldfish and animal crackers, we got to sit and relax, but Avery made sure she sat right next to me.

I watched the bigger kids, they were probably nine or ten, on the tennis court, drilling. Running forehands and backhands. Watching them brought me right back to being there, those long days of tennis camp. The strong rubber smell of tennis balls, the heat from the court searing the bottoms of my feet, even through my tennis shoes. The *thwack thwack* sound, bits of ball fuzz flying. I was nine again.

I'd been at tennis camp all day, but now I was lying on my bed reading. I was still wearing my tennis shorts. I smelled like dirt and sweat, and my hands were sticky from the racquet grip. I was procrastinating taking a shower because I was at a really good part in my book—the main character was just about to solve the murder mystery. Before I could get to the best part, Scotty came into my room. Part of me really wanted to tell him I was busy, that I was reading a really good book. But the other part of me was so excited that he'd come into my room. To be with me. He was sixteen. Normally, I didn't get much more than a "Hey, what's up?" from him, but when he came to my room, he wanted to be with me.

"What'cha reading?" he asked.

I shrugged, holding the book up. By now, I knew he didn't really care what I was reading.

"Where's Deb?" he asked. Scott always called Mom Deb, even though she was practically his mother. I guessed it would be weird if he started calling her Mom, since he had a mom, even if he hardly ever saw her and he called her Judy anyway.

"She went to the Club."

"She leaves you home alone now?" he asked.

I shrugged. "I'm responsible."

"Where's Gav?" he said.

"Jonathan's."

"Do you want to hang out?" he asked, still standing in the doorway. It was what he always said when he wanted to do something. I was tired. I'd spent all day at Marwood with dumb catty girls who just wanted to talk about their crushes on boys and their new nail polish. I didn't have crushes on boys. I didn't wear nail polish. I wanted to read, to be in someone else's world. I just wanted to be alone.

But again, it was Scott.

"Okay," I said. He closed the door and sat on the edge of my bed. I folded down the corner of my page.

I'd done everything wrong that day, and I'd felt so completely useless.

I cursed Sebastian under my breath for making me think about this stuff. With my legs stretched out in front of me,

I felt grass prickle the backs of my thighs. I focused on the little kids—most of them couldn't sit still even though they were captivated by Miss Liz's silly version of *Little Red Riding Hood*. I watched Avery's face change from glee to fear as the Big Bad Wolf showed up. And then the craziest thing happened. Without even hesitating, Avery climbed onto my lap and pulled my arms around her as if it were the most natural thing in the world.

At twelve o'clock, the parents and nannies came to pick up the kids from camp. Avery ran into Darren's arms. He looked exhausted, holding the baby, carrying a diaper bag and now Avery's backpack.

"My mother-in-law bailed on me again," he said. "She has no idea what a pain in the you-know-what this is for me. Now I have to put them in the nursery here. They hate that."

"Can't blame 'em," I said.

"I guess you'd know, huh?" Darren said. "How'd she do?"

"She did great. She took a little while to warm up, but then she had a good time. She didn't want to go in the big pool, only the kiddie pool."

Darren sighed, exasperated. Being a pool hater myself, I said, "Swimming isn't all it's cracked up to be."

"I know," he said. "But Kevin was the captain of his college swim team, and you know, the pressure!" At this point, Avery was pulling him by the arm and yelling, "Come onnn, Daddy! I wanna go home now!" I was glad to get off the swimming topic. "Bye, Avery," I said. "See you tomorrow."

"Bye," she said.

Darren looked at me curiously. "Do you babysit?"

"Um . . ." It was an interesting question. *Do* I? No. *Would* I? Sure. It would mean more money I'd use when and if I ever got into Berkeley. It would mean I wouldn't have to be home with Mom so much this summer. And I imagined that hanging out with Avery wouldn't be so bad either.

"Sure," I said.

"I'm dying here," he said as the baby pulled his sunglasses off and jabbed him in the cheek with them. "Maybe a couple of afternoons a week? Just so I can finish stuff up here."

"Yeah, sure."

He put his hand under my chin. "You're a good girl, Miss Macy. Oh, I know you pretend with the hair and the sarcasm. But you are just so good."

I couldn't help smiling. "Don't tell anyone. I have an image to protect."

Darren finally gave in to Avery's tugging and turned toward the nursery, waving backwards at me.

Once all the kids were picked up, Rebecca draped her arm over my shoulder.

"Let's do a last meal lunch before Juice Paradise."

"Okay," I said, reluctantly. I wanted to sit underneath my oak tree and reread Sebastian's letter and remember my visit with him. But making excuses to Rebecca was often more trouble than it was worth, so I agreed to eat.

We went to the outdoor snack bar and ordered burgers and fries. I signed it all to my mom's account number and then we found a table.

"There's your mom," she whispered. Out of the corner of my eye, I saw her walking from the tennis courts to the main building, her blond ponytail swinging, her toned legs brown underneath her bright white tennis skirt. Evidently, she'd gone straight from cardio to tennis. Her face was tight and her eyes were far away. Even though she wasn't looking in our direction, I ducked.

"Jeez," Rebecca said. "This is going to be a long summer."

"No, it's not that bad. Just weird, I guess. She was actually pretty cool this morning when I told her I'd be working here."

"So you told her?"

"Only out of necessity. We were leaving the house at the same time."

My phone buzzed with a text.

CHRIS: Hey what's up?

"Who's that?" Rebecca said.

"Chris. He started at his dad's law firm."

My phone buzzed again.

CHRIS: U there? I'm bored.

"So," she said. "When are you going to tell me where you were yesterday?"

I wasn't going to keep my visit to Sebastian a secret. I didn't have anything to hide.

"I visited Sebastian at the hospital."

"Um, *that* is not what I was expecting you to say. And why in the world did you do that?"

I knew she'd have a dramatic reaction. Drama was what she did best.

"Take it down a notch," I said. "This is serious."

"Okay . . ." she said, drawing out the *ay*.

"Remember I talked to him at your house that night? And then he went straight to the hospital the next day, so I thought maybe I—I don't know. Anyway, his mom put me on his visitor list, so I went. It was weird. I mean, have you ever been to one of those places? It was bizarre. Depressing. He didn't try to kill himself, by the way. He's just depressed and he's an addict. I'm not sure if I'm allowed to tell you that. Maybe I shouldn't have."

"Oh my god," she said. "Can I talk?"

I nodded.

"What the hell?" she said. "This is the first I'm hearing about this? You're freaking me out. Who is this guy? Do you even know anything about him?"

"It's Sebastian Ruiz, Beck. We go to school with him. He's in my English class."

She shook her head.

"I don't think so, Mace. I don't think you need this. This sounds big. I mean . . . this guy's in the psych ward. He's like, mentally fucked up. No. Not good."

"Excuse me?" I said. Rebecca hadn't ever really talked to me like that before.

"That didn't come out right," she said. "I just don't understand why you would want to take that on. I mean, if it were me or Chris in the psych ward, that would be one thing. But you don't even know this guy."

She looked up at me and her eyes looked hurt.

"What's happening here?" I asked. "Are you jealous?"

"No!" she said. "It's not that. It's just scary. Too real and like, so big. Jordan had a girlfriend once—she was really unstable, and she ended up killing herself. I mean, it was way after they broke up, but still. I don't want you to get hurt." Jordan was Rebecca's second oldest brother.

"It was just one visit. It's okay. Don't worry."

She wasn't completely wrong. I didn't know how stable Sebastian was. And I didn't know how much I could handle. But it was the *real* that made me know it wasn't just one visit. I knew I'd go back.

"So, what's the deal with Juice Paradise?" I asked, desperate to change the subject.

"I don't know," she said, frowning slightly. I could tell she was trying to decide whether to let me out of this conversation.

"Let's blow it off," I said. "You don't need it."

"Hollywood, Macy. Hollywood does not tolerate fat girls." And with that, I knew she had let Sebastian go. For now.

"You don't have an ounce of fat on you, Beck."

"I am not skinny," she said as our burgers arrived, dripping with grease, the plates spilling over with perfect McDonald's-look-alike fries. "Not skinny enough for Hollywood." She stuck a fry in her mouth. "Yum! This is the best last meal ever!" This was probably our tenth "last meal" together.

CHRIS: U there?

"Just text him back," she said.

"Fine."

ME: Hey. @ Marwood still. Lunch w R.
CHRIS: How was 1st day?
ME: Not too bad.
CHRIS: Hope kids didn't tire u out too much for tonite. ;)

Instinctively, I grimaced. I didn't want the flashbacks, the stuff with Sebastian to affect things with Chris. I wanted to still be a make-believe normal girlfriend. Everything had been headed on the track to just fine.

ME: Not sure yet bout tonite.
CHRIS: LMK. Say hi to R.

"He says hi," I said to Rebecca, putting the phone down.

"Hi," she said, her mouth full of fries. "You going to tell him about Sebastian?"

"Why wouldn't I?" But I hadn't thought about it before that moment.

I should have thought about it. Chris was my boyfriend. He had been for six months. Even though it wasn't something I'd been looking for, I *had* said yes, and now I had to live with it, because the alternative meant losing him, and I had never lived without Chris in my life.

When we were eight, Chris and I created a short-cut through the woods behind our houses. By zigzagging through the tangle of trees and thorns, we shaved minutes off our time to get to each other, which meant more time to play knights and ride our bikes. By sixth grade, we'd worn a pretty good path through the woods and had erected a decent fort with a tree branch roof where we could sit and pretend we were cool. We'd never shared our fort with anyone. It was just for us.

Our fort had always been our place for friendship and talking and games. But six months ago, things changed. It was December, a clear night, not too cold. Neither of us had been ready for the night to end after one of Rebecca's bigger Saturday night parties, so we agreed to check in for our curfews and then sneak out to our fort. We each brought a couple of beers. We were lounging around, rehashing the party, giving odds on how long it would be until Cody realized Rebecca was totally in love with him.

"I saw you hanging out with Cameron Levinsky," Chris said suddenly, fiddling with a bottle cap.

"Mm-hm," I said, taking a swig of my beer, letting the bubbles tickle my throat. I'd hooked up with Cameron that night. We'd found our way into one of the bedrooms and had very quick, mediocre sex. I'd had sex with him before once or twice. He was a decent guy.

Chris took a deep breath and let it out slowly.

"Why do you screw all those losers?" he asked.

My body tensed. "I'm not sure I understand the question, Chris." I was ready to get up and walk away. And he knew it.

"I mean, you let these guys take advantage of you, and you are so much more than they are."

"Who says they're taking advantage of me?"

"Well, aren't they?" he asked.

"No."

"It just seems like you pick these guys who are totally not interested in a relationship. What do you get out of it?"

"Sex," I said.

"Don't you want more?"

"No." Sex was what I was good at. Sex was where the high was. That first moment when I knew a guy wanted me made me feel powerful and special. Even if it was only for a few minutes and then it all sucked after that, it was worth it. What was the point of being with the same person all the time? Once that moment was over, the power was gone, that feeling of being special was gone. Who needed that?

"Even with the right guy? You wouldn't want more?"

"No," I said.

"Are you sure?" he asked. And then I got where he was going. And I knew that once he said something, there would be no turning back. I wanted to stop him, but I froze, and he kept talking. "Even if that person were say, I don't know, maybe, *me*? You wouldn't want something more?"

I laughed because I was nervous. I really didn't mean to laugh. It was just what came out of my mouth.

"Screw you, Macy," he said. He sprang to his feet and got about ten yards away before I even registered that he was leaving.

"Wait," I said. "At least help me clean up before you go."

He came back, swiping at beer bottles and caps, sticking them in his pockets.

"I shouldn't have laughed," I said. "I didn't know you felt that way."

"Of course I do. We're not kids anymore, Macy. We're together all the time; we like hanging out; everyone thinks we're together anyway."

"So we should go out because everyone assumes we already are?" I asked.

Why *hadn't* I thought of Chris as an option? Because Chris didn't fit my mold. He didn't just want sex. Chris was a good guy. He was relationship material. I'd always pictured him with some cute brunette with a neat ponytail and a perfect smile who was on the yearbook committee and would hang on his every word. I'd never pictured him with me. I was not relationship material. I was not a good guy's girlfriend.

"No . . ." he said, like I was an idiot. "Not because everyone assumes we already are. But maybe we should try it because we want to."

"How would that even work? What if it didn't work? Then we would lose our friendship," I said. I was warming up to the idea because I was starting to get that feeling: Chris wanted me and it felt good.

"We have to set ground rules. We have to be honest. And we have to promise no hard feelings if it doesn't work."

I let that sink in. But then a thought crossed my mind.

"Chris. Do you just want to get in my pants? Because you could've just asked. I'd be up for that. You don't have to sugarcoat it with the whole 'make an honest woman out of me' thing."

He picked up the battery-operated lantern we had for our night visits and held it up to look at me closely, searching my eyes for something.

"You're serious, aren't you?" he asked.

I thought it was a rhetorical question.

"Are you, Macy? Are you serious? I can't tell."

"Yes," I said, looking down at my feet.

"You are so fucked up."

"Thanks," I said.

"Look. I'd rather hang out with you than with anyone else. Plus, you're hot. I think about you naked all the time. You've never thought about me that way? Never ever?"

Of course I'd thought about sex with Chris. Many, many times. With his soft blond hair, bright blue eyes, chiseled features, and built chest and shoulders, there was no question he was hot. But he was Chris. And sex with Chris would mean having a real relationship. And I had never thought of having a real relationship with him, or anyone else, for that matter.

"Well, maybe not never *ever*, but I didn't think it was cool, thinking about having sex with your best friend."

"Maybe what they say is true," he said. "Maybe guys and girls can't really be friends."

He put the lantern down, moved closer to me until we were only a few inches apart, and put his hands on my waist.

"Wait, so this is happening?" I asked. "Like, now?"

He pulled away.

"Only if you want to," he said. "I don't want to twist your arm or anything."

"Okay. But serious rules. I don't want to tell anyone for a while. Until we figure out if it works."

"Got it." He pulled me to him. "Is this okay?"

I nodded. He kissed me. Once, like a peck. I giggled. Then he pressed his lips on mine and started really kissing me. I cleared my mind and kissed him back. It felt good. And then I remembered it was Chris. I giggled again.

"Is it too weird?" he asked, his forehead against mine.

"I don't think so. Is it for you?"

"It's amazing," he said. "I could do this all night."

We kissed again. I reached for the button of his jeans.

"Whoa." He took my hand. "What's the rush?"

"No rush," I said, and we kept kissing. But sex was always a rush with me. Trying to get it done before getting caught in a bedroom at a party, the woods, the backseat of a car, a bathroom with a long line.

For a second, I wondered if he was stopping because he didn't really want me enough. That he'd come to his senses and realized I was not girlfriend material. But he kept kissing me and telling me how happy he was, so I had to believe him. I vowed I would let Chris slow me down. I would let him teach me to take my time.

We didn't have sex that night, or the next or the next. It was two weeks before Chris finally allowed it. And even though we eventually came clean about being a couple, I was totally opposed to PDA, so we *never* kissed in public.

Fast-forward six months, and nothing much had changed. Chris was still my boyfriend. I missed the thrill of a new conquest occasionally, but Chris almost made up for it with his enthusiasm. Every now and then, I'd have eye contact with some guy at a party—someone I'd hooked up with before or maybe not—and for a moment I'd feel that tingling, the anticipation of possibility. And then, after a few minutes, I'd remember that sometimes Chris made me feel like the most important person in the world. And the idea of betraying him would make me clutch my heart as if it were breaking.

But since that Saturday on Rebecca's porch with Sebastian, I was feeling that anticipation of possibility again, and this time, nothing could make it go away.

After Juice Paradise, I dropped Rebecca off at her house.

"Thanks for coming," she said, glumly.

"Sorry, Beck." The juice regimen was way too expensive—you had to pay to join and then pay each day for the six disgusting juices they'd give you.

"I just wish I hadn't eaten that burger now."

"Beck, you're going to drive yourself crazy. You loved the shit out of that burger." My fingers itched to put the car in gear and get home to my tree.

Rebecca gathered her things and looked at me curiously.

"Aren't you coming in?" she asked.

"No, I'm gonna head home."

"Come on," she said. "Jordan just forwarded me a bunch of stupid videos. You can't make me watch them alone." She looked at her phone. "He says 'I peed in my pants, then died. Can't miss these, sis.'"

"Sounds promising," I said. "Tomorrow."

She looked at me with her pouty lips and sad eyes— the look she always gave me when I wouldn't do what she wanted. I was so susceptible to those damn, lonely, pathetic, sad eyes, but I stayed strong.

"Too bad the juice place blows," I said. "I saw something about that Master Cleanse diet all the starlets are doing. You make the nasty shit yourself. I'm on the case."

"Okay," she said. I waved as I drove away, and she walked slowly up the porch stairs to her empty house. I headed toward home where I could think about Sebastian under the quiet of my oak tree.

CHAPTER SEVEN

The breeze was warm in my hair, and the trunk of my oak tree was rough against the back of my neck, but I liked being able to feel it. I pictured sitting with Sebastian on the porch swing again, and in my fantasy, he'd take my hand and I'd put my head on his shoulder, and we would swing back and forth in silence. I held his letter in my hands. I'd already memorized practically every word, so I stared at his drawings. And then I closed my eyes, imagining his face, his lips, his raspy voice. I shivered the same shiver from that night at Rebecca's when we looked at each other. How was it that I read this depressing letter from Sebastian and I felt excitement? It didn't make any sense. But I knew why. Because Sebastian felt that connection—the same one I felt.

With my eyes closed, I wrapped my arms around his middle, holding him tight, whispering, "It'll be okay. I'm here. Everything's going to be okay." It felt good, to hold him like that in my awake dream. To feel powerful and to know that I could make him better, help him fix this huge thing that had broken him. But why was I that person? I stared at the letter again, his handwriting, how he'd written my name and thought of me. And then I closed my eyes again.

"Macy!"

"What?" I yelled, startled. I stared at Gavin, not really registering he was coming toward me. For a second, I was in two worlds at the same time, and I didn't want to pull away from Sebastian yet.

"Mom's looking for you," Gavin said.

He held his hand out to pull me up. Even at only fourteen, he towered over me—super tall, super skinny. I noticed some dark peach fuzz above his upper lip. He had to start shaving soon. Dad hadn't been around to show him how, and Gavin would never ask Scott. Who knows what Mom was thinking? Poor guy was forced to have his big sister teach him how to be a man. He was in for it.

"What's that?" he asked, pointing at the letter.

"Nothing." I stuffed it in my pocket.

"Doesn't seem like nothing."

"Watch it," I said as we entered the house.

"Mom?" I shouted, my voice echoing through the two-story entranceway.

"In here," Mom called from the kitchen. She was leaning over the center island, flipping through the mail. Could there be something from Sebastian?

"There was a message for you on the machine," she said. Sebastian? Was he allowed to use the phone? Was he home already?

"It's from Darren." Mom studied my face. I looked at her blankly. "Something about Avery and babysitting. He couldn't find your cell number."

"Oh, okay," I said, a little disappointed that it hadn't been Sebastian.

"You're babysitting?" she asked.

"Sure, why not?" Scott can take her for every dime, but me? I get judged for trying to *make* a little money.

"Well, I'm just so surprised. I didn't even know you liked kids. And now you're a camp counselor *and* a babysitter."

"So, now you know. I like kids." Well, I seemed to like one kid, anyway.

"Why do you always have to be so nasty, Macy?"

"Because you're constantly being nasty to *me*, Mom." Out of the corner of my eye, I saw Gavin duck into the family room. He always disappeared when Mom and I fought.

"I don't see it that way. I'm just trying to have a conversation with you, but fine, Macy, forget it."

She chucked the mail on the counter and left the kitchen.

I took some loose strands of hair and twisted them into a dreadlock.

Gavin slunk back into the kitchen.

"What was that all about?" he asked.

I shrugged.

"Why are you guys always fighting? She's not that bad, you know. She just asked a question."

"Coming from her, it's always more than just a question."

He nodded as though he understood, but I knew he didn't. My relationship with Mom was complex. His wasn't.

I looked Gavin in the eye.

"Gavin. I'm going to tell you something very important. Are you listening?"

"Yes," he said, staring back at me.

"Seriously, listen carefully."

He nodded anxiously.

"You look like a freak with that mustache. We have to shave it off today."

He picked up a magazine from Mom's pile and threw it at me. I ducked just in time.

"Screw you," he said, his voice cracking.

"I'm serious. Go get your wallet. We're going to CVS."

He stood still, staring at me.

"Go!" I shouted, and he loped off to his room, his body bearing a close resemblance to a skeleton in a science classroom.

I listened to the voice mail.

"Hi, Deb," Darren's voice said. "I know we haven't talked in a while. I'm actually looking for that sweet, blond, dread-locked girl of yours. You know the one. I can't find her cell number. She said she'd babysit Avery and Ben. Have her call me, would you? Thanks."

Gavin came back into the kitchen. He'd brushed his hair and changed his shirt.

"Oooh, handsome!" I said. "Who are you dressing up for? Gotta girlfriend at CVS?"

"Shut up!" he shouted and blushed. The blush gave him away. Now that he was hormonating, he was discovering the feminine mystique. Without a doubt, Gavin had a crush.

In the car, the air felt good blowing through my hair.

"What's the latest on Bot Boy?" I asked. Gavin was writing a novel about a boy who's half robot and has to make a diffi-cult decision—whether to be a robot and have the knowledge to save the world or be human and have the love of the girl next door.

"Hiatus," he said, frowning.

"Why?" I tried to push some more loose hair behind my ear. Now that I'd washed my dreads a few times, they'd started to come untwisted. I'd have to do some work on them.

"Will you get my sunglasses?" I asked. "I think they're on the floor." I heard a crunch. "Yeah, that's them." He picked up the mangled glasses.

"Maybe if you weren't such a slob . . ." he said. I grabbed the glasses from him and used them to push back my hair.

"Maybe if you weren't such a tool," I said, punching him. He just stared out the window. It was too close to home. One of the jock boys' favorite things to call him. "So, why haven't you been writing?" I asked.

"Writer's block, I guess."

"What do you do all day then? You're just in your room farting around?"

"Yeah, pretty much," he said.

"That's beyond lame, Gavin. It's summer. Where's Jonathan?"

"Camp in Maine."

"Eliza?" Eliza was Gavin's friend since preschool.

"Um, I don't know. Working, I think?" I detected something. I snuck a peek at him. Some pink on the neck. Yes, that was it. Eliza worked at CVS. Gavin had dressed up, brushed his hair, and blushed for her. While she was the frizzy-haired, braces-wearing, plain-Jane type, Eliza was smart and had a sarcastic vibe that I liked.

"Hmmm," I said. "Well, you have to get out of the house more. I can take you to Marwood if you want. You can hang by the pool, get some chow and stuff. Then I can take you home after camp."

He rolled his eyes. "Just what I need. Jeremy Lent and Brent Chase and the boobsie twins."

"The boobsie twins?"

"Yeah," he said. "Sadie Brown and Lila Patino. We call them the boobsie twins, because we know Jer and Brent only hang out with them 'cause of their big boobs."

"Huh." I got the best insight into boys' minds from Gavin, now that he was going into high school.

"Hey, do you think Mom and Dad are okay?" Gavin said. "I mean, do you think they're like separated or something?"

I'd been avoiding thinking about that, and I was good at avoiding thoughts. But I knew Gavin hadn't learned that trick.

"I don't think so," I said. "But it does seem like Dad's been away more than usual lately. Given the recession and everything, you'd think an investor would have less work, not more. And Mom seems extra bitchy lately."

"I think she seems sad," he said.

"Whatever."

"Is it weird that I miss him?"

"No," I said. "I can't believe he missed first-day-of-vacation breakfast. Let's call him now." I pressed DAD CELL. We heard one ring and then his voice mail.

How long had it been since I'd seen him—or even talked to him? A week? More?

"Hi, Dad, it's us," I said after the beep.

"Hi, Dad," Gavin said.

"We're just calling to say hi. Give us a call."

After I hung up, Gavin and I were silent. I pulled into the parking lot at CVS and caught Gavin checking himself out in the side mirror before we walked in.

The automatic doors slid open.

"The stuff is back here," Gavin said and made a beeline for aisle six.

"Oooh!" I said, staying by the front of the store. "Smarties are on sale."

And there she was. Just as I knew she would be.

"Eliza!" I exclaimed. "I'm so surprised to see you here."

She was leaning her elbows on the counter, reading a magazine. She stood up.

"Holy amazing hair, Macy! How's your summer? Hotter than balls, huh? I've got fifteen more minutes on this god-damned infernal death shift."

I did a double take. Even though I knew she'd been declared a serious loser by the middle school popular patrol, she was looking good. Braces off, frizzy hair in a braid. Cute little boobs in a tank top with pink bra straps peeking out. The red CVS apron cinched tight around her little waist. If Gavin didn't claim her now, for sure the hormonal boy vacuum would suck her up this fall.

"Watch your language, little missy," I said. "These virgin ears of mine."

She stuck her tongue out at me, and I smiled.

I walked toward the middle of the store and found Gavin studying shaving lotions.

"Eliza's here," I said.

"Oh really?" he said, unsuccessfully feigning surprise. "I didn't know she was working today."

"Yeah, well she is. She said she's off in fifteen minutes. And she's super hot. Temperature-wise. And looks-wise too. Don't you think?"

Gavin rolled his eyes at me.

"I think she needs to cool down. Maybe you do too. I'll take you guys to Ben & Jerry's, if you want. What do you think?"

"Shut up," he said, and I saw his neck get a little pink again.

"I want ice cream," I said. "Don't worry, I won't tease you guys. See if she wants to come."

He glared at me, but he went to the front counter, empty-handed.

I grabbed one of those semi-electric razors and shaving cream with aloe and followed him.

"Oh, hey, Eliza," he said, his voice cracking. "I didn't know you were working today."

"Gavin," she said. "Why didn't you call me back yesterday? I had to go to that stupid art show with my mom all alone. You totally screwed me."

"I, um, I . . . I got really into my writing, and I . . ."

Oh man, Gavin was so out of his league. At fourteen, Eliza was already too much woman for him.

"I'm just messing with you, G," she said.

"Um," he said. "When do you finish here? We're going to Ben & Jerry's if you want to come."

"Hell yeah," she said, looking at the clock. "Close enough."

She rang up our shaving paraphernalia and handed me the bag.

"I gotta just tell boss lady I'm going," she said, untying her apron. "Be right back."

I raised my eyebrows at Gavin. He was in big, big trouble. It was all over his face.

At Ben & Jerry's, I pretended to get a text so I could let Gavin and Eliza hang, but also so I could be alone with my thoughts. Sebastian. He was a constant buzz in my head. I was functioning with only half a brain. The other half was like this: Sebastian, Sebastian, big lips, brown eyes. Sebastian, raspy voice. Sebastian, addict, vulnerable, needs me.

What was I doing? Fantasizing about a guy in a mental institution? There were so many things wrong with that. Not to mention, the whole I-had-a-boyfriend thing.

I called Darren.

He picked up, and I heard the baby screaming in the background.

"Hi, it's Macy."

"Avery hasn't stopped talking about you. Did you put some kind of love potion in her apple juice? Ben! Oh shit, sorry. This baby is the devil. Damn, I shouldn't have said that to you. Really, he's an angel. I swear. It's just with me. He likes to torture me when he knows I have work to do. . . . Forget everything I just said. You still think you can babysit?"

"Sure," I said. How devilish could a baby be?

"Excellent. Can you do one o'clock Friday?"

"No problem," I said.

We hung up. Two jobs. Obsessed with a depressed institutionalized addict. And because I was confused about who I was for a minute, I texted Chris.

ME: Workin hard?
CHRIS: Yeah. But thinking bout u.
ME: U 2.

CHRIS: Can u hang tmw nite?
ME: Sure.

Okay. I was Macy Lyons, loved by a handsome boy who wanted to have sex with me.

Back inside Ben & Jerry's, Gavin and Eliza were at a table—Eliza sucking on a straw from her chocolate milkshake, Gavin eating Cherry Garcia with a spoon. I recognized the look in poor Gavin's eyes, which were trying desperately to keep in contact with Eliza's but couldn't. He was in lust, maybe even in love. He was probably afraid that if he looked her in the eye, she'd know how he felt. And Eliza was oblivious. All chitchat and banter and sarcastic laughter. The table was covered in splotches of old ice cream and pieces of napkin, but they didn't seem to notice or care. I ordered myself a chocolate peanut butter on a waffle cone and sat down with them. I stared at Gavin's mustache. What was I thinking? Would I even know how to tell him what to do with that thing?

My phone rang. I pulled it out of my shorts pocket. Dad. I went out to the parking lot again.

"Hi, Dad," I said as I chewed on a frozen chunk of peanut butter.

"Hi, Mace." He sounded far away, but his voice immediately made me feel better, calmer.

"Are you back in town?"

"No, I'm still in Chicago," he said. "How you doing?"

"Okay, I guess. You coming home tonight?"

"No, hon. I've got to go to Miami tonight for the rest of the week."

"Oh. It's just that you're totally MIA, Dad." I was whining now. I couldn't help it. "You missed vacation breakfast."

"I know, sweetie. I'm so sorry. I feel horrible about that." He cleared his throat. "You finish up school okay?"

"Yeah." What was I supposed to say? I spent the morning of my last day in a psychiatric ward waiting room?

"You guys okay?"

"I don't know. Mom's . . . well, Mom's acting like Mom. Um, Gavin needs to shave, and I don't know what the hell to do."

"Oh boy. I knew that day was coming soon. Can he hold out 'til the weekend maybe?"

"No, Dad, he looks like a skeletal gorilla."

He laughed. "Well, then, you can supervise. It's easy. Just tell him to be careful around that upper lip area."

"Dad?" I wanted to tell him about Sebastian, that I was all jumbled up inside and I didn't know which way was up. But I'd never talked to Dad about anything guy-related really— not even Chris—and right now, while he was away and distracted by work, wasn't the right time to start.

"Hmmm?" he said.

"Nothing."

"Okay, well, I have to go. Tell Mom I called."

"You haven't talked to Mom?"

"My meeting's about to start. Tell her I'll e-mail my itinerary when I can. I have to go. I love you, sweetie. Say hi to Gav." And then he hung up.

I went back inside. Gavin looked up.

"What's wrong?" he asked.

"Nothing. That was Dad. He says hi."

"Why didn't you let me talk?"

"He had to go. He said he'd be home this weekend."

"Is your dad away again?" Eliza asked, noticing Gavin's sad face and looking at him curiously.

"Yeah," Gavin said.

"Are you guys done?" I asked, eyeing their empty cups. "Let's go." I took one last bite of my ice cream and threw the rest in the trash.

"Hey," Gavin yelled. "I would have eaten that!"

"Sorry. Would you like me to retrieve it for you, Oscar?"

He gave me the finger.

"Nice," I said. "You're so welcome for the ice cream."

When we got back in the car, Eliza must have sensed the change in Gavin because she stayed quiet. He didn't say a word or look at her.

"Talk to you later, G?" she said, opening the car door when we reached her house.

He nodded and watched her walk away.

"You could have at least said good-bye," I said as I started driving.

He smacked his forehead. "I'm such a moron."

"Don't worry about it. It's just Eliza." I punched him on the shoulder, hoping to lighten the mood, but he just stared straight ahead.

We pulled into the garage. Mom's car was there. A wave of dread washed over me.

"I'll meet you in your bathroom," I said. "Start running the hot water." I shoved the bag with the shaving stuff at him.

I went looking for Mom. I hoped she wouldn't be in the mood to kill the messenger because my message would sting.

CHAPTER EIGHT

I heard Mom's voice in the study.

"Hi, Rob. Call me as soon as you can," she said. "I promised Harry I'd send him the tax forms tomorrow but I can't find them."

I stood outside the study door. Why would Dad call me and not her? Maybe something *was* going on in their marriage. I waited another few seconds before entering so she wouldn't know I'd heard her. She looked so small sitting in Dad's giant desk chair. There were papers and envelopes strewn across the normally spotless desk. Mom had the mouse in her hand and was frantically clicking away.

"Hi, Mom." She straightened up quickly. Her hair was coming out of its ponytail. She was chewing on a pencil—hard—I could see the teeth marks from where I was standing.

"Hi," she said. "What's going on?"

"Not much."

Mom took a deep breath as though trying to reorient herself. I wished I could just turn around and walk away. Mom didn't look like her usually bitchy self, so I wasn't inspired to upset her.

"Did you talk to Darren?" she asked. "Are you going to babysit for the kids?"

"Yeah."

"You were so cute at that age. I know you won't believe this, but you wore a purple tutu to camp every day. You refused to take it off, even to go in the pool. Finally, this sweet counselor—oh, what was her name? Melissa, I think. Or was it Marissa? Anyway, the last day of camp she convinced you to take it off. I can't remember the story she told you—something about a princess needing to save a unicorn or something. Whatever it was, it worked."

"Yeah, well, I'm not so into princesses or unicorns these days, Mom. Or pools."

Mom put her pencil down and sighed. She pressed a finger in each of her temples.

"Anyway," I said. "I got a call from Dad. He's going to Miami tonight. He'll send you the itinerary."

"Oh," she said, fake cheerfulness in her voice. "When did he call?"

"About half an hour ago."

Mom's eyes watered. And then I felt a little sorry for her. She cleared her throat and started in on the mouse-clicking again.

"Thanks for letting me know," she said.

I went up to Gavin's room. He was lying on his bed reading an Iron Man comic. I heard the water running in his bathroom.

"You ready?"

"Whatever," he said.

"You're all bent about Eliza?" I said. "Just call her later and it'll be cool. Come on. Let's do this thing."

I opened up the fancy new razor and put a washcloth under the hot water. Gavin didn't move from his bed.

"Gavin. It's now or never. I'm doing you a favor."

"Whatever," he said. "Why do you think you can help me shave? You're a girl."

"Don't be a loser, Gavin. It's not going to hurt."

"Fine," he moped, entering the bathroom.

Damn, he was tall.

"Hold on," I said.

I got a chair from his room and brought it into the bathroom.

"Sit," I said.

He sighed heavily like it was a great hardship, but he obeyed.

I took the hot washcloth and pressed it against his dark peachy-fuzz mustache and the first inklings of a beard.

"Ow!" he yelled. "That's too hot!"

"Man up. You have to soften your skin before you shave. It gets the pores all ready." His eyes teared up, but I kept the washcloth pressed to him.

I started foaming the shaving cream into my hand. Just as I was about to spread it on his face, he grabbed my wrist.

"I'm not a baby," he said. "I can do this myself." His eyes were intense. Angry. Poor Gavin.

"Suit yourself," I said. I smeared the foam onto his out-stretched hand, and he spread it all over his face.

"Am I doing the whole thing or just the mustache?" he asked.

"You're the man. Apparently, I'm no help."

He picked up the razor, checking it out, then he clicked on the buzzy part and seemed impressed. I took out my phone and snapped a few pictures of him all lathered up.

"For Dad," I said.

"Okay, here goes," he said and scraped the razor along the right side of his face. Then he rinsed the razor in the running water and tapped it on the edge of the sink, just like Dad. Just like Scott. *Tap tap tap.*

I heard the tap tap tap *of Scott's razor against the sink as I walked by his room.*

"Macy, is that you?" he called out.

"Yeah."

"Come in, talk to me while I shave," he said.

"Okay," I said, coming into his room. I stood at the door to his bathroom. He wore a white towel around his waist and his face had white shaving cream on one side.

I shivered. I looked in the mirror and shut the memory down, blinked it away, though it was taking more effort than usual.

"I don't know about this part," Gavin said. The razor hovered above his lip. He'd finished both sides of his face.

"You want me to do it?" I asked Gavin.

"No, I can."

"Dad said to be careful above the lip."

"Great, thanks, Dad," he said.

He took a deep breath and started shaving, making little strokes and then getting bolder. We were both concentrating very hard. I was shadowing my hand along his. I couldn't help myself. It reminded me of when I saw Aunt Carrie feeding my cousin Dylan when he was a baby. Aunt Carrie would open her mouth every time she put the spoon in Dylan's mouth. It was this weird instinct thing. I wished Gavin would've let me do it. I would have been so gentle and careful with him.

"Yo yo! What up!" Eliza's shrieky voice came from Gavin's room.

We both gasped, startled. Eliza bounced into the bathroom, looked at Gavin, half-shaven, me with my hand hovering over his, and then she burst out laughing.

"Ow," Gavin said.

"I just couldn't miss out on this ceremonious occasion. I rode my bike right over, and when your mom said you were upstairs, I was scared I missed it all! I know you didn't invite me, G, but screw you. Oh my god! Is that blood?" Eliza suddenly looked pale.

A thin line of blood trickled down the side of Gavin's lip to his chin.

"Shit!" he yelled. "Shit shit shit!"

"Ohhh," said Eliza. "I gotta lie down."

She disappeared into Gavin's room.

I grabbed a handful of toilet paper and pressed it against Gavin's lip and chin. He looked near tears.

"It's okay, Gav," I said. "This happens all the time."

I peered under the toilet paper. It wasn't too bad once the blood was cleaned off—just a small nick.

He allowed me to finish the rest of the mustache for him. I was good at it. And, despite the piece of toilet paper I'd stuck to the cut, he looked pretty smooth. Quite handsome for a robot-loving skinny-ass man-child, in fact.

We found Eliza lying on Gavin's bed, her arm slung over her eyes dramatically.

"I'm sorry, G," she said, when she heard us coming. "I can't stand the sight of blood. Was that my fault? I didn't mean to scare you. I just . . . I don't know, you seemed so bummed, and I came by to cheer you up. I brought you gummy worms. See? They're over there." She pointed at his desk.

"Thanks. That was really nice of you."

Gavin sat down on the edge of the bed, far away from Eliza. I gestured for him to move closer and gave him the thumbs up.

Eliza sat up slightly, leaning on her elbows, checking him out.

"Nice," she said. She touched his face. "Smooth." She touched the little piece of toilet paper on the side of his lower lip. "Ouchy."

My exit cue. Fourteen-year-old geek budding romance would suffer with an audience.

CHAPTER NINE

On Tuesday afternoon I sat on my bed with Sebastian's letter on my lap. The letter was wrinkled from all the times I'd opened it and folded it back up, but I'd tried to keep the drawings as smooth as possible. It had been two days since I'd visited him in the psych ward. I knew I wanted to go back, but I couldn't shake the feeling that maybe Rebecca was right. Maybe I should just walk away. And besides, he hadn't *asked* me to come back. Maybe he didn't want me to. But I kept thinking about what he'd said—that if he'd gotten a ride with me that night, he wouldn't have felt so alone. Maybe I wouldn't have either.

The doorbell rang. I shoved the letter in my desk drawer and ran downstairs. I opened the front door to Chris.

"Hey," I said.

He was still dressed in his work clothes—khakis and a blue button-down shirt. "Sorry I didn't check before coming over. I know you hate that. But my phone died on me."

"No problem," I said. In fact, I was relieved to have the distraction.

"Should we see a movie tonight?" he asked. "There's the new Leo one. It got pretty good reviews, I think."

"I can't. My presence is required for dinner. Scott's coming over with Yoli."

"She's the hot smart one?"

"Yeah."

"Maybe I should stay and check her out," he said.

"Sure," I said, realizing that having Chris by my side when Scott was around might help. I hadn't seen Scott for a few weeks, and if anyone could make things seem normal, it would be Chris. Even though Scott had tortured Chris throughout our childhood with chubster jokes, they got along pretty well now.

Chris followed me into the kitchen. The counter was overflowing with grocery bags. I opened the refrigerator to get us some chocolate milk.

Mom came sweeping in with more bags on both arms. Her face was flushed.

"Hi, kids. Can you get the rest of the bags from my car?"

Chris hopped up and ran out to do her bidding. I reluctantly started emptying the bags, which she'd put on the kitchen island.

"Can Chris stay for dinner, Mom?"

"Of course," she said with her fake smile. Mom thought I was settling with Chris, that he was too comfortable. And I had to give it to her—the whole "boy next door" thing *was* pretty nauseating. But he was handsome and polite, so she liked him.

Chris came in with the rest of the bags. It looked like we were cooking for the president. Mom had clearly gone to at least five different markets to get what she needed—fish, organic vegetables, dessert. Dad wasn't even expected home. This was all for Scott and Yoli.

Mom rushed around the kitchen, barking orders at us.

"Macy, wash the lettuce. Chris, would you please shuck the corn out on the patio? I'm just going to run up and get dressed. I'll be right down."

I unwrapped the lettuce at the sink, pulled apart the leaves, and let the water wash the specks of dirt away. Through the window above the sink, I watched Chris set to work shucking corn. He was intent on his task, and every now and then he'd look out at the backyard and take a deep breath in his endearing but aggravating stop-and-smell-the-roses way.

Gavin came into the kitchen. His cut from shaving yesterday was just a tiny dark spot now, barely noticeable.

"Hey," I said. "Where's Eliza tonight? Maybe you should invite her over for dinner."

"She's meeting Sara. They're going to the Leo movie." Sara was Eliza's other friend. I'd only seen her once, and once was enough.

"We were just saying we want to see that," I said.

"I asked Mom but she gave me the whole *Scott's coming* speech."

"Yeah. The world stops when Scott graces us. Gotta kiss the ring."

Gavin snorted and grabbed a cracker off the counter. "What's she making?"

"Tuna steaks, corn, some fancy rice thing. Pie from the bakery. She spent like a thousand dollars at the cheese shop."

"At least we'll be eating well. Is Yoli coming?"

"Yup," I said.

"But no Dad, right?"

"No Dad," I said.

"No Dad," he repeated.

"He'll be here this weekend."

"Chris is here?" Gavin said, noticing him through the window.

"He's staying for dinner. He's Mom's little helper tonight."

"I guess that's good for me," he said.

"Like you've ever helped with anything in your life."

"I'm just smarter than you guys, that's all," Gavin said.

"If by smarter, you mean a complete loser, then, yeah, you're much, much smarter."

He punched me in the arm.

"Ouch!" I said. "I'm gonna get Chris to beat you up."

"I'm soooo scared."

"Chris!" I yelled. "Gavin punched me! Beat him up!"

Chris came in, jumped in front of Gavin with his hands on his hips and puffed his chest out Superman-style. "Hold it, villain," he said in a deep voice. "I must avenge my love, the sweet Lois Lyons. And there is only one way to do that." He put Gavin in a headlock and gave him a noogie.

"Seriously?" Gavin said, trying to suppress laughter. "That is so . . . I don't even know, like, lame. What are you, captain of the football team or something? Do better."

But I knew Gavin loved it. Considering Scott had completely ignored him his whole life, Chris was like the big brother he never had. And Chris was always telling me how chill he thought Gavin was. I had a sudden pang that I hadn't asked Chris to help with Gavin's shaving experiment. They both would have liked that.

"Gavin, change your clothes. We're having a nice dinner tonight," Mom said, entering the kitchen in all white, perfect subtle makeup, and light floral perfume. Clearly she was trying to impress hot Yoli. Gavin looked down at his vintage *Empire Strikes Back* T-shirt, his jeans hanging on to his non-existent hips for dear life.

"What's wrong with this?" he asked.

"A collared shirt please."

Gavin groaned. Mom glanced at me and looked away. I guessed my prairie skirt and gray tank top passed muster. Unless she was avoiding a fight in front of Chris.

"Okay," Chris said. "What's next?"

"If you could unwrap the pie and put it on a tray to heat up later, that would be great. And wash the grapes for the cheese platter," Mom said, dumping ginger sauce she'd bought for the tuna into a saucepan.

The phone rang.

"Macy, get that?" Mom said. "I have to stir."

Caller ID said it was Scott. I passed the phone to Mom without answering.

She shot me an exasperated look as she took the phone from me.

"Hi, Scotty," she said. "Are you on your way?"

Then she listened.

"Oh," she said. "Uh-huh, yeah, okay." Then, "It's okay. Of course." Then, "Maybe tomorrow then."

Inevitably, Scott had cancelled. Eight times out of ten, he cancelled.

"They're not coming?" I asked after she hung up.

"He had a late night last night."

It was always a lame excuse, too. He never even tried to make up something good. Getting hit by a cab, anything would have been better. But I breathed a sigh of relief that he wouldn't be here.

"What am I going to do with all this food?" Mom said. Her shoulders fell.

"I'll invite Rebecca," I said.

Mom nodded and turned her back to us to stir the sauce.

ME: Scotty strikes out agn. Come eat food meant 4 him?

REBECCA: Yes! Be over soon.

"She's coming," I said.

"Good," Mom said. "I can finish up here. I'll call you when dinner's ready."

Mom was back to cooking alone mode. Now that it wasn't a dinner party, cooking was therapy.

Chris and I went out to the patio. We sunk into the wicker couch's plush pale green cushions that Mom covered every night to make sure they stayed perfectly clean. The sun had that summer evening glow that made everything look brighter than it was.

"My dad's got me working on this really cool case," he said. "I mean, I'm just photocopying and typing stuff, but it's cool."

"What is it?" Sometimes, I loved to just sit back and listen to Chris talk. He could take mundane happenings and weave them into stories. And he knew how to emphasize all the right parts with his voice—a benefit of hanging out with actors.

"Well, the case isn't that interesting really, but the people involved are. This rich guy died and his four grown children are fighting over the will. But the thing is, they're not what you'd expect. They all have valid reasons for fighting the will. At least, *I* think they seem valid. It's really sad, actually, when you think about it. Even when this case is over, how are they ever going to be a family again? You can't just move on from something like that. Like, can you imagine the next Thanksgiving?" He drew a box in the air with his fingers to make a TV screen. "Silence, silence, 'pass the gravy please,' silence, silence, 'I hate you, I'll never forgive you,' silence, silence, 'pass the salt.' 'No, that's my salt shaker, I won it in court.' 'Fuck you.' 'You too.' Silence, silence. 'Turkey's great this year.'"

I laughed a little. I'd been listening, but competing thoughts jockeyed for position in my brain—grown-up charming club-owner Scott, sixteen-year-old Scott, Mom's disappointment over the absence of Scott.

"Tough audience," Chris said.

"Sorry. Preoccupied," I said.

"Are you okay?"

"Yeah," I answered quickly. "I guess it just bugs me how my mom gets so upset. She sets herself up every time." I left out the part about how she would never be that disappointed if I didn't show up somewhere.

"You mean Scott? She'll get over it," he said.

I rolled my eyes. It wasn't about Mom and how she'd get over her disappointment. It was that no one saw Scott for who he really was. Behind all that charm and good looks was . . . maybe something bad. He was convincing. Even *I* had trouble believing that he maybe wasn't all he seemed.

"You don't get it," I muttered. No one got it.

"What?" Chris said. "I said the wrong thing?"

"Don't worry about it."

"Now *I* don't get it. I'm the bad guy? I don't understand why it's that big a deal. So Scott's unreliable and selfish. So what? What else is new?"

"She just always says it's okay," I said. "She never gets mad."

"Look. Later she'll be eating full-fat ice cream out of the carton. Why would she get mad when he gives her an excuse to do *that*?"

I had to give him a quick smile for that one.

"But I want her to get mad," I said. "At *him*."

"He's just a fuck-up, Mace. She's gotta know that deep down. She just doesn't want to believe it. Let her live in her fantasy world."

This was Chris's way of saying that he got it, but he thought I should just let it go. Let it roll. That was his philosophy, one I had tried to follow, but lately, things weren't rolling off me as smoothly as they used to.

Through the window, I could see Rebecca entering the kitchen from the side door. She said something to Mom, helped herself to some grapes from the cheese plate, and then came out to the patio, closing the door behind her.

"Hello, lovebirds," she said. "Mom-o seems sad."

"No Scotty-boy makes Mom a sad Mom-o," I said.

"What was tonight's excuse?"

"Poor Scotty was *way* too tired from working *so* hard at the club last night," I said.

"Yeah, working so hard boozing it up and getting laid," she said.

My phone rang. A number I didn't recognize.

I answered.

"Macy?" It was Sebastian. I knew his voice the second I heard him say my name.

"Hold on a sec," I said, my heart pounding. I turned to Chris and Rebecca. "Be right back."

I walked quickly into the house, up the stairs, and sat on my bed, out of breath.

"Hi," I said into the phone.

"Hi, it's Sebastian."

"I know," I laughed. "I didn't know you could call."

"Yeah, I get to use the phone a couple of times a day. And since my mom put you on my list, I have your number."

I was still trying to catch my breath. I couldn't believe he'd called me.

"Sorry about the puking," he said. "That sucked. There's nothing worse than watching someone blow chunks."

"Unless you're the one blowing chunks," I said. We both laughed a little.

"They've had to experiment with my meds a lot to get the right mix. I guess that wasn't the right one."

"So, you're feeling better?" I asked.

"Much," he said. "How are you? What are you up to now?"

"Well, my cousin just cancelled out on dinner at the last minute, and so the world has stopped."

"Why? What's his deal?"

"Well, the sun rises and sets for him, so I think my mom is crying on her makeup table right now."

Sebastian laughed. "I'm sure he doesn't deserve to be such a source of heartbreak."

"No, but also sort of yes. My aunt was a deadbeat mom and my parents took over, so I guess he's got some of that abandonment-slash-entitlement thing going on. It's hard to explain."

"You don't have to explain to me. I totally get it."

Of course he did. That's what I was starting to realize. Sebastian had this way of getting things that other people didn't. And he didn't necessarily think I should just let it roll.

"I knew someone a long time ago," he continued. "He was violent, abusive, cruel. Everyone made excuses for him because he'd had a tough life—his mother died and his father beat him. But I've met this guy here who's got the same history, and he's great, not a violent bone in his body. It's made me realize how wrong it was to excuse that man I knew and let him get away with the horrible things he did. But you know what? I think people want to excuse assholes because they can't accept that someone they love chooses to do bad things. And the truth is, sometimes assholes don't need an excuse to be assholes. They just are."

"Yeah," I said. "I think I'm starting to figure that out, I guess."

"So, um," he said, his voice suddenly sounding nervous. "Do you think you'd want to come by again?"

"I'm sorry I haven't sooner. I wasn't sure if—"

"No, it's okay," he said. "I won't be here much longer—a week probably—but it still feels like forever. Don't worry if you can't make it."

"I can come tomorrow," I said, excited. "I'll come at four."

"Okay." I could hear him smiling.

After we hung up, I exchanged my gray tank top for a black three-quarter sleeved V-neck, and headed back to the patio.

"Who was on the phone?" Chris asked.

Here it was. Confession time.

"Sebastian Ruiz."

"The suicide guy?" he asked. Rebecca's face screwed up a little.

"He didn't really try. That was just a rumor," I said. "He's in the hospital. I visited him the other day."

"Wow," Chris said. "Why didn't you tell me? Is he okay?"

I looked at Rebecca and raised my eyebrows at her, my way of saying, "See?"

"Um, he's doing much better."

"I didn't know you really knew him," he said.

"Not that well. He was in my English class. He doesn't have a lot of friends."

"Dinner's ready," Mom called from the kitchen.

"I love when your mom cooks," Chris said, rubbing his stomach. "Especially when I'm starving." He put an arm around me and his other arm around Rebecca and led us into the dining room. We had to squish to fit through the door—a three-headed beast.

"What's up, stud?" Rebecca said to Gavin as he sauntered in and took his seat. He blushed. Rebecca loved embarrassing him. But the game lost some of its fun when it turned out to be so easy. He grunted.

"Wow, are these tomatoes from Rob's garden?" Rebecca asked. At the start of junior year, Mom and Dad had asked Rebecca to start calling them by their first names, which still didn't roll naturally off her tongue.

"Yes," Mom said. "They're doing well this year." I know she wanted to add, "because I'm the one tending to the garden," but she didn't.

Everyone was quiet for a little while, concentrating on eating. Just when it was about to get uncomfortable, Rebecca filled the silence with talk of music and movies, and the rest of us joined in while Mom acted like she was listening.

"Mom, can I go to a late movie tonight?" Gavin asked.

"How late?"

"Nine-fifteen."

"It's okay with me," she said. "But I think I'll go to bed early. Can you get a ride home?"

"Eliza or Sara's mom can take me home."

"We'll pick you up," I said, looking at Chris and Rebecca. "In fact, let's all go to the movies."

"Yes, let's," Rebecca said, grinning evilly at Gavin.

"I'm in," Chris said.

Gavin groaned.

"What's wrong?" I asked Gavin. "We're gonna cramp your style? Ruin your moves? Don't worry, we won't sit with you and your girlfriends."

"Whatever," he said, pushing the tuna steak around on the plate with his fork.

"What are you talking about?" Rebecca said. "I'm totally sitting next to Gavin. I want to share popcorn. It'll be so romantic."

"No way," Gavin said. "You probably don't wash your hands after you go to the bathroom."

"Moi?" Rebecca said dramatically.

"Gavin! Rebecca, leave the poor boy alone," Mom said, smiling a little. "Fine, you can go. Just clear the table first."

"This was really delicious," Chris said. "Thanks."

Mom's smile was thin.

After Chris, Rebecca, and I cleaned up dinner, we left Mom steaming milk for a cappuccino. Chris and Rebecca went outside to wait while I found Gavin in his room, furiously typing on his MacBook.

"What are you doing?" I asked.

"Writing," he said, not looking up.

"It's time to go."

"Coming."

He stood but didn't stop typing.

"If you're motivated, you don't have to go, you know," I said. "I'll tell Eliza how she inspired you so much, you had to stay home, driven to write. A true artist. Giving up his love, his true love, for his work."

He closed the computer and walked past me.

"Will you stop with the Eliza jokes?"

"Touchy, touchy," I said.

"What was that letter you were reading the other day, huh? I've seen you with it a lot. It's some kind of love letter, isn't it? And I'll bet it wasn't from Chris. Or maybe it was from Chris. Should I ask him?"

"I don't know what you're talking about," I said as calmly as I could, though I felt panicky.

"Leave me alone about Eliza," he said.

"Deal. But I have no control over Rebecca."

We went downstairs, and the four of us got into my car. I drove to the theater, all the windows down, warm air surrounding us. Rebecca teased Gavin in the backseat, tickling his neck with her finger. He slapped it away.

"Hey wait," I said. "You said Eliza was going to the early movie."

"Yeah, it was sold out."

"Well, shit, then this one will be sold out too," Rebecca said. "We should've gotten tickets online."

"They got *me* a ticket," Gavin said, snickering.

"You can hitchhike home," I said.

After parking, we ran to the theater. We got tickets, but there were no more seats together. Gavin found Eliza and Sara, who had saved a spot between them, right in the center of the theater.

He saluted us as he sat down. I turned to Chris and Rebecca. "You guys wanna bag it?"

"No," Rebecca said, inching her way past a man with long legs to a seat on the end. "I've been dying to see this. We'll do something else after."

"Come on," Chris said, taking my hand. "Let's go to the front row so we can sit together."

"I don't want to get a neck cramp," I said. Suddenly, I wanted to sit by myself, surrounded by strangers, no need to talk to anyone.

"I'll sit there." I pointed to a lone seat toward the center of the theater. "And there's one for you." I nodded toward another spot on the other side of the aisle.

"Okay. I'll see you after," he said, squeezing my hand.

I made my way to the seat next to an older woman. As I sat, I knew that her distinctive citrusy perfume would always remind me of this movie and this moment.

I thought about Sebastian, the way I felt talking to him on the phone tonight, like some truer version of myself, if that were possible. Sebastian was making me *feel* things, and I didn't want that. But I also did. I *so* did.

The lights dimmed to black, and the previews started. I suddenly felt exhilaration and fear. This was nothing like the easy feeling I had with Chris, and it was nothing like the urgent need for sex I'd had with all the guys before Chris. This was something different.

I'd never believed in the concept, but was this what it felt like to discover your soul mate? Whoever Sebastian was to me, my feelings were only getting stronger. I actually put my hand on my chest to feel my heartbeat speeding along. The previews ended, and the crackly crack of the feature movie started. I took a moment to listen to myself, to realize that something was happening. And, for the moment at least, I was okay with that.

CHAPTER TEN

"Glad you're back," Rashanna said, ushering me past the community room. I saw through the glass that everyone was pretty much where they were the last time I'd been here. The anorexic girl and the huge overalls guy were playing a game at the table. Two kids were watching TV, and the blond boy, who I now knew was Sebastian's roommate, Luke, was sitting on the window ledge scribbling in a notebook. A man stood in the corner, probably another nurse or some sort of attendant. Maybe one of the kids was on suicide watch.

Rashanna led me into the visitors' room, which was bathed in bright sun.

"Hi," Sebastian said, standing up. He was wearing jeans, a soft-looking white T-shirt, and Converse—the kind with no laces. He looked good. Really good. I felt a tingle travel through my body.

"Hi," I said. We both sat down.

"I'll be in the nurse's station," Rashanna said, closing the door.

"I went outside today for a walk," Sebastian said. "Outside privileges are hard to come by. You have to be extra good."

"So you've been extra good then?" I asked.

"It was my reward for opening up some in group yesterday."

We looked at each other. There was a new comfort level between us after the last visit, after talking on the phone. Something about this place accelerated our friendship.

"Was it hard?" I asked. "Opening up? Talking about personal stuff to strangers?"

"Oh yeah," he said. "Big time hard. Strangers or not, I don't like to talk about personal stuff that much anyway."

I nodded.

"But I promised Rashanna and my mom that I'd try, so I did."

"Was it like what you see in the movies? The therapist and everyone sitting in a circle and they keep making you talk until you just break down and start crying?"

He laughed a little. "Actually, it wasn't that far off. I didn't cry, but once I started talking, they didn't leave me alone. Man, they just kept at me like I was their onion to peel."

"Did they get through any layers?"

"Maybe one or two," he said. I wanted to know what he'd told them, but I didn't ask.

He lifted his hands to put in his hair, and they were shaking. Really shaking, like an old man. He held them out in front of him.

"Wow," he said. "Jesus, look at that."

"Are they always like that?"

"Just the last couple of days. Maybe still withdrawal from the drugs, maybe the new antidepressants, just, everything, I don't know." He put his hands back on his lap and they seemed to still again. "I haven't been sleeping well. Luke was up all night."

"Did something happen?" I asked.

He shrugged. "He's so messed up. He makes me feel like a poseur for even being here. He's paranoid schizophrenic or something."

"So, what does that mean? Does he see things?" I asked, staring at his fingers, which were now resting comfortably on his knees. Though still grayish, they looked long and strong, like they would play a mean bass or something.

"Yeah, sometimes," Sebastian said. "He told me about when he was sent here. His parents went out of town, and he refused to sleep because he had these terrible nightmares. He bought paint and stayed up painting the inside of his house bright orange to keep it sunny even at night, so it would never have to be night and he'd never have to sleep. He didn't sleep for five days straight. When his parents showed up, he was sitting there in this bright orange house, babbling and going nuts." Sebastian looked at me now, his eyes filled with wonder and sadness. "He's really smart, though. It's sad when you see someone like that and you know it's like, the chemicals in his body are just totally out of whack."

"That sucks," I said, which seemed like a stupid thing to say.

"It was the poster," he said, "of the solar system. Last night. He started seeing things on it. He thought that aliens made me put the poster up as a way to get to him. He thought they were coming for him and that I was in on it."

"Holy shit." My throat felt hollow. "Did he do anything to you?"

"No. He was just yelling a lot. They sedated him. He doesn't remember any of it."

"I'm sorry. I wish I hadn't brought it," I said. I put my head in my hands and tried to erase the image.

I heard him shift in his chair. He put his hand on my knee.

"I shouldn't have told you. It was sweet that you brought the poster. I love it. Come on."

I looked up at him.

"He's really sick," he said. "It's a sickness."

"Do you think you're sick?" I asked.

He shook his head slowly. He took his hand away from my knee—I missed it.

"Maybe a little. I think sometimes all this mental stuff is chemical and sometimes it's more about what's happened in your life. I know I'm more prone to depression and using drugs to cope, but I don't know."

"So, what's happened in your life then?" I asked.

"What's happened in yours?" he snapped.

I wished I could take it back. I wanted to be Sebastian's breath of fresh air, not another one of his pushy counselors. But I also hadn't come to be treated badly. I stood quickly, and my chair made a loud scrape on the floor.

"I'm sure our time is almost up. I'll go find Rashanna," I said.

Sebastian took my wrist in his hand. There was no anger, no desperation in the gesture. Only warmth and apology.

"Please sit down. I'm sorry."

I sat down, fighting the urge to cry. I felt so damn vulnerable with him.

He turned to face me. His body was so long, thin, beautiful in its unique way. I instinctively turned toward him too. He put his elbows on his knees and bent his head down so our faces were at the same height.

"My dad was the asshole I told you about on the phone. A mean alcoholic. It's no story you haven't already heard a thousand times. He used to hit my mom when he got really drunk."

I cringed.

"When I was seven, he threw a chair at her and I ran in front of it, and it got me in the head." He pointed at the scar on his eyebrow, the one I'd noticed the first time I met him under my oak tree.

"Jesus," I said.

"Like I said, not really an original story."

"Is anyone's?" I asked.

"I don't know. It just seems so cliché."

"So now you're critiquing your life like it's a plotline in a movie?"

His lips turned up a bit in a half-smile. "Anyway, my mom had enough. So we left Madrid. Now I realize how brave that was. My mom didn't know anyone here. She had one distant cousin living in Queens, and he set her up with all the right paperwork and everything to get through the legal stuff and transfer her nursing degree. Then she ended up getting the job at the hospital, so we moved here."

"Have you heard from your father?" I asked.

"Nope. Never."

"Wow. I'm sorry."

"It's okay," he said. "I'm really okay with that. I realized that I could wish and wish, but he would never change. I know we're better off not hearing from him."

I nodded.

"I used to get in these moods when I was little," he continued. "My mom would call them my 'little funks.' It made sense, given the way we were living back then. But then we moved here. It was kind of like we were this team, taking on the world. She worked a ton, but it was still just us and I felt so free. And then she married my stepfather. When Sofia was born, I was excited. I never had a brother or sister. I loved having this smart, little person who was completely connected to me. But my mom and stepfather worked full time, and Sofia wasn't an easy baby, and they just didn't have a lot of time. It wasn't their fault, but I was odd man out. . . . This is so dumb."

"No, it's not," I said. "It's not dumb at all. Go on."

"My moods came back. And they weren't so little. They felt like heavy blankets that I couldn't shake off. I started taking painkillers from my stepfather's medicine cabinet from when he broke his toe. I guess it was my way of self-medicating. The pain meds kept me numb and made me feel sort of looser and free. After that, I found a guy by the train station who could get them for me. For a while, it wasn't hard to get. And then when it got harder, I did some stupid shit to keep up my supply. The kind of stupid shit you could go to jail for."

I could tell from his expression that asking specifics about the stupid shit he did was out of the question, so I didn't.

He let out his breath and closed his eyes. I wanted to touch his face, right at the top of his cheekbone, but I kept my hands in my lap.

"Is that what you shared in group?" I asked.

"Pretty much. I thought I started doing drugs because I was bored and felt sorry for myself, and it was fun to get high. But the therapists and the people in group say that I have depression, and I always have. We just didn't realize it when I was younger because when you see your mom getting the crap beaten out of her every day, being depressed seems like an inevitable outcome. But leaving Madrid didn't make it go away. It's not just a bad mood I can get over."

A fly buzzed by my ear. It moved over to Sebastian, so I waved my hand over by him, and my finger brushed his face, near where I'd been itching to touch him. He smiled at me.

"Thank you for telling me," I said. "I know that wasn't easy."

"Do you ever feel like you're completely alone?" he asked.

I nodded.

"Sometimes it's lonely even when you're in a bigger family," I said. "Lonelier even."

"The asshole-slash-not-asshole cousin?" he asked.

"Well, yeah, I guess. I mean, we've always gotten along pretty well, but my mom lets him off easy. Unlike me. I can't do anything right in her eyes."

"I doubt that," he said.

"It's true. He sucks up a lot of air whether he's in the room or not, you know? And I get it, he's cool; he's pretty cool to be around, but it makes me feel kind of, um, second-rate, I guess."

"Hard to imagine," he said. "You seem pretty first-rate to me."

He smiled, and I felt fluttery in my stomach.

"Can I ask you a question?" he asked. Now I was panicked. He seemed to be able to read me so well. Did he guess something about me?

"You can ask," I said, quietly. "Can't guarantee I'll answer."

"Smartass," he said. "Why are you coming here to see me?"

I was relieved that he hadn't asked more about Scott, but then I felt nervous, like I had to give a speech at school and I hadn't prepared. I had no answer.

I shrugged.

"Is it because you feel sorry for me?" he asked.

"No. It's not that at all."

"Do you feel obligated?"

"No! Do you want me to stop coming?"

"No way," he said. "I just feel sort of guilty, like you have your life out there, so why are you coming here?"

I owed Sebastian honesty. I felt like that was really the only thing he asked of me.

"At first, I think it was because I was afraid I was the last person to see you and I could have stopped you, so I wanted to know. And, also . . ." I started fiddling with one of my dreads, pulling at it, twirling, faster and faster.

"What?" he asked, so quietly I almost didn't hear.

"I don't know," I said. "It was like that day when we talked. You understood parts of me even *I* don't understand. And I didn't get how. Is that weird?"

He smiled. "No. I felt the same way about you."

"Since that night, things are different. I don't know, I can't explain it," I said.

"Me too." He put his hand on mine. I never felt warmth like this when Chris touched me.

Just then Rashanna came in, and Sebastian quickly took his hand away. Shit, we'd broken the no contact rule. Would I be allowed back?

"Did you have a nice visit?"

We both nodded. Our moment was over, but it lingered in the air. Rashanna pretended to ignore it.

"One sec," she said and stepped into the hall to talk to another nurse.

"I can come again on Friday, if you want," I said to Sebastian. "After babysitting. . . . Ugh, what was I thinking? I have no idea what I'm doing."

"How old?" he asked.

"A four-year-old girl and a one-year-old boy."

"There's only one thing you need to know," he said. "Pay very close attention to what I'm about to tell you."

I nodded.

"If crying, insert ice cream," he said.

I rolled my eyes and laughed. "Thank you so much for that sage advice."

Rashanna returned to the room.

"Okay, Sebastian," she said. "Lunch is in ten minutes. Come on, Macy."

Sebastian veered off into the community room, and I heard someone say to him, "Hey, man. Is that the girl?"

What did he mean by *the girl*? Did Sebastian talk about me?

I followed Rashanna down the corridor and through the double doors to the reception area.

I sat in my car and felt the sun on my face through the windshield. It was the same sun as the one that had been in the visitors' room, but it felt different here. Bigger. Inside the psych ward, even the sun seemed imprisoned. But Sebastian was happier today. Despite the poster disaster and his lack of sleep, some of the dullness had lifted from him. I closed my eyes and tattooed his flirtatious smile onto my memory. There was no doubt in my mind that we felt exactly the same way about each other, and that was an amazing feeling.

I reached behind my neck to untie my bandana. I shook out my dreads and caught a glimpse of my eyes in the mirror. They looked different somehow. Same color—greenish-brown—same dark eyeliner and mascara, but something was different. There was something extra—a lightness, or maybe it was an absence of heaviness. I felt the change now, rising in me from my chest and spilling out through my pores.

CHAPTER ELEVEN

I pulled into Darren and Kevin's driveway at 12:57 p.m. on Friday. Their house wasn't right in town like Sebastian's; in fact, it was only a few minutes from mine, but it still seemed worlds away. It was a real family neighborhood with paved roads and houses far enough apart to be private but close enough together to feel like you're not alone. Almost every house on the road had a swing set in the backyard, and there were no electronic gates like mine at the end of driveways.

I knocked lightly. Darren opened the door almost immediately and put his finger to his lips.

He was holding the baby, who was asleep on his shoulder.

"Let me just put him down. Avery's in there." He gestured toward a room off the kitchen as he crept up the stairs silently. The glory of gay-party-Darren was long gone. Instead of leather couches and sleek glass tables, the sitting room had bright primary-colored plastic chairs and toys that sang nursery rhymes when you touched them. A wooden coffee table that once may have been nice was now camouflaged in soft smushy material to protect the kids' heads from pointy corners. Mom probably hadn't been here since Avery was born. If she had, she'd probably run out screaming.

Avery was lying on her stomach on the floor, turning the pages of a giant encyclopedia of snakes. Her hair was in a messy bun—more hair out than in—and she was wearing blue shorts and a yellow T-shirt. She'd told me at camp that she never ever *ever* wore pink. Pink was silly.

"Hi, Avery," I said. She looked up at me.

"Where's Daddy?"

"He's upstairs with Ben. What are you looking at?"

She didn't answer. She kept flipping through the book. She wasn't the same kid as at camp. Here, she was in her own territory. She was boss. I could tell right away I had no control here. I knelt down next to her. I liked snakes about as much as I'd like getting stuck with a hot poker in hell, but she'd thrown down the gauntlet and now I had to win her over. I wanted the Avery who'd snuck her way onto my lap the other day.

"Wow," I said. "That one is gigantic. Is that an anaconda?"

Avery looked at me and rolled her eyes. Yes, this four-year-old actually rolled her eyes at me.

"Cobra?" I asked.

"An anaconda is a constricting snake and a cobra is a poisonous snake," she said, matter-of-factly. Okay, we were warming up here.

"Huh," I said. "So then, by definition, anacondas aren't poisonous?"

It seemed like she was trying to figure out whether I was teasing her or was actually just an idiot. She must have decided on the latter because she began to explain.

"Constricting snakes *squeeze* their prey until they *die*." She balled her hand into a fist very dramatically. "Poisonous snakes *bite* their prey with their fangs and the venom comes out of the venom sac and *kills* them." Now we were getting somewhere. I could learn a few things from Avery. Could I get my hands on a venomous snake and put it in one of Mom's spandex capris? I was deciding whether it would be appropriate to ask Avery which way she'd prefer dying when Darren walked into the room.

"Okay!" Darren said. "Ben is down. He should nap about two hours. There's a bottle for him in the fridge. Help your-self to anything. I'll be at Marwood finishing up all the crap piled up on my desk. Call me if you need me!"

Avery looked alarmed. "Are you leaving, Daddy?"

"Yes, Ave. I told you that Macy was coming to play with you."

"But you have to stay *here*, Daddy!" She was whining now.

"It's okay, Avery," I said. "We'll have fun. We can draw some awesome snakes!"

Darren gave me a thumbs up. He quickly kissed Avery and then rushed for the door. "Call me if you need me," he said again. The door closed and I heard the car start up and go.

Avery's lip quivered.

I prayed she wouldn't cry. Maybe it was just a quivering lip thing that would go away.

"Come on," I said. "Let's get back to the snakes."

"Daddy!" she wailed and the tears burst out of her eyes. "Daddy!"

She ran so fast, I barely had time to blink. I ran after her as she opened the door, but before she could make it outside, I closed it and turned the top lock.

Holy shit, she ran so fast, she almost got away. What if she'd gotten out into the street? I couldn't even go there.

I knelt down next to her and put my hands on either side of her face, which was bright red and streaked with tears.

"Avery, it's okay. Your dad's only going out for a little bit."

But the tears and wailing kept coming as we stood there—to the point that I wanted her daddy too. I alternated between confusion about how to handle the situation and heartbreak for her abandonment.

"Avery, come on. Let's play." But she wouldn't stop. The way she was crying, it seemed like it could go on forever. I didn't want to call Darren only minutes after he'd left. I could handle this. And then I remembered Sebastian's advice: *If crying, insert ice cream.* I went to the freezer and scooped some ice cream into a green bowl with tractors on it. I grabbed a spoon and carried the ice cream over to Avery, who was now pressing her nose against the glass of the door, as though the harder she pressed, the more she could will Darren to come back.

"Avery?" I said quietly.

"I just want my daddy. I don't want you!"

"I know," I said. "But maybe you want some ice cream?"

"No!" She sniffled again. But then a miracle happened— she turned slowly and peered into the bowl.

"Chocolate *is* my favorite," she said, still sniffling but calmer now. "How did you know that?"

"I guessed. It's my favorite too." Truthfully, it was the only kind of ice cream in the freezer.

"Okay," she said, walked over to the table, climbed up on a chair, and waited for me to bring her the bowl. While she ate it, the tears dried on her cheeks. I'd have to thank Sebastian later for his simple, yet genius, plan.

"Macy?" Avery asked, chocolate smeared around her mouth like a beard.

"Yes, Avery?"

"Do you have two dads, too?"

"Nope," I said. "Just one."

"Do you have a mommy?"

"Yes."

"What's her name?" she asked.

"Deborah. But everyone calls her Deb."

"Is she pretty?"

"Yes, she's very pretty," I said.

"Is she nice?"

"Some people think so."

"I cry whenever Daddy goes away because I love him so much and he loves me. And I want to be with him all the time," she explained frankly, licking ice cream from her lips.

"Yeah," I said. "I feel the same way about my dad." I had a vague recollection of wanting to be with my mom, too—long, long ago.

"Macy?" Avery asked. I was learning that kids liked that, to say your name to make sure you were listening. It was a smart trick, considering how often adults only pretended to be listening.

"Yes, Avery?"

"I wish all snakes were poisonous snakes," she said.

"Why?"

"Because I like them better."

"Cool," I said. "Well, then, I guess we could *pretend* all snakes are poisonous."

"So there could be a boa constrictor with fangs and venom?" she asked, excited.

"Sure, why not?"

And this was how the next hour and a half went. Conversations about snakes and about Avery missing her dad. Avery slithering around on the floor and hissing like a snake. Building a Lego snake. Reading the snake encyclopedia. I was bored to tears, but she was cute, and the stuff she said was pretty funny. At around three o'clock, the baby started to make little googly-goo noises upstairs.

Avery followed me to Ben's room. When I opened his door, I was greeted with the foulest odor I'd ever encountered.

"Oh, man, that is just *wrong*," I said as Ben smiled and reached his arms out for me. I picked him up, turning my head to the side.

"Peee-yew," Avery said. "Ben made a stinky poop."

"He sure did," I said, paralyzed.

"Aren't you going to change his diaper?" she asked.

"Uh-huh." I hadn't even seen a diaper since Gavin was in them.

Sebastian had not prepared me for this. Ice cream wasn't going to fix this situation.

Avery pointed at a table with a super soft-looking pad on top, so I lay Ben on it. Changing his diaper was like trying to put a sweater on a rabbit—he immediately rolled over until he was on his hands and knees, laughing. When I'd finally finished, I held up the dirty diaper and looked at Avery.

"Garage," she said.

With one arm, I hoisted up Ben, and with the other, I held the dirty diaper way out in front of me and made a bee-line for the garage.

After I washed my hands about twenty times, Ben sat on my lap, pensively drinking his bottle and watching Avery push a tractor around the coffee table. Ben rested his head on my chest. It was all so simple. A happy baby equaled a long nap, a giant shit, and a bottle of milk. A happy kid equaled tractors that go, all kinds of snakes, and someone to listen to her talk. Life was uncomplicated for them—black and white, yes and no, good and bad. For little kids, all problems were solvable. So then what happens later on? When does everything get so complicated?

I breathed in Ben's sweet baby smell and felt my eyes burn. Nothing would ever be simple for me.

When Ben started to squirm, I put him on the floor to crawl around. I pictured Sebastian's doodle eye, always watching out for me. And I felt it now. But who was watching out for *him*? Me? My heartbeat sped up. Was it fear that I was starting to care so much about Sebastian? Or was it that Ben had pulled himself into a standing position and looked like he may topple over at any second? I ran to sit behind him.

At around three thirty, I heard the key in the lock.

"I'm home," Darren called. "How'd it go?"

"Great," I said.

"Avery? Hi, I'm home." Avery was still pushing her tractor, not looking up. Darren picked up Ben, who was reaching for him.

"She had a little trouble after you left," I said. "So I gave her some ice cream."

"Perfect. Sorry she was a toughie."

"It was great—we had fun," I said. I didn't want Darren to think I couldn't handle a four-year-old crying, even though, for a minute there, I had questioned my ability.

"So again on Monday, maybe? I'll just add it to your paycheck, if that's okay with you. And tell Deb I—never mind, sweetie. I won't make you be my messenger."

He took my chin in his hand and stared into my eyes. "You're a good girl."

I rolled my eyes at him. "I'm not seven, Darren."

"To me, you are, love. And you're a good person. You always have been. Always. You know that, right?"

I looked at him curiously. "Um, I—why are you saying that?"

"Because, sweetie. I'm not sure that anyone's really making sure you know that lately. Oh, shit. That was probably so out of line."

I gulped.

"You remind me of me at your age," he said. "I wish someone had just said to me, 'Darren, you're a good person.' That's it."

"Okay, well, I guess I'll see you Monday at camp," I said, making my way to the door before any tears tried to bubble their way up. "Bye, Avery."

"Bye," Avery said, but she didn't look up from her tractor. Ben goo-gooed.

I heard Darren mutter, "Ah, shit, Darren," under his breath.

I got in my car. What had Darren meant by that? And why, suddenly, did I seem so transparent to everyone?

I rolled down the windows and drove slowly. It seemed like every house had one of those yellow plastic men out front with a flag, telling cars to SLOW DOWN.

I pulled over and stared at one of those yellow men. *Slow down*, he was saying to me. Just *slow down*. I watched the yellow man's white flag flutter in the breeze. I took a few breaths. And then I started to drive toward the hospital. To Sebastian.

CHAPTER TWELVE

Back in the psych ward, I was starting to feel like a regular. The receptionist greeted me by name, and as I followed Rashanna through the hallway, I felt a certain confidence in my step from knowing where I was going.

I could see Sebastian sitting in the visitors' room, his long legs stretched out in front of him and crossed at the ankles. He was rubbing his glasses on his T-shirt, focused on the task of cleaning them. He looked up when I got to the door and for that one second, I was able to take in his eyes, naked without the barrier of his glasses. I felt myself heat with the thought.

"So? How did it go?" Sebastian asked, putting the clean glasses back on. I sat across from him in my usual chair. Rashanna smiled, closed the door, and then went into the community room.

"Your advice totally came in handy," I said. "Though it does nothing for changing diapers."

He laughed.

"She's a cute kid," I said. "She likes snakes and tractors."

"Well then she and my sister will hate each other. Sofia is all about pink and sparkles."

I shrugged. "Pink snakes and sparkly tractors?"

"We could make it work," he said.

"You look really tired," I said.

"That good, huh? And here I wore my best outfit and everything." He was in the gray sweatpants with a white T-shirt.

"Just sayin' . . ." I said. "It looks like maybe you didn't sleep well again last night."

He nodded. "I don't sleep well here in general. I want to be back in my own bed."

"When will that be?" I asked.

"Soon. They think I'm almost ready."

"That's great news!" Sebastian outside of here. What would that mean for me?

"Mmmhmmm," he said, closing his eyes. He was quiet, so I stayed quiet too. We were like that for so long, I thought he might have fallen asleep.

"Should I go?" I whispered.

His eyes flew open. "No. I was just thinking."

"About what?"

"About what I was going to say that day at Rebecca's. You asked me in your letter, and I never answered."

I'd forgotten I'd written that, but I did still want to know.

"What was it?"

"I was going to ask you if you still had hope."

"It was a question?" I asked.

"Don't sound so disappointed," he said. "What . . . did you think I was going to tell you the meaning of life or something?"

He smiled slyly, and I couldn't help smiling back.

"Or maybe about a new theory of relativity you came up with. Then I could have stolen it, sold it, and become rich and famous."

He laughed.

"Nope, nothing so monumental as that. I'd just wanted to ask if you considered yourself an optimistic person. And I wanted you to say yes. Because I didn't consider myself that way. Not at all. But for a minute that night, talking to you, I felt like, this awe-inspiring wave of hope and possibility. Like maybe I wasn't completely alone. Isn't it ironic that I felt hope that night? Given that I came here the next day?"

He stared straight out the window, not looking at me.

I tried to catch my breath. How could *I* have given Sebastian hope when I was fighting to stay afloat myself? But I couldn't say this to him. I couldn't crush what little he had, even if the hope he got from me was just an illusion.

He looked at me now, the fluorescent light reflecting off his glasses, but his eyes behind them were dark and powerful.

"I vaguely know that was way too intense to say," he said. "But this place is like a vacuum where the real world doesn't exist, so you just lose all sense of what's appropriate."

"I think we're way past that," I said.

He smiled and nodded.

"Hopeful," he said. "What do you think?"

"You still want an answer," I said.

"Well, I'm guessing you aren't coming up with a new scientific theory. That's my job apparently. Come on, talk to me about hope."

"Okay. I think I might be somewhat optimistic. That day, I'm not sure how I would have answered, to be honest. I'm not sure I would have even understood what you meant."

"But now you do," he said.

"Yeah, now I do, I think."

Just then, Rashanna came in.

"Sorry to cut you two short," she said. "How you feeling?"

"Good," Sebastian said.

"Like to hear it. Say your good-byes. You have group in fifteen minutes."

He nodded, not enthusiastically.

The three of us walked into the hallway.

Suddenly, a loud piercing scream came from the community room.

"They're here! Don't move!" Through the glass door, we could see Sebastian's roommate, Luke, screaming at the top of his lungs. He jumped from the window ledge, where he'd been sitting when I came in, to the floor and then he crouched.

Sebastian started to move toward him.

"Don't move! I said don't move!" Luke shouted. Sebastian inched backward, reaching out and gently pushing me so I was behind him. Luke's eyes were crazy, moving around and around all over the place.

Rashanna and the man who'd been standing at the door rushed over to Luke, but he jumped between, frog-like, and landed back on the floor, still in a crouched position. His eyes settled on Sebastian and then on me.

"They're here," he whispered loudly. "She's not who she says she is." Then he ran toward the doorway. I stood frozen against the wall, Sebastian's body squarely in front of me.

Rashanna and the other guy ran after him and another nurse came in the door. The three of them grabbed him and lifted him off the ground as he kicked and screamed.

"No! No!" he shouted. "You don't understand. They're here to kill us. Unless we stop them. Sebastian! Don't let them take me! Sebastian!"

The staff quickly took him away, and after a minute, I couldn't hear his shouts anymore.

The room was silent except for a few of the kids saying "Holy shit" and "Where are they taking him?"

Sebastian turned around and put his hands on my shoulders. I didn't think my heart would ever slow down, but the weight of his hands soothed me. What had just happened?

Rashanna came back into the room and told everyone to calm down, that everything would be okay. It was time for group, and the therapist would talk about what had happened.

"You guys okay?" Rashanna turned to Sebastian and me and put a hand on each of our backs.

We both nodded.

"Luke'll be alright," she said to Sebastian. "You'll talk in group. Head there now, okay?"

Sebastian tried to smile at me, but it wouldn't come.

I wanted to say something, to say the right thing, whatever that was, but now his eyes were empty.

I followed Rashanna down the hall. I didn't turn back; instinctively, I knew he needed that privacy, that he didn't want me to see him as shaken by Luke's outburst as he was.

When we got to the double doors that led to the lobby, Rashanna put her hand on my elbow.

"It's hard," she said. "Some days are harder than others."

"I feel horrible," I said. "That poster. I never should have brought the poster."

"If it hadn't been the poster, it would've been something else. Don't even go there."

"Is that—can that be bad for Sebastian's recovery? I mean, Luke is his roommate. I know he cares about him."

"I've got his back, don't worry."

"Will you ask him to call me when he can?"

She nodded. "Sure I will."

She turned and went back inside.

The elevator got down to the lobby, and I pushed my way out to the sun and the fresh air, the surreal feeling familiar from the last two times I'd come. Even though Sebastian said he'd be going home soon, my heart felt heavy in my chest as I walked out, aware that I was now free. Outside. And he was still stuck in there. Inside.

CHAPTER THIRTEEN

When I pulled into my driveway, all I could think about was getting to my oak tree to sort out what had just happened at the hospital. And then I gasped. Standing in front of me was Chris.

"What are you doing here?" I asked as I got out of my car, leaving it parked in the driveway.

"Nice," Chris said. "That's how you greet your boyfriend?"

"I was just surprised to see you. I thought you didn't get out until six." I took his hand but I was annoyed that he was there. I needed to be alone at my oak tree.

"A big case just wrapped up, so my dad sent me home early," he said. "Where were you?"

"I was babysitting Avery and Ben." I couldn't tell him about my visit to the hospital because then I'd have to talk about it, and I just couldn't. Not now.

"Oh, right. That was today. How was it?"

"Avery totally freaked out when Darren left, but after she calmed down, it wasn't so bad." I thought of Sebastian and the ice cream.

Chris looked at me curiously.

"I thought you said the babysitting was until four," he said.

Now he decides to remember details?

"I stopped at the hospital to see Sebastian on my way home." I couldn't lie to him. Chris and I had known each other for so long, and we didn't lie to each other.

Chris looked away. "I thought that was just a one time thing."

"Well, he doesn't have many friends. I think it's nice for him to have someone from school, a familiar face. It's a really depressing place. His roommate totally freaked out, and, I don't know," I said. I was talking too much.

He nodded. I could tell he was trying really hard not to be jealous, not to say anything that would give away that he was.

"He won't be there much longer," I said.

"That's good." He cleared his throat. "So, he'll be back."

I hadn't realized what that would mean until he said it. Sebastian would be back.

"He's clean now," I said. "He probably won't go to parties."

"Bummer."

Then he switched gears and grabbed me around my waist.

"I thought about this the whole train ride home." He kissed me. "Is anyone home?"

"I don't know." I hoped someone was home. I wasn't in the mood. I thought about stopping him for a minute, but saying no never came easily to me. Saying no was always more trouble than it was worth. Saying no meant telling him why, telling him how I was feeling. And I just couldn't do it. Partly because I didn't even *know* how I was feeling.

"Well then, let's go see," he said.

We walked in the side door. I peeked into the garage but Mom's car wasn't there.

"Hello?" I called out.

There was a note on the kitchen counter.

Kids—Scott's cooking dinner tonight. Please be home by 7.

I looked at my watch. Almost two more hours. Forget until then. Just forget everything until then.

Chris followed me upstairs. I looked in Gavin's room. His comforter was bunched up at the end of his bed; his laptop was closed. Everything was quiet.

"I guess no one's home," I said.

"Good." He nudged me into my room, closed the door with his foot, and then pushed me onto my bed. He pulled off my shirt and unzipped my shorts. I tried to get myself into it, unbuttoning his shirt, unbuckling his belt. But mostly, I was thinking about getting it done so I could be alone again and hopefully talk to Sebastian about what had happened with Luke.

I kissed Chris back, but I wasn't into it. I immediately felt so guilty—and something else, something more familiar. I was doing something I didn't really want to do and I felt powerless. Confused. Worthless.

I felt myself spiraling, falling off a cliff, trying to grab hold of something—anything—as my mind kept spinning. It wasn't just about Chris. Something in me was changing. Sebastian, the psych ward, Mom, Avery and her innocence, little girl me, Scott, Scott, Scott.

Chris collapsed on top of me.

He was getting heavy, so I gently pushed on his shoulders. He lifted himself up on his hands and looked down at me, scrunching his eyebrows.

"Hey, are you okay?" he asked. "You seem kind of far away."

"I'm good." I turned my head and kissed the inside of his forearm.

He smiled. "What should we do now? You want ice cream?"

Sex and ice cream, and all is good. Just like baby Ben with his nap and bottle.

"Sure," I said.

"Let's go to my house. We have rocky road."

It was comforting to hand over control and let Chris decide where we'd go, what we'd eat. I needed him to do that for me every now and then.

We cut through the woods. As we walked by our fort, Chris straightened a branch on its roof.

"We should really do some renovations," he said.

He took my hand and we interlaced our fingers. We'd been holding hands like that since I was five, getting on the bus for the first day of kindergarten, hopeful and scared at the same time. Chris had grabbed my hand to reassure himself as much as me. Now holding hands meant something different—sex, love, whatever it should mean—but it still felt the same to me. Comforting, a united front against the perils of the world. It was just beginning to dawn on me that soon after kindergarten my life at home had become perilous. I'd never really thought so. But seeing Avery, how innocent she was, was bringing out something in me, a realization, a new kind of anger. I pictured Avery's small body, her mind that was focused on snakes and tractors, not even aware of the things I'd known when I was just a little older than her. I instinctively squeezed Chris's hand, feeling the emotion rise up in me. He squeezed back.

We got to the end of the path in the woods and found the honeysuckle bush that marked where the gate to Chris's backyard was. He pushed the bush to the side and I sucked in its sweet smell as I bent down and walked through. Chris's yellow house rose up in front of us. The planters on his deck still held the dried-up chrysanthemums from last fall. Theresa, Chris's mom, would put something in the planters whenever she'd remember—whatever was right for the season—mums in the fall, evergreens in the winter, pansies and geraniums in the spring and summer. More often than not she'd forget, and whatever was there the last time she planted stayed there for months and months. But no one seemed to care. Not like at my house where the times for changing plants were marked on Mom's calendar, and when the day arrived, Mom would call Eduardo and say, "Hi, Eduardo. It's time for the 'insert name of flowers here.' And while you're doing that, please clean the gutters, and the fence out back is missing a post, and can you please make sure the rhododendrons out front are trimmed? They're a mess. Thank you." Then she'd hang up and later that day it would be so.

Chris and I stepped through the always-open gate, walked along the overgrown stone pathway, and tramped across the deck. Chris slid open the sticky sliding door to the kitchen. I immediately felt what I've always felt in his house: be who you are comfort. No judgments, no criticisms comfort. Check your attitude at the door comfort.

Chris opened the freezer door, which was haphazardly littered with photos of Chris and his brother, Joseph, and even a picture I'd drawn when I was eight in scrawly orange and red crayon of Chris's family plus me, all holding hands.

He took out a quart of rocky road and I got out the giant bowls that said ICE CREAM in pink and green block letters. As I pulled open the silverware drawer for spoons, Lady, their ancient golden retriever, lumbered over and stuck her nose in my butt. I pushed her away gently.

"Come on, Lady," I said.

I scratched behind her crusty ear. And then Peaceboy, who looked like a perfect replica of Snoopy, trotted in with nails clicking on the tile. He sniffed at Lady's tail and she nudged him away, wanting me to continue the scratching.

I scooped ice cream into one of the bowls. A tiny swirl of steam rose as the cold met with warm air. I realized it was the second time I'd done this today. The ice cream had worked magic on Avery's issue, but I doubted its powers could fix mine.

"Hi!" Theresa said, rolling up leashes in her hand. "What a spectacular day. You're here early."

"It was slow. Dad sent me home," Chris said.

She put the leashes right on the kitchen counter, where I knew they'd stay until the next time she walked the dogs. I wished Mom could've seen that. She'd have a heart attack.

Theresa sat on a stool at the kitchen counter. She put a hand through her curly mess of black hair and wiped a single drop of sweat from her natural makeup-free face. She wasn't pretty like Mom, but she wasn't un-pretty either.

"Macy," she said, looking at me.

"Hmmm?" I tried to push the brain freeze from my forehead with my palm.

"Chris said no Nantucket, huh?" Her dark blue eyes searched me.

"Nope. Not 'til August anyway."

"What about your job?" she asked.

I shrugged. "I got a job at Marwood. Camp counselor. And I'm babysitting for Darren Roth's kids."

"You didn't tell me," she said to Chris, raising an eyebrow at him.

It was Chris's turn to shrug.

"Avery is such a doll," Theresa said. "I still haven't met the baby. Did you know Darren and Kevin built a place near us on the Cape? It's stunning. Chris, remind me we should have them over, introduce them to some people in town."

Just then we heard a loud *clatter-clang-bang*.

"Peaceboy upended the dog bowls again, I think," Theresa said. She gave Chris a look and he went to check on the dogs.

Theresa kept staring at me until I was almost uncomfortable. I let a chocolate chip dissolve on my tongue as I sat, waiting for her to say something.

"You okay?" she asked.

I nodded.

"You sure? It seems like something's up with you."

Theresa could say these things without sounding all mom-ish. She'd always been more like a peer, a friend. But in the end, she *was* a mom. Chris's mom.

"I'm good," I said.

I could tell she didn't believe me, and I wondered if Chris had told her about Sebastian. But if he had, she probably would've just asked me about it directly.

"You should come to the Cape with us," she said.

Just then Chris came behind me, put his arms around my waist, and rested his chin on my shoulder. The only thing worse than PDA was PDA in front of a parent, even if it was Theresa. I worked hard not to recoil visibly, but his chin on my shoulder felt like an uninvited guest.

"We've got my sister and her kids coming up this weekend, so that'll be too crazy, but how about next weekend?" Theresa suggested.

"You should come," Chris said.

"Okay. I will."

Theresa smiled, satisfied.

"Well, I'm off to pick up Joseph from camp. Be back soon," she said. And then she left.

My phone buzzed with a text.

MOM: Come home in 10 min.

I groaned.

"What?" Chris asked.

"Scotty dinner. The prodigal prince returns to court, and the queen must have her attendants surrounding her at the royal palace." I clapped my hands twice quickly. "Come, come, ye serfs, come hither for the feast!"

"Well, by definition, if your mom is the queen, then you, my dear, are the prin*cess*." He clapped twice, too, and bowed with flair.

"Hardly," I said. "Maybe Cinderella, sweeping up ashes while her evil cousin takes all the glory."

He studied my face.

"You'd look good with ashes, dirty girl. Let me make you dirtier. Come, Cinderella. We have time for one more." He tugged my hand, pulling me toward the stairs.

"I have to go," I said.

"I'll come with you."

"No, not tonight." I yanked my hand away.

"What's with you?"

"Nothing!" I snapped. "Maybe I don't feel like being a dirty girl. Maybe 'dirty girl' is a fucked up thing to call someone you like." I didn't know where this was coming from. Chris usually made me feel respected and sweet. I cursed myself for having let my guard down with him, letting him make me feel like a real girl, like girlfriend material. I *was* a dirty girl. The glass slipper would never fit.

"I was trying to be funny," he said.

I shrugged.

"I'll walk you back home," he said.

"It's okay. I'll call you later."

I left his house and made my way toward the prodigal prince charming waiting at mine.

CHAPTER FOURTEEN

I took the long way and walked home slowly, kicking the rocks in the road. I pulled out my phone to see if I'd missed a call from Sebastian, but there was nothing. As I turned into my driveway, I saw Scott's new BMW parked at the top.

Everyone liked Scott when they met him. He was good-looking and funny and charming. He was the one person I still felt like I wanted to impress. I hated that, and I hated myself for it. It made me feel exactly like what I used to be—an annoying little sister.

When I walked in the front door, I immediately smelled food cooking—meat, garlic, roasted tomatoes, the inevitable thick sauce. Scott was the only one of us who'd taken an interest in cooking, so Mom taught him everything she knew. He learned well: his cooking was even better than hers. It sucked that everything he made always smelled and tasted so damn good.

"Hey, Mace!" Scott said as I entered the kitchen. He kissed my cheek, and I felt that well-known mix of excitement and disgust. Even at twenty-four, he still had his pretty-boy face, and it was flushed from the heat of the stove. His dark hair was, as always, coiffed with just the right amount of gel to make it look perfectly done but not overdone. He wore designer jeans and a black collared shirt. His shoes—some kind of soft leather loafer—probably cost as much as a semester at Berkeley.

Gavin came in the door behind me, a backpack slung over his shoulder.

"Hey," I said to him. "Where've you been?"

"Eliza's. Hey, Scott," Gavin said, sliding onto a counter stool. "What's in the pot?" Gavin was an easy conquest when food was in the mix.

"It's coq au vin. Apology stew." He gave us a crooked smile. "I made it at the apartment, so I'm just warming it up, but I'll give you a preview. How about you, Macy? You want a taste?"

"Nope. Thanks," I said and went up to my room.

I threw myself onto my bed and turned on the red lamp. I loved the soft pink glow it made on the walls. My own impossible rose-colored glasses.

I heard a knock on my door. My entire body froze.

What'cha reading? You wanna hang out?

"Come in," I said, but every muscle in my body was tight.

Mom opened the door. Ironically, I was relieved to see her.

"Dinner's almost ready," she said. "Come down."

"I'm not really hungry."

"Are you feeling sick?"

"No," I said.

"Then come down now," she said, her voice more stern. "And I need you to finish setting the table."

She looked like she was going to say something else, but she turned to leave.

There was no fighting her. I went down the stairs as slowly as possible. I could hear Super Mario Brothers music from the family room. Gavin was at his games again. And I was setting the table again.

"So, tell me about the summer, kiddo," Scott said to me as he seemed to glide from the stovetop to the sink. "Deb said you got a job? Gotta hand it to you, you are the responsible kid."

What was he trying to do with the whole *kid* thing? I was seventeen now, no longer a kid. A kid is what I was back then, when I was seven, eight, nine, ten, eleven.... But not now.

"Yeah. I'm a counselor at Marwood."

"Nice," he said as I reached into the cupboard for plates. "Darren still there leading on all the poor women who think they can turn the gay man? I heard he settled down."

I grunted, trying to convey the message *Do not engage with me.* But he seemed oblivious to my hostility.

"Man, he *hated* me. He and Deb used to get in the biggest fights about my behavior." He used air quotes for *behavior.*

Now I perked up. "Really?"

"Yeah, I don't even remember what stupid things I did, little pranks or whatever, but he would get so pissed. Not you, though, you were pretty good. What happened to *you*? What's up with the rebel hair?"

I looked at him, speechless.

"Just kidding," he said. "It looks good. Very hip, the dreads. Really."

"Thanks." I could never tell if he was patronizing me or being sincere.

After pulling out forks, knives, and napkins, I went into the perfectly quiet dining room. I set the table for four, using my handy mnemonic to remember which side was which: fork and left have four letters, knife and right have five. My face burned a little. Did Scott think my dreads were stupid? And then I tried to convince myself that his opinion no longer held any power over me. My dreads were awesome. Trendy or not, my dreads spoke. They were strong. They were mine. I touched them gently, almost an apology for doubting them.

"About five minutes!" Scott called out. "Deb, you opening wine?"

"Coming!" Mom yelled from the basement steps. She came into the kitchen and put a bottle on the counter.

"Perfect," he said. "Stags' Leap cab is one of my favorites. Rob won't miss it?"

Mom shook her head and looked at me so I knew I was meant to set the table with wine glasses. Wine with dinner most nights, unless Mom was cleansing. I carefully took the crystal glasses out of the china cabinet in the dining room, two at a time, and placed them on the table. Despite being underage, Gavin and I were allowed to drink wine with dinner too. It made Mom feel European and sophisticated.

Gavin came in from the family room and took his seat, clueless to the whole "girl sets the table while boy plays video games" stereotype in action. Scott poured wine into each glass, carefully turning the bottle to catch every last drop. Mom folded her hands under her chin and smiled.

"This is great, Scott," she said. "It's so nice to have all of you home." Her smile faltered a second when her eyes passed over Dad's empty chair.

Scott lit the candles and served each of us. He heaped coq au vin on our plates, added Parmesan risotto, roasted asparagus, and warm sourdough bread.

"So, why couldn't Yoli come?" Gavin asked Scott.

"She's got an opening at the gallery tonight. It's a big one. Lots of good publicity."

"You're not going?" Mom asked.

"Nah. I hate those things. I can't stand those pretentious artsy-fartsies and the cheap wine and cheddar cheese cubes," he said. Mom looked down at her plate. I knew what *I* was thinking—*what a selfish jerk-off*—but could Mom have been thinking the same thing about perfect Scotty?

"Guess who was at Tarantula last night?" Scott said. Tarantula was the velvet-roped club in Tribeca he imagined he owned, even though Mom and Dad had paid for his miniscule stake in it.

"Who?" Gavin asked, like he actually cared about celebrities. He must have realized no one else was going to take the bait. Certainly I wouldn't, and Mom still seemed to be reeling from Scott's abandonment of his super-awesome gallery-owner girlfriend on perhaps the most important night of her career.

"Leo," he said. "He has a new girlfriend. A model from Venezuela. Nobody could keep their eyes off her, and it was driving Leo absolutely insane. He kept trying to move into a dark corner so people would stop looking at her. But I really think he was just pissed that *she* was getting all the attention. Finally, I broke down and gave the poor sucker the VIP room."

"We saw his new movie the other night," Gavin said, looking to me for backup. "Not bad."

"Phenomenal," Scott said. "Best acting he's done yet. Really. I smell Oscar."

Just then we heard the garage door. Mom, Gavin, and I all sat up straighter and looked at each other. There were footsteps, and then Dad appeared in the dining room. He looked just as startled as we were.

"Hi, everyone," he said.

"Dad!" I couldn't help sounding like a kid. I jumped up and gave him a big hug. He looked tired, with stubbly uneven beard growth and saggy eyelids.

He took a clump of dreads in each hand. He looked surprised and then sad.

"Wow, things are different. What's this?" he asked.

"The hairstyle suits her," Mom said, shockingly coming to my defense. Then she got up and gave him a quick kiss. "Honey. I didn't know you were coming home tonight. We would have waited for you."

"No, no, it's okay," he said, ruffling Gavin's hair and clapping Scott on the back. "My flight got in late so I missed my dinner meeting in the city. I figured I'd come home and see you guys, take tomorrow off. Let me take a shower. I'll be down in a minute." And then he went upstairs.

Mom sat back down, her lips in a tight thin line.

"What's up with Rob? He looks like shit," Scott said.

"He's been traveling the last couple of weeks," Mom said.

"Man, he works hard. But I guess it's all worth it for this." Scott gestured his hand around the dining room, meaning the house, the kids, all of our expensive habits. He forgot to point at himself, the most expensive habit of all.

Mom got up and brought in a plate, silverware, and wine glass and set them at Dad's place. She hesitated before sitting down again.

Did Dad hate my new hair? Again, I had to convince myself that I'd created my dreads for myself, to be strong, to be different. It was okay if not everyone liked them. Even Dad.

Scott talked about events he was planning for the club while Mom looked off into the distance, and I focused on eating, hating that I was savoring each bite of Scott's meal.

Then Dad came down. He looked like himself again. Handsome, clean-shaven, his dark hair wet and slicked back. He had on khakis and a navy blue polo shirt.

He took his usual seat at the head of the table and served himself food.

"I'm starving," he said. "I've been eating crap all week. This is great, Scott, thanks."

"It's nothing," Scott said. "My pleasure." But nothing was ever nothing with Scott. Dinner had to be a buttering up for something. Most likely another loan—especially with him showing up last minute and without Yoli. He wanted something.

"And I brought some Scotch for after dinner," he continued, looking at Dad.

"Sure," Dad said. "So, Gavin, Macy, what have I missed? Well, other than your new hair." He smiled at me. "I was surprised to see such a big change, and I wasn't even gone that long. But Mom's right. It looks great. You look like a flower that's just bloomed. Beautiful, sweetie."

I tried to hold in my smile unsuccessfully. Dad liked my dreads.

"So, tell me the happenings. Tell me all."

"Gavin's in loooove," I said. Gavin shot me the finger and snarled.

"Hey," Dad said. "A guy has a right to keep his feelings private. Gavin? Just let me know when you want to have that birds and bees talk I've been trying to have with you." Gavin made gagging sounds.

"Macy's been partying every night," Gavin said.

"Tattletale," I said. "Not true."

"Hold on a sec," Dad said. "I was gone for, what, ten days? And, somehow against the rules of nature, instead of growing up ten days, you have regressed about five years. When I was growing up . . ."

"Blah, blah, blah," I said. "We know, you and your brothers were best friends, respected each other and your parents. You never told on each other, no matter how horrible the crime."

Dad sighed. He looked at Mom. "I think I'm being made fun of." Everything felt normal. Almost. But the vein by Dad's temple that popped out when he clenched his teeth was at attention. And Mom was quiet all of a sudden, almost shy. I knew something wasn't quite right, but at least Dad was making an effort.

"Deb," Dad said, looking at her across the table. "Did you get your hair done too?"

"It was getting too blond," she said.

"It looks good," he said. "Has anyone challenged you on the ladder?"

"No. I guess everyone's scared of my backhand." She laughed, but it wasn't real. She twisted the diamond ring on her finger.

"Hey, let's all go for a walk after dinner," Dad said. "When was the last time we did that? A night walk with the whole family. Let's do it."

We all looked at him like he was crazy. Because he was. Probably the last time we'd gone for a family night walk was, um, never.

Gavin was the first to speak up. "Good idea, Dad, but nah."

"I have plans, Dad. But nice idea. Really." I rolled my eyes at him.

"Come on, guys," he said. "Why are you all such naysayers?"

"I'll walk with you, hon," Mom said.

"Me too," Scott said. "I'll even hold hands with you and look at the stars."

"To quote you kids, 'Whatevs,'" Dad said, and he seemed genuinely annoyed. He stood up and brought his dishes to the sink. Gavin and I exchanged a look. I wasn't positive what his look said, but mine said *What the fuck?*

Mom looked at the dishes on the table and then at me—my cue to start clearing. Scott had followed Dad into the kitchen and was talking quietly to him by the sink.

"Excuse me," I said, pushing past them to load the dishwasher. They moved into the family room. Then Dad turned on the TV and flipped the channels until he got to the Mets game. Scott opened up his bottle of Scotch.

I slammed the dishwasher shut and went to my room. Having Dad home again was different. Maybe because Scott was here. Maybe something was actually different about Dad. But it didn't completely ruin the fact that he was back, and I could breathe a little better now.

CHAPTER FIFTEEN

On Saturday morning, sleep left me, but not suddenly. It took its own sweet time, like it wasn't really sure if it wanted to go. I tried to hang on to it, to stay inside the dream I'd been having, which—even though I couldn't remember what it was—I knew was good. I lay still and closed my eyes again, trying to capture what had caused this feeling, this peaceful, sweet, easy, and oh-so-rare feeling. But it was gone. It had retreated like a turtle back into its shell.

For a moment, I got a childlike thrill when I remembered Dad was home, like when I was little and he'd come home after a long trip. He'd make up for having missed a game or recital by spending time with me tossing around a baseball or something. But then I remembered that I was seventeen and that wasn't going to happen this time. And the knowledge that the day ahead held nothing much of anything and that everything basically sucked replaced that momentary peace I'd had.

I got up, brushed my teeth, did some dread maintenance, and made my way downstairs, letting my nose guide me to the coffee. Mom was horrified I drank coffee. She said I was way too young; she didn't start drinking it until she was twenty-five, and even now, she only drank one, maybe two cups a day. Some days, though, the smell of coffee was the only thing that got me out of bed.

But today, on my way downstairs, I was stopped mid-step by an argument in the kitchen.

"It's not that much," Mom said.

"I don't give a shit how much it is, Deb," Dad said. "I don't want to give him another dime."

"He's our nephew," Mom said.

"He's not a baby anymore. He's a man. And he needs to start acting like one."

"It's an investment, Rob."

"Right." Dad laughed. "An investment in a new club that's going to be the hottest thing. Just like the others, right? How much money has he paid us back? Huh, Deb?"

"He will," Deb said. "He's just getting on his feet now."

"He has no feet. He doesn't need feet. He has a boat—a yacht, actually—and he sails it in a never-ending ocean of my money."

"That's a good one," Mom said, actually laughing.

Dad sighed in defeat. "I don't feel like fighting about it, Deb."

"This will be the last time," she said. "What do you want to drink tonight?"

"You choose."

"You trust me?" Mom said, and I heard her open the basement door. "Wow, that's a first."

She disappeared into the basement.

"California!" Dad called down to her. "French has been giving me a headache."

As I got to the bottom of the stairs, I heard Mom call up, "So, then what you really meant was that it's my choice, but only if it's what you want."

"Very funny," he called back to her.

"Hey, sweetheart," he said when he saw me.

"Hi, Dad." I leaned into him. He kissed the top of my head. I took a mug out of the cupboard and poured myself a cup of coffee.

"You slept late," he said.

"Well, what else is there to do on a Saturday?" I was hinting for Dad to invite me to do something.

I searched for something to eat.

"I'm sorry about Nantucket and vacation breakfast," he said.

I looked up from the cereal cupboard. Dad looked miserable.

"It's just not the best time to go right now," he continued. "I know Mom said it was because of Scott's classes, but it's also my work schedule and some cash flow issues. Things are stressful right now."

"Is the business okay?"

"It'll be fine. This market is scary for everyone, but it's all going to be fine. Everyone just has to tighten their belts for a while. So I have to connect with all my clients to reassure them, and face-to-face is always better."

I guess that explained the long hours and extra traveling, but if he was so tight on cash, I didn't get why he'd agreed to give Scott another loan.

Dad put his arm around me and I breathed in his fatherly, spicy aftershave.

"You feel like tossing the ball around a bit?" he asked.

"Really?"

"Sure. Grab the mitts and I'll meet you out back."

I nearly jumped for joy. Dad was home.

I spent the rest of the weekend hanging out with Gavin and Dad, my companion, my friend, my Mom-translator and buffer. Mom called Scott to ask him to come home again, but, to my relief, he never called back.

And I didn't hear from Sebastian.

On Monday, Dad left for work and I was pretty mopey. Until I checked my e-mail.

From: SebastianRuiz513@bmail.com
To: macythegreat@bmail.com

I'm home. I got out yesterday. Do you want to try to meet later? My mom said I could have the car for an hour in the afternoon. Like 4 p.m.? McDonald's?

I tried not to think about Sebastian all day, about why he hadn't called me all weekend, about what it would be like to see him again outside the psych ward. My brain went back and forth between joy and panic. Joy: I was so happy that Sebastian had made it out of the hospital. Panic: I had to see him out of the hospital. Joy: I got to see him! Panic: Would it be weird seeing each other? We hadn't even talked since the Luke thing. All day at camp, I was a nervous wreck, my foot shaking every time I had to sit still. Rebecca eyed me curiously, but it was too hectic for her to ask me what the hell my problem was. Somehow I made it through the rest of the workday.

At exactly four, I turned into the McDonald's lot and parked between a Range Rover and a Mercedes. Even the rich and famous love a Big Mac once in a while. I got out of the car and hoisted my bag further up onto my shoulder. The toe of my sandal got caught in a mini pothole, and I stumbled. Once I'd steadied myself, I looked around to see if anyone had noticed. It doesn't matter who you are; everyone looks like a fool when tripping. But no one had seen. I opened the door, the cold air-conditioning smacking me in the face. I searched the tables. It was late afternoon on a Monday, so there were just a few old ladies having coffee and french fries and a couple of moms watching their kids run around on the indoor jungle gym. No Sebastian in sight.

I slid into a booth and stared out the window at the cars.

"Hey," a quiet, low voice startled me. Sebastian.

"Hi," I said. I stood up and we sort of hugged, but I was halfway in the booth and he was so tall that it didn't really work. I laughed nervously.

He sat across from me, put his long fingers on the table. He was still skinny and pale, but he was less grayish. The brown of his skin had returned some.

"Hey," he said again, with a self-conscious smile.

"Hey," I said. "Why didn't you call?"

I hadn't meant it to sound so aggressive, but it had.

He looked down. "Sorry."

"I just meant, um, about getting home. That's great. . . . Is Luke alright?" I asked.

"Maybe a little better."

He wouldn't look at me. What was happening?

"You want some coffee?" he asked.

"Yeah." We both started to stand. "I'll get it," I said.

"Okay." He pulled a few dollars out of his pocket and handed them to me.

"What do you want in it?" I asked.

"Just black." We avoided each other's eyes. Where was the connection? Was it gone? Or was I just nervous? I walked to the counter. After everything I thought we'd had at the hospital—and the connection was just *gone*?

I got the coffees and carried them back to our table. Sebastian drummed the table with his fingers.

"So?" I asked as I put the coffees down and slid into my side of the booth. "What's it like being home again?"

"Thanks." He lifted his cup and took a cautious sip of the piping hot coffee. "Home's good, I guess."

I hesitated, unsure how much to ask. "Is your mom being cool?"

"She's pretty freaked. She thinks I'm pissed at her for sending me there."

"Well, aren't you?"

"Yup."

"Yeah," I said. "Not surprising."

"The therapists say I have to let that go, though. She was only doing what needed to be done."

He looked out the window. A few cars were inching along the drive-through. Every time a car pulled up to the window, a bodiless, faceless arm reached out to hand over a package of food.

"What about Sofia?" I asked.

"Sofia's so cool. She's all, lemme show you this new toy, and come play with me and stuff. She's cute."

"That's nice," I said. That's nice? That was the best I could come up with to keep the conversation alive?

My shoulders were tight with frustration, sadness, even anger. It felt like we were two strangers. There was something about Sebastian that I'd needed, that I'd gotten from the visits, from our phone calls. But now, in the real world, it wasn't the same.

"Your hair looks good," he said. It was the first time he was seeing my dreads without a bandana wrapped around them.

"Really? Thanks."

"It's a good look for you," he said.

"You don't think it's too, you know, too . . . *too*?"

He laughed. "Well . . ." he said. "It *is* kind of a statement."

"Oh, really!" I said. "And what's it saying?"

"It's *trying* to say 'I'm a badass chick, don't mess with me.'"

"And what's it *really* saying?" I asked, trying not to be offended.

"It's really saying 'I want you to think I'm a badass chick, but really I'm soft as a little chickie. Bawk bawk!'" He flapped his arms like a chicken and I couldn't help laughing. He looked ridiculous with his giant, skinny arms.

"Look at *you*!" I said. "With your little specs and buzz cut, thinking you're fooling everyone like 'I'm all clean-cut and studious,' but I know what *you're* hiding under there."

He raised an eyebrow. "Yes, you do, as a matter of fact."
Then it was silent as we both sipped our coffee.
"Sorry," I said. He waved the air, brushing it away.
"You know," he said, quietly. "I kinda wish . . ."
My phone buzzed with a text.
"It's my brother, Gavin," I said. "Hold on a sec."

GAVIN: Can u pick me up?
ME: Where?
GAVIN: Eliza's.
ME: Trouble on lover's lane?
GAVIN: Can u come or not?
ME: B there in 20.

"Everything okay?" Sebastian asked when I looked up.
"He needs me to pick him up. I'm his chauffeur this summer."
"Where's your mom?" he asked.
"Probably the gym, like always."
"Everybody's got their vice," he said. "You have to go now?" He seemed relieved, and I felt it too.
I looked into his eyes again. There. I felt a little something, but still not like before.
"I should," I said, putting the lid on my coffee. "I'm sorry to cut out so early. It's just that he's kind of needy lately. I don't want to leave him hanging."
"I get it," he said. "It's cool. We'll talk later."
"Yeah. See you later."

I walked out of McDonald's as fast as I could and didn't look back. I got into the car and drove. After a few blocks, I pounded the steering wheel with my fist.

"What the hell am I doing?" I yelled. The sound of my voice bounced around inside the car. All the feelings, the need, the connection, all gone in a few minutes? I wanted to cry for letting someone in that deep. I wanted to cry because I could finally admit to myself that I'd been hoping for something more—even though I didn't deserve it. But I couldn't cry. I'd taught myself not to cry a long time ago.

Right before the turn onto Eliza's road, I pulled over and put the car in park. I took off my seatbelt, rested my hands on the steering wheel, closed my eyes, and took four slow, deep breaths. For years, I'd seen Mom do that to keep herself from falling apart when Gavin and I used to run around the house yelling and causing chaos. I opened my eyes and stretched my neck so I could see my face in the rearview mirror. No tears, no smears, no smudges. All good. I took one more breath, buckled my seatbelt, and pulled back out onto the road.

I turned into Eliza's driveway. Gavin sat on the front stoop. When he saw me, he pulled out his earbuds.

"Hey," he said. He gestured toward the house. "I just thought I'd wait out here for you."

He jumped up and got in the car.

"Did something happen?" I asked as I put the car in gear.

"Not really. Sort of. Yeah," he said, crossing his arms over his chest and looking out the window. "She kicked me out."

He looked so pathetic, all long and skinny and grumpy, I couldn't help laughing.

"It's not funny!" he said.

"What happened?"

"I don't want to talk about it," he said. "But it's kind of opposite of what you're thinking."

"I'm not thinking anything. What am I thinking?" I looked over at him. His face was flushed. "Oh! That you tried to go too far! Like you're some made-for-TV movie asshole? Not likely, I'm sure."

He rolled his eyes at me.

"Opposite of that . . . Oh my god! *She* wants to hook up and *you* don't?" I couldn't even imagine a fourteen-year-old boy, or a boy of any age for that matter, turning down a chance for a sure-thing hookup.

"I'm not talking about it," he said.

"You have much to learn about the ways of women, young apprentice. Worry not, my son. For I am here to lead you to the truth." I used my best Confucius voice.

But Gavin looked seriously wounded.

"Gav? Are you really upset? What's going on?"

Then he broke. No tears shed, but they were in his voice, which cracked every few words.

"How am I supposed to know what she wants? Or how to even start things? I don't know what the hell I'm doing. I mean, look at me. I'm a freaking loser. I am not Scotty. Jesus, at my age, he was probably fooling around with every hot girl in his grade."

I cringed, staring at the road.

"You are nothing like Scott, thank god," I managed. "But know this: you are awesome and that smart girl Eliza knows it. She wants to be with you, and it doesn't have to be any more complicated than that. Believe me, she doesn't know what the fuck she's doing either. You guys can do whatever you want, as long as it's okay with both of you." I paused. "Holy shit. Now *I'm* in the made-for-TV movie. Am I the preachy mom or the cool big sister?"

"Big sister, hold the cool," he said.

"A-hole." I shoved his arm. "You can always talk to Chris."

"Oh, beautiful. Sex tips from my sister's boyfriend."

"And . . . we're home," I said, pulling into the garage.

"If you tell anyone about this, I'll kill you," he said.

"Who would I tell?"

He looked at me like I was an idiot.

"Oh, come on," I said. "Rebecca? It would destroy her. You think I want to clean brains off her bedroom wall? No thanks, bro. It's our secret."

"Wow," he said. "You are really fucked up."

"It must run in the family."

As he got out of the car, my phone buzzed with a text. From Sebastian.

"I'll be right in," I said to Gavin. He shrugged and went into the house.

SEBASTIAN: That was all wrong, wasn't it?

Of course Sebastian would text in perfect grammar.

ME: I guess?

SEBASTIAN: It was a lot of pressure. I was really nervous.

I smiled. There he was. Honest Sebastian.

ME: Yeah. Me too.
SEBASTIAN: I was going to say, before you left, that I wished we had met up somewhere else. Somewhere other than McD's. It just didn't seem to fit us. Can we try again? Somewhere else?

Us.

ME: Yes.
SEBASTIAN: Tonight? We can meet in the park.

He was trying to preserve what we had. I had been ready to give up, but he was still trying.

ME: OK.

CHAPTER SIXTEEN

I wanted to wear my orange and red tie-dyed tank top to meet Sebastian, but I couldn't find it and I was going insane. I pulled everything from my drawer, and finally, there it was on the very bottom, hiding under a lime green shirt. It was the same lime green V-neck with lace trim I was wearing when I lost my virginity.

It was fall of sophomore year. A warm September night. Excitement was in the air. A new year. New beginnings. No more being a freshman, no more being lowest on the totem pole. I knew enough to know there was really no such thing as new beginnings, but I was still naive enough to hope I was wrong. I got dressed more carefully for the party that night. I chose the lime green top because I thought it looked girlie and sexy on me, and that's the look I was going for. I was tired of all the making out, under the bra, hand down the pants. I wanted something real to happen. I almost didn't care who it was with. My latest hookup had been Jason Capalongino, a junior. He played lacrosse but he was a bench warmer, so he wasn't quite good enough to be in the jerk-off jock crowd. He had long hair that curled out of his lacrosse helmet at the bottom, so when I'd walk by the field on my way to the bus, I'd always recognize him. After the initial rush I'd gotten from knowing he wanted me, and after that first-kiss euphoria, the rest was just bad kissing and groping. But it was still always worth it for those first moments—the realization that the guy wanted me and the anticipation and moment of the first kiss. In that second, I felt completely pure and cherished and in control. That's why I kept going back for more of the making out with Jason Capolongino, with Mike Danforth, with Grayson DePenta, with Austin Lee, and all the other guys. But I was ready to have sex. And since Jason was the last guy I'd kissed, he was as good a candidate as any.

When Rebecca and I got to the party that night, Jason was with another girl. I didn't like Jason enough to really care that he was tongue wrestling with someone else, but I was pissed that my plans were ruined.

Rebecca and I partied hard that night. We did shots of Bacardi and played quarters with the guys from the band when they went on their break. When we finally realized we were a little more wasted than we'd planned, we stumbled out of the party, leaning on each other for support. She was carrying a bottle of beer.

"Hey, drinking in public is illegal, you know," I had said.

"Underage drinking is illegal too," she replied. "You don't see me going all straight edge, do you?" Then she laughed and spit beer out all over the place, including on my lime green top.

"Oops, sorry," she said, still giggling and trying to wipe off the beer with her hand. She was really just pawing at my boobs. I gave her boob a good honk in return.

"Ow!" she screamed. And then she squeezed mine. And then we cracked up and ran home, practically sideways, laughing the whole way. When we got into her house, we plopped down on opposite ends of the couch with her brother Charlie, who was a senior, in the middle. Jordan and Tony, her other two brothers, had already moved out. Jordan was at one of the state colleges and Tony was in the army.

"Hey," Rebecca said to Charlie. "Where were you? I thought you said you were going to the party."

"Nah," Charlie said. "Didn't make it." He was in his usual uniform of ratty-looking plaid shirt, worn jeans, and hiking boots. "Good party?"

"Yeah," Rebecca said, grabbing the remote from him and flipping through channels. My head had started to spin so I got a glass of water from the kitchen.

"Jess wasn't there," she said to him.

"I don't care."

"I know that's why you didn't go. And she wasn't even there."

Charlie shrugged.

I'd forgotten that Charlie and Jess had just broken up. They'd been going out for three years.

I brought my water back to the couch, took a few sips, and then put it down on the coffee table. Rebecca immediately grabbed it, pounded the rest, and then lay her head down on the cushion. Within minutes, she was breathing slowly and heavily, passed out.

Charlie took the remote off her lap.

"What should we watch?" he asked me.

174

"Something brainless, I guess. I'm pretty wasted," I said.

"I'm toast too."

"By yourself?" I asked.

"Some of the guys were over for a while before they went to the party."

I was sitting pretty close to Charlie at this point. Rebecca took up a lot of the couch in her sleep, so Charlie had to keep moving over to get away from her curled-up feet. I'd always thought Charlie was cute, but he was never an option. Ever since I'd met Rebecca, he'd been practically married to Jess. I looked at Charlie closely while he tried to find something to watch. He had some scruff on his chin and cheeks. The white T-shirt he wore underneath the plaid shirt had a beer stain on it. His light brown eyes looked tired and sexy. His hair looked not-so-recently washed. The scruffy lumberjack look. I was digging it.

"This is good," I said as he got to *Real World*.

"Seriously?"

"Brainless," I said.

"Right." And then he noticed me looking at him. Our faces were inches apart. I could smell the beer on his breath. I leaned toward him, feeling that anticipation. *Does he want me?* And then he kissed me. *Yes, he wants me.* I deserved good things like this cute guy wanting me. His kiss was hard and sure, and the tingle shot straight to my toes. We started making out and his hand went up my shirt, the lime green one with the lace trim.

"Let's go to my room," he whispered, like he suddenly realized that his sister was passed out on the other side of him. I nodded and we went to his room. Within minutes, we were naked and fooling around. And I felt so powerful because he kept saying, "I want you so bad."

He opened his drawer and got out a condom.

"Is this cool?" he asked. I nodded.

We had sex. It hurt some, it felt sort of good, but mostly it was done. It didn't last very long, and he apologized afterward.

"Sorry for what?" I asked.

"That I couldn't last long enough for you to . . . you know . . ."

I didn't think a guy would even notice or care about that.

"It's okay," I said. And, *maybe next time*, I thought. But we both knew there would probably be no next time. He fell asleep almost instantly, his breath hot on my neck. What was it with these Maronis? They were narcoleptics. I got up, gathered my clothes and tiptoed into Rebecca's room. I put on a T-shirt from her drawer and climbed into her bed. Unlike the Maronis, I couldn't just fall asleep; instead I lay there thinking. I was no longer a virgin. My body had finally caught up to the rest of me. Thank you, Charlie Maroni. I tried to assess what I felt, what my body felt, which was . . . pretty much nothing.

Charlie and Jess got back together a few days later. We never hooked up again. But after that, I was free to have sex with anyone who wanted to. And lots of guys wanted to, as it turned out. And then when Chris and I started going out, I tried my best to feel *something*. Sometimes I could be right there in the moment, feeling how good it was to just be loved by Chris. And then, I'd be back. Just me. Watching us have sex.

Now I held the lime green shirt up against myself in the mirror. It would be a nice look for tonight, but I didn't want any history interfering with my night with Sebastian. I stuck with the orange and red tie-dyed tank and black gauzy pants. I checked my dreads—perfectly ratty but also perfectly in place. I heard Gavin's heavy footsteps coming up the stairs and into his room. I expected the door to slam, but it closed somewhat gently. He was making an effort after Mom begged him to stop being so hard on her doors. I added one more touch of mascara.

When I got halfway down the stairs, I heard angry whispers coming from the family room. Mom and Dad were fighting again. I stood still, listening, not wanting to but unable to stop myself.

"Again, Rob?" Mom said.

"I have to," Dad said.

"Where to this time?"

"San Francisco, Seattle, and then a conference in Phoenix. I'll be back next Monday."

"You're never here. Ever. I'm taking care of everything," Mom hissed.

"Oh, so you're taking care of *everything*, huh? How do you squeeze *everything* in between the gym and getting your nails done?" Harsh, Dad, even if it's true.

"Are you fucking kidding me?" I had never heard Mom swear like that before. I wanted to run away, but I needed to hear the rest of Mom's answer. And, boy did I hear it. I could tell that her teeth were clenched, even through the whispering. "You made me quit my job, remember? I could have been running that place by now. And when all the kids went to school, you still wanted your clients to think you were so good that you didn't need your wife to work. Nineteen-fifties bullshit. So, what could I do? Goddamn nothing, that's what. The gym, tennis. This is your doing, Rob. And don't fucking forget it."

"Whoa, Deb," Dad said in an *I've got to calm this crazy bitch down* voice. "I didn't know you were so miserable."

"Yes you did. You just didn't care," she said. "It's always like this. You're never here but then you swoop in, play a little ball with the kids, and they'll still worship you. And I'm here doing everything, and they treat me like shit. I know you're trying to escape, and I don't even know if I care anymore. I'm going back to work."

"Of course I care. I'm sorry you're so lonely and trapped here. I think you *should* go back to work. I've always thought that, but the time never seemed right. I guess now it is."

"Yeah, now," Mom said, her voice bitter with sarcasm. "Now. In the middle of a recession. It's a perfect time to find a job. Especially when I've been out of the workforce for seventeen years doing nothing but getting my nails done."

"I'm sorry," Dad said quietly, sweetly.

"I need you to care," Mom said, her voice muffled. Probably Dad was hugging her now and she was talking into his shirt.

"Deb, I do. So much."

Mom breathed a few times.

"Let's go out," he said. "You want to go to the movies?"

"Yes, let's do that," Mom said.

I waited a few minutes until I thought it was safe to go down. I found Mom and Dad huddled over the counter reading movie reviews.

"I'm going out," I said.

"Home by twelve," Mom said automatically.

I nodded, unable to look at her now that I knew how miserable she was. And why.

"Have a good time," Dad said.

"Thanks." I closed the door behind me, forcing myself to leave what I'd just heard behind me, especially the part about Dad wanting to escape. Did he really not want to be with Mom—with us? She was right. He was never home much growing up, but when he was, he was totally *Fun Dad*. Was it all an act? I didn't want to think about it. So I didn't.

As soon as I got in my car, I felt a wave of something pass through my body. Excitement, exhilaration? Now that the initial awkward meeting with Sebastian was over and we were going to start again, I couldn't wait to get to him. This bubbling feeling was so new, I didn't know what to do with it. I started driving, rolled down the windows, and screamed. But a happy scream, not like earlier in the day when everything sucked. Now there was promise.

I pulled into Leonard Park. It was deserted at nine o'clock at night. In fact, it was probably illegal to be here at all. My car was the only one in the lot, so I figured I'd gotten there first. But as I walked toward the swings, I saw Sebastian was already there, sitting on one of them, swaying slightly back and forth.

"Hi," he said as I got closer. A wood chip lodged itself in my sandal, but I didn't want to stand there shaking my foot to get it out, so I ignored it.

"Hi," I said. "How did you get here?"

"I walked. It's not that far."

But I knew where he lived, and it must have taken him at least forty-five minutes.

I sat on the green swing next to him, gripping the cold, rusty chain. I reached into my sandal and pulled out the chip scraping the arch of my foot. I pushed my feet on the ground, but my legs were too long for the little swing, so I had to put my knees together and splay my feet out. Sebastian's legs were stretched out in front of him, his heels pushing on the ground. In the distance, behind the sandbox, monkey bars, and jungle gym, I could see the outline of the Rec Center where I'd been forced to play indoor sports in the winter. A vision of six-year-old Chris chasing me around the path on his Batman scooter popped into my head.

The air felt a little damp even though it hadn't rained. I wished I'd brought a sweater. It was dark, but I could see Sebastian's features, the white of his teeth, the shine from his wire glasses. He reached over and took my hand from the chain. He squeezed once with his long fingers and then let go.

"I'm glad you came," he said.

"Me too."

"I know today was so weird. I just . . . after everything, and then the whole McDonald's thing. You know. It didn't seem quite right for what we have going on," he said.

I nodded. And then, without permission, my mouth opened and words came out.

"What *do* we have going on?" That's not how I meant it to sound. Like an insecure girl trying to figure out where she stood. Or worse, a bitchy girl who was pretending she didn't know something was going on.

"Good question." He laughed a little nervously. "I've been in the psych ward for three weeks. Nothing is normal there, so I don't know what's normal here anymore. What *do* we have going on?"

"I don't know," I said. "But I was upset today when I thought whatever it is was gone."

I swallowed hard. I was glad it was dark out because I felt so vulnerable. I didn't want him to see me like this.

"Me too," he said.

"It's weird for me. To get upset." Again, the words spilled out of my mouth like I wasn't in control of them. I felt shaky, opening myself up to him, and I wasn't sure how to stop it, or if I wanted to.

"I get that sense about you. You're very strong. Too strong."

"Too strong?"

"Just strong enough?" he said quickly, smiling. He paused. "I should've called you after the thing with Luke. But I started thinking, and I felt all this pressure to try to help him and I totally couldn't. It was like this extra burden. And then I realized that was exactly the position I was putting you in, so I didn't want to do that to you. But then I missed you."

"I don't feel burdened," I said.

He let out an audible breath.

"Listen," he said. "I know there's something here. But we really can't get into that kind of relationship right now."

I felt a sting in my chest hearing him say it aloud, especially after all I had just admitted. A guy who didn't want me. It hurt. It hurt a whole fucking lot. I hated myself for thinking I deserved something more. And then I hated myself for thinking I didn't deserve more. I was drowning in a pool of lose-lose self-hatred, but I didn't want him to see that. I straightened my shoulders, gripped the chain of the swing tighter.

"I'm not trying to be all like *I know you want me*," he said. "But I want us to be honest. Relationships are roller coasters, and I'm so fresh off the addiction thing, they're afraid that if anything happened, I'd go right back. Plus, I have to steer clear of the drinkers and druggers, so I can't really hang with your friends. There are a lot of rules. And, well . . ."

He paused, like he didn't want to continue. But then he did.

"I totally screwed up the last, well, only relationship I had. It was bad. I mean, super horribly bad. I can't be in that situation again. I never want to hurt anyone like that again. So, that's it." He took a deep breath. "I know this sounds so lame, but can we be friends?"

Now the pain was stronger in my chest, a warm burning that made my eyes blur.

"We already are," I said, trying to be light, but it still hurt. "And I have a—you know—I'm with someone." I couldn't say *boyfriend*. And certainly not to Sebastian. It seemed so . . . small.

"Chris Holtz," he said.

"Uh-huh."

"He seems like a nice guy." I could definitely hear a smirk in his voice. He thought Chris was dumb. That's what he was thinking.

"He is," I said. No matter how I was feeling about Chris, I didn't want Sebastian to sense my own doubts.

Sebastian nodded.

"To be honest," he said. "I'm totally jealous."

Jealous. He *did* have feelings for me.

"Tell me what it's really like being home," I said.

"Well, I'm back in the place where I'm an addict. It's bizarre to wake up in my bed and know that I won't be having a pill today. Or a line, or a smoke, or a drink. Nothing. I've always woken up in that bed hoping I wouldn't, but knowing I would. And now I know I won't. And it's awesome. But it's also scary as shit. I mean, my existence has been thinking about when I can get to wherever I need to be so that I can have my next hit of whatever. And now, I can't think that. So, I don't know what to think about."

I didn't tell him that I used to feel that way with sex—when could I get my next fix of a new guy wanting me, kissing me. I'd lived without it since I'd been with Chris.

"Nothing will keep me busy long enough," he continued. "I have to finish the work I missed from the last couple of weeks of school, but I know that won't take me long, so I've been postponing that. I already read one book today. I took a long walk. Obviously," he said, gesturing toward the road he'd come from. "I saw you this afternoon. I'm seeing you now. I have to keep my mind occupied every second so I don't think about when I'm going to get my next high."

I nodded again. "It's going to take a while," I said, praying I could say the right thing, but also knowing that if I said something wrong, he'd let it slide. "It seems like it's a game of patience. With time, but also with yourself. You can't be too hard on yourself. It's okay if you have a thought about when you can get your next high. It's just that the next thought will now have to be *Oh yeah, I'm not doing that anymore. So, when's the next time I get to see Macy?*"

He smiled. "Yeah. Just what I need. To transfer my addiction to you. But, you're right. The therapists all say not to be hard on ourselves. The truth is, I'm so fucking scared I'll have to go back there. And I really don't want to."

"Did you hate it?" I asked.

He looked up at the dark sky. "Yes and no. Yes for obvious reasons. I was there against my will. I had to go to therapy all day long, the food sucked—all that stuff. But also no, I didn't hate it because I learned so much about myself, and I was surprised by how much people can genuinely care about someone they barely know." He started swinging a little more. "Rashanna cried when I left."

"Really?"

"Yeah," he said. "That was tough. You know, you think of the staff there, and this is what they *do*, kids like me in and out every day, and then I leave and she's crying and I'm like 'how can you do this job?' I was afraid she was crying because she knew I'd fail, but she said it was the opposite, that she was crying because she knew I'd succeed and she'd never see me again."

"Wow."

He nodded and swallowed. "I guess I was a good patient. She said a lot of the kids, they're so damaged and when they leave, they're just going back to their same messed-up family situations. And she knows she'll see them at the hospital again. This one thirteen-year-old girl Michele had been living on the street for months. They had to cut off all her hair because it was infested with bugs and nasty stuff. I think she showered like ten times before she was clean. But there was this look in her eyes like . . . no matter how clean they got her—showered and off the drugs—she'd seen things no one should ever see, and they could never scrub that out of her. She's who Rashanna meant, like beyond repair. . . . I hope I don't have to go back."

"You won't," I said, trying to stop myself from imagining what this girl Michele had seen. "But if you do for any reason, it will be because you need it. It helped you."

"Yeah, it did. I know I've got to change things. I hope I can change things."

This connection with Sebastian, feeling the way I imagined you're supposed to feel when you're in love—connected, honest, exhilarated—made me feel that hope of change. But the feeling dissolved in an instant as soon as I remembered that Sebastian and I wouldn't have a chance at it.

"What are you thinking about?" he asked.

"Um . . . just what you said, the hope of change," I said quickly, hoping he couldn't read the sadness in my voice. "It sounds really good."

"It sounds good in theory, I know. But in reality? It sucks. It's just discipline and hard work and watching minutes tick by." He rubbed the fuzz of hair on top of his head.

"So, then. What are you going to do . . . to keep yourself busy? Can you get a job?"

"I'll try. I have to do the outpatient program and Narcotics Anonymous, so I'd have to find something that works with the schedule. I won't be babysitting Sofia as much as I thought. I have to 'earn back their trust.' But my mom's friend works at the library. I might be able to get some hours there."

"That would be good," I said.

We swung back and forth again on the swings, out of sync for a while, and then we were swinging together, right in rhythm.

"Oh, I almost forgot," he said suddenly. "I made something for you." He pulled a piece of paper that was folded into quarters out of his back pocket and handed it to me. I unfolded and tilted it to catch some of the light from the parking lot. It was a drawing of me, and it really looked like me. A lion burst from the top of my head, its mane falling down and then combining with my hair. The lion was roaring, but didn't look scary; it looked sweet, in a way, like it was smiling really wide. The whole drawing was done in black pencil, but parts of the lion had been shaded in some yellow and brown.

"Oh my god," I said. "This is incredible."

Sebastian looked down shyly.

"I drew it before. You know, before I saw your dreadlocks, so it's still got your wavy hair. I know the lion is kind of dumb," he said. "Because Macy Lyons, you know—lion—it's so obvious, but there's something about a lion that makes me think of you. They're tough and they're leaders, but they're also soft and sweet-looking. I guess it's what I was trying to say earlier—I feel like I can see a softer side of you that maybe not everyone gets to see."

"You do," I said. "I do feel like you see me differently than other people do."

"And," he said, "you see me differently than other people do too. It's like you don't even know me but you have faith in me. You trust me with myself."

We sat in silence for a few minutes.

He took my hand and intertwined his long thin fingers in mine. The touch of his palm against mine was thrilling in a way that it never was with Chris. We stayed like that for a little while, and then I took our clasped hands up to my face and put the back of his hand against my cheek. He moved his finger slowly back and forth on my skin. And it felt amazing, the softest touch of his finger on my face. And I knew for sure I was falling in love with him because nothing had ever felt so good in my entire life. He gently took his hand back, pulled out his phone, and looked at the time.

"I really should go," he said. "My mom is watching me like a hawk. I just got let out for a bit on parole."

"I'll drive you home."

"I think I want to walk. It's good for me to walk."

I nodded, disappointed. We stood and walked across the wood chips to the parking lot. Sebastian opened the driver side door for me. It would have been the moment for a kiss, but we both knew it wasn't going to happen.

"Thanks for meeting me," he said.

"You know I want to see you."

"Feels good to know that," he said, smiling.

He leaned toward me, kissed me softly on the cheek, then turned and walked toward the road.

I watched him, his jeans low on his hips, his long arms dangling by his sides. He put his hands in his pockets.

I got in the car and started the engine. My phone buzzed. I searched my pockets, but it was nowhere. And then I found it wedged between my seat and the console. I'd missed five texts.

JASMINE: It's me, Rebecca. Fone out of juice. Where r u?

CHRIS: R u at party in Pound Ridge? Call me.

JASMINE [REBECCA]: Where r u?? 911!

CHRIS: I need to talk to u.

CHRIS: Where r u??

CHAPTER SEVENTEEN

Rebecca's "emergencies" were rarely emergencies. Chris, on the other hand, never sent me an *I need to talk to u*, so I called him first, but it went to voice mail.

"What's going on? Call me back," I said.

I called Jasmine's phone next, and Rebecca picked up on the first ring. I could barely hear her; the noise in the background was deafening: music, laughter, shouting.

"Where are you?" I asked. "It sounds like you're in hell."

"I am in hell," Rebecca yelled into the phone. "I need you here now."

"And where is this particular version of hell?" I asked.

"Hold on a sec," she said, and then I heard her saying "excuse me, excuse me," obviously pushing through a crowd. And then it was quiet. "I'm outside now. I'm at a party. Some girl name Jacqueline. Yes, it's pronounced like that—Shak-u–*leen*. Some French girl."

"Uh-huh," I said. "And?"

I put my phone on speaker and started driving, pulling out onto the road. Sebastian must have been walking fast because I couldn't see him anymore.

"*And*, I'm in trouble here," Rebecca said. "Cody dragged me to this horrid prep school party. I tried to resist, but he

189

was insistent. And now he's gone MIA on me, and I have no idea where he is. Probably screwing a skinny chick somewhere." She sniffled.

I tried to make my voice sympathetic. "Oh, Beck. Maybe he's just out smoking or something."

"I'm outside right *now*. He's not out here. I'm telling you, he's gone. He completely ditched me. Will you please come get me? I feel like such a loser," she said.

I pulled into the supermarket parking lot. If I was going to pick her up, I'd have to turn around. "Isn't there someone there who can take you home? What about Jasmine?"

"Jasmine's hooking up. Everyone is completely out of their mind wasted. No one is even close to going home, even if I would get in a car with them."

I looked at the clock on my dashboard. 10:40 p.m.

"Okay," I said. "Where does this little french fry live?"

"Shit. I don't even know where I am. Hold on." I heard her going back inside and asking for the address. I put my head on the steering wheel, wishing I hadn't called her back. But . . . who knows what would've happened if I hadn't.

"Pound Ridge," she said into the phone. "42 Fox Run Road, just past the lake."

"Seriously?" That was a hike and a half.

"Please," she whined. "I need you."

I pictured her puppy dog eyes, and I couldn't resist her this time.

"Wait outside," I said. "I'm not going inside to look for you."

"Thank you, thank you! I'll be out front. I promise."

It wasn't like this was the first or the second time this happened. It was all the time. Cody would take Rebecca to a party, and then he'd go find another girl and leave Rebecca by herself. Or they'd hook up, and then the next day, he'd say it had been a mistake. Of course, she only wanted the guy she couldn't have. And now I was about to torture myself in the exact same way by agreeing to be "friends" with Sebastian, when I knew full well I was starting to have seriously serious feelings for him.

After twenty minutes of driving and searching for the house number in the pitch black, I finally pulled into the long winding driveway. French Jacqueline lived in a quaint, little country house tucked into the woods. About twenty cars were parked along the driveway, mostly huge SUVs. As I had suspected, Rebecca wasn't outside. I texted Jasmine's phone, hoping Rebecca still had it. I was not going inside.

ME: Beck? I'm here.

As I finished the text, Chris called.

"Hey," he said. "Are you with Rebecca?"

That was not what I was expecting. "I'm about to be. Why? Aren't you at that client dinner with your dad?"

"Yeah, I'm still here."

"Okay . . ." I said. "So, what's the emergency?"

"Cody texted me."

"And?" I asked.

This was also not the first time Chris and I had both been dragged into the whole Rebecca/Cody drama.

"You're not going to believe this," he said.

"I already know," I said. "He screwed with her. Made her come to this party and then dumped her. Again."

"He didn't dump her," Chris said.

"No? Then why did she call me to come get her?"

"Cody's locked in a bathroom on the third floor," he said.

"What?"

"Yeah," Chris said. "He texted me that he went to the bathroom up there, and the lock got stuck and no one's been up there. He said he tried Rebecca a thousand times, but she won't pick up."

I sighed. "Damn. I guess I have to go in. So then what? He didn't ditch her? He wants to be more than friends?"

"Seriously? Who knows what he wants? Just go rescue the bastard."

"Fine," I said. "But you owe me."

"*They* owe you. They owe *us*."

"Fine. I'll take care of it. Go finish your dinner," I said.

"Alright. Call me later, okay?"

"Okay."

After my quiet night with Sebastian, having to go into a drunken sweat-fest was the last thing I'd wanted to do. I walked up to the front door. A blue stone walkway had been placed in fresh mulch. I made giant steps, trying to step only on the flat circular stones. A little fishpond gurgled off to the side. It seemed like it would be a good place to sit and try to find peace. Like my oak tree. I wondered if French Jacqueline ever sat for hours like I did. Maybe we could be friends, she and I. My phone buzzed.

CHRIS: He says get paperclip to push the lock.
ME: *Groan*

I put my phone in my pocket and stared at the front door, which was giant and heavy, covered in wood grain and knots, like it had been salvaged from an old horse barn. I pushed it and found the inevitable mess of loud-smelly-drunken people. I scanned the crowd for any ex-hook-ups that I'd need to avoid. All clear.

"Macy! Hey! Where've you been?" Jasmine shouted. She was sitting on a couch with her arm draped around the neck of a guy I didn't recognize. She came over and hugged me, drenching me with the mixed odors of beer and sweet perfume. As usual, she looked perfectly put-together—her brown hair blown long and smooth, makeup applied so perfectly as to look nonexistent, every item of her clothes fitting just right on her model-perfect body. No one should look like that.

"I feel like I haven't seen you in forever! Where've you been?" she asked.

"I've been around," I said, scanning the crowd. "Have you seen Rebecca?"

"She was just here. Maybe she's in the kitchen." The boy on the couch was beckoning to her with a come-hither finger.

"He is so hot," she said to me. "He goes to Andover."

I nodded, pretending I cared.

I entered the kitchen. Cute little painted flowers were spaced out on every few tiles on the floor and behind the stove. The refrigerator was a retro mustardy yellow. Heavy wooden beams ran across the low ceiling and matched the old barn door at the front of the house. I wanted to live in this kitchen. It was small, cozy, comfortable. Not like my kitchen where the ceilings were so high that you couldn't even chew without an echo. Jacqueline's kitchen table was a long thin rectangle with chairs that had soft flowery cushions on it. Everything felt very Euro-country, but in an authentic way. Nothing was trying too hard.

I found Rebecca sitting at the table, drinking a beer and staring out the window. People were sitting all around her laughing and telling jokes, but she just looked pathetic sitting there. I came up behind her and put my arms around her neck.

"Hi," she said. "Oops, I didn't wait outside."

"It's okay." I sat in the chair next to her. I didn't feel any particular urgency to rescue Cody. He deserved to wait.

Her mascara had smudged a little below her eye. I licked my finger and wiped at it.

"Gross," she said.

"You look like a rabid raccoon."

"Let's get out of here," she said.

"We have to do something first."

"What?"

"You'll see," I said. I led her out of the kitchen toward the staircase. I didn't recognize many people at this party. It was a different crowd—not quite mainstream, but not quite edge either. Maybe Euro.

"Where's the French chick?" I asked Rebecca as we started up the stairs. The carpeting was navy blue with specks of tan in it and the wood on the edges was dark. I was curious who lived in this house, the kind of house that made me want to be an architect in the first place. What lucky girl had parents who cared more about warmth and comfort than big and fancy?

"I don't know," Rebecca said, sullenly. "Why are we going up here?"

I didn't answer, just kept walking up another flight of stairs to a small third-floor room with slanted ceilings. The same dark wood beams as in the kitchen stretched down on either side, holding up the ceiling. The room had been made into a study, with a dark green rug, soft lighting, a simple wooden desk, and a wooden chair. Two red leather armchairs sat facing each other with a small table in between. I yearned to sit at the table in the daylight and look out the window to what I knew would be trees—tons of them. Instead, I went to the desk and found a paper clip. The only door in the room had to be the bathroom. I knocked on it.

"Oh, thank god!" Cody's voice shouted. Rebecca's mouth dropped open.

"What the hell are you doing?" she whispered loudly at me. "Torturing me? You want me to catch him hooking up? Are you trying to prove something?"

"No," I said, straightening the paperclip. "He didn't ditch you tonight. He's been locked in this bathroom since you last saw him." I stuck the small wire in the tiny hole of the knob and jiggled until I heard a little pop. The door swung open.

"Cody?" Rebecca said quietly, peering into the bathroom, as if she didn't believe me. Cody was standing in front of us, his phone in his hand. He *looked* like he'd been locked in the bathroom for a long time. His hair was a mess, like he'd been tugging at it in frustration.

"What the hell?" she said. "Are you okay? I thought you ditched me."

"Beck, you know I wouldn't do that," he said, putting his arm around her. "Thanks, Macy."

"Wait!" Rebecca said. "How did you know he was in here?"

"I called Chris," he said. "He called Macy."

"Why didn't you call *me*?" she said.

"I tried."

"Oh, yeah," she said. "My phone is dead. I'm such an idiot."

"At least you're a hot idiot." He kissed her.

"Okay, then," I said. "All's well that ends well."

"Um," she said, her face bright, her eyes smiling. "Maybe we should stay."

Cody put his arm around her waist.

"Yeah, I've been locked in the bathroom all night," Cody said. "I need a drink."

I felt the momentary urge to stay, if only to meet the elusive French Jacqueline, but when I realized it was getting close to midnight, I fought it. It wasn't worth the inevitable blowout with Mom.

"Turning into a pumpkin, have to go," I said. "But have fun, guys."

I started back down the stairs.

"Talk tomorrow," Rebecca said. "Love you!"

As I got to the bottom step, I could hear the *slurp slurp* of them making out.

On my way to the front door, I waved to Jasmine, still on the couch with her Andover guy. Once outside, I looked back longingly at the murmuring fishpond, the house, everything I imagined it to be.

CHAPTER EIGHTEEN

That night I dreamed of the country. Not the New York City suburban country, where we lived, but real country, where seeds were planted and things grown and harvested. Fields and fields of vegetables. Cows being milked, tractors, horses, the works. A thick, sturdy log cabin with one simple room just big enough for cooking, eating, and sleeping. Furnished only with a table and chairs and a bed. I lived in that house. When I woke up, I felt oddly refreshed. And then I looked around my room, which Mom had decorated—silky blue and brown striped comforter, twelve-foot ceilings with giant crown moldings, custom-made blue and brown paisley roman shades, plush beige wall-to-wall carpet, a walk-in closet, the door to my private bathroom with matching blue and brown towels and shower curtain. I wanted to throw it all away and move into that log cabin. Or at least into French Jacqueline's house.

After the kids had all been picked up from camp, I turned on my phone for the first time since I left for Marwood in the morning. It buzzed incessantly with texts.

CHRIS: U @ camp alred?
GAVIN: Bored. U comin home?

CHRIS: Going to Mets game. Call me.
SEBASTIAN: Can you do something today? I have an idea.

Intrigued, I texted him back.

ME: What is it?
SEBASTIAN: Secret. When are you free?
ME: Rest of day.
SEBASTIAN: 2pm. But can you drive? I don't have full car "privileges" back yet.
ME: I'll pick u up. Where r we going?
SEBASTIAN: Dress comfortably. See you at 2.

When I got home, I listened in at Gavin's closed door. Silent. I wrote him a note *Gone fishin'* and put it on the floor outside his door. I got dressed in a short flowered skirt and a black tank top. Downstairs, I slipped on flip-flops and went out to my oak tree until it was time to go.

I pulled up in front of Sebastian's house. Before I could put the car in park and get out—I didn't want to honk for him— the front door opened and Sebastian came out. He was all sported out in long basketball shorts, a white athletic-type shirt, and sneakers. He shouted something inside the house, closed the door, and jogged toward the car. He looked really cute, all tall and thin and grinning at me. A huge smile spread across my own face in response.

"Hey," he said, as he got in the car. And then he looked me up and down.

"*That's* your interpretation of comfortable clothes?" he asked, taking in my tank, skirt, and flip-flops, but I happily noticed his eyes lingering on my legs.

"Yes, this *is* comfortable," I said.

"No, no, no, my sweet mistaken girl. This. This is what I meant by comfortable," he said, gesturing at himself. "Shorts, sneakers."

"But these are the very definition of comfort," I said, lifting up a flip-flopped foot and smiling.

"But you can't run in those," he said.

"Well, that's okay, I don't run."

"Ah, but you're running today," he said, pointing at me.

"Ah, but I'm not," I said, pointing back at him.

"You didn't know I was on the cross-country team, did you?"

"Um, no," I said. "And if by cross-country, you mean like you enjoy driving to California and back, that's great and all, but I don't see how you'd have the time."

"Ha, ha. I'm a runner."

"How nice for you," I said, but I was surprised. "But how are you a runner and a . . ."

"A druggie?"

"Yeah. That."

"I know. It's a weird combination, but I *am* very good at it."

"Again, how nice for you."

"Come on," he said. "We have to go back to your house now so you can change. We're going jogging."

"Not a chance in hell."

"You'll like it," he said. "I promise."

"Let's see, the last time I ran was in eighth grade when they made us run forever as fast as we could. I seem to remember feeling like someone had reached into my throat, squeezed my heart, scraped the roof of my mouth with a dull razor blade, and then put my legs in a vice. So, hmmm, I don't think I'll like it."

"You'll see," he said. "You'll like it. Now drive."

"Yessir," I said, saluting his faux-bossiness. I started driving, aware of his large body in the small seat just inches away from me.

Jogging? Mom jogged. I didn't jog. But if Sebastian jogged, *then* what? The world was completely upside down now—Mom wanted to work, Dad was more MIA than usual, and Sebastian was a long-distance runner.

We pulled into my driveway and went into the kitchen.

"Um, wait here, I'll be right back," I said. He was so tall that the giant room with soaring vaulted ceilings didn't even make him look shorter.

He slid a stool out from the counter—the heavy iron made a scraping sound on the tile—and he perched half his nonexistent butt on it.

He could have come up to my bedroom, but something stopped me from inviting him. It's not like I cared about propriety for Mom. At this point, she wouldn't have even cared if a guy were in my room. But instinct told me being in a bedroom together would be too tempting for me.

I ransacked my room. I'd never voluntarily run before in my life, but somehow Sebastian made me want to do things I didn't usually do, like laugh hysterically and cry and . . . jog. I found an old pair of school gym shorts, faded red with a small pointy-nosed fox on the bottom. I didn't own a sports bra, so I took out the rattiest bra I had and tightened the straps as far as they'd go, then slipped on one of Dad's shirts I'd stolen to sleep in—light blue with yellow writing: BLEU RIDGE SUSTAINABLE FARM—SUSTAIN THIS! Now for sneakers. I rummaged through the closet until I found them. I hadn't worn them since we were required to take gym class in tenth grade. I ran into Gavin's empty room and grabbed his Star Wars baseball cap, the one with crossing light sabers. I stretched it as far as it would go over my dreads and galloped down the stairs, enjoying the soft cushioning of the sneakers.

As I approached the kitchen, I heard voices—the Spanish-speaking voices of Sebastian and Mom—bouncing off the high ceiling. Mom had always claimed she spoke fluent Spanish, but I'd never heard her until now. But—wow—she was gabbing away. And Sebastian's voice in Spanish was different than in English. It was just as raspy but had a slightly lower pitch. It was hot that he could speak two languages. Mom was looking intensely at Sebastian, talking to him like he was an adult. She had never looked at me like that.

I stood in the doorway to the kitchen, listening to the *r*'s rolling off Sebastian's tongue, until finally Mom saw me and switched to English.

"What are you planning to do after you graduate?" Mom asked him. I stepped into the room, unsure of my place in this strange adult-like conversation. Sebastian looked at me and smiled, but Mom was waiting for him to answer.

"I don't know yet," Sebastian said, also switching to English, so smoothly it was as if he didn't notice. And then I wondered which language he dreamed in. I wondered if he dreamed about me. "I still have some stuff to work out, but I've considered applying to schools in Spain."

Sebastian hadn't mentioned this possibility to me, and I hoped that it wasn't true.

"That would be amazing," Mom said, a far-off look in her eyes. "How wonderful to bring your experience back there."

"I'm ready," I said, cautiously. Mom snapped out of whatever European fantasy world she was living in. I could tell by the way she sized me up that she was not pleased with what I was wearing, but thankfully she didn't say anything.

"What are you guys up to?" she asked.

"We're going for a—" Sebastian started.

"Nothing," I jumped in quickly. If Mom knew I was exercising, I wouldn't hear the end of it.

"Okay, then," Mom said, her voice cold and distant as she turned to open the refrigerator. "Have fun doing . . . nothing. Should I expect you for dinner?"

"No," I said.

"It was nice to meet you, Sebastian," she said.

"You too. Bye, Mrs. Lyons."

We went through the garage to my car. He got into the passenger seat slowly, his knees pushed up against the glove compartment.

"So, where are we going?" I asked.

"To the reservoir."

I started the car, revving the gas.

"So," he said after I started down our driveway. "Why are you so nasty to your mama?"

"Are you *kidding* me? You mean why is *she* so nasty to *me*?"

He shrugged.

"What?"

"It's just that she seems pretty cool. She's interesting. Come on, she did public relations for the US team in the Barcelona Olympics."

"Oh."

"You didn't know that?" he said.

"I guess I knew she'd done something Olympic-related, but I never really knew what."

"God," he rolled his eyes at me. "That woman *knows* shit."

"Whatever," I said, refusing to give in, but I felt kind of guilty for never asking Mom more about what she'd done before I was born.

"You're so stubborn, you know that?" I felt him looking at me and I heard the smile in his voice, and I shivered. I wanted to touch him so badly. I felt the skin on my hand go all prickly on the gearshift, itching for him to touch it.

"Pull over here," he said, pointing at the art museum parking lot. "We'll park here and walk over to the path."

I pulled into a spot. A huge banner for the museum's Chinese photography exhibit flapped in the wind.

We got out of the car, and I held my keys since I had no pockets. Sebastian took them and put them on top of my front tire.

"What if someone takes them?" I whispered, looking around.

"Never happens," he said. "It's a rule of running."

"How could you possibly know that?" I whispered again.

"I just do."

He put his hand on my back as we walked toward the path. His touch felt hot on my already-warm back.

"First we have to stretch," he said, moving his neck from side to side and bending his gangly body toward his toes.

I laughed, but I copied everything he did.

"Loosen up," he said. "Bend, twist, get your blood moving. Jog in place." He moved his knees up and down while he rolled his neck and shook his arms by his sides.

"You look ridiculous," I said, and then he exaggerated the movement, making his skinny legs spring off the ground and almost touched his knees to his chest.

He cocked his head to the side, with a mock-curious look.

"You makin' fun o' me?"

"Yup," I said.

"Come on," he said, so I did what he was doing, and I looked ridiculous too, and I didn't care. We both bent over laughing.

"Okay, all warmed up. Let's go."

I started running slowly. He ran next to me, clearly at a crawl's pace for himself, but he didn't seem to mind. We were silent. I heard the rhythmic sound of our feet on the dirt. My breathing almost immediately got loud and heavy. After what felt like forever—the taste of metal in my mouth, the fast pounding of my heart—I stopped.

"Phew," I said. "Okay, you're right. That was great. Can we go back now?"

He laughed and looked at his watch. "We've been running exactly three minutes and twenty-three seconds."

"Seriously?" It felt like it had been at least fifteen minutes.

"We're going to run twenty minutes," he said.

"I don't feel like it," I whined. "Can't we just go get a cheeseburger?"

The truth was, I didn't really care what we did. I just wanted to stay near Sebastian.

"Nope," he said. "Twenty minutes." And then he lightly smacked me on the butt.

"The football smack?"

"It works in every sport. It's very motivating," he said. His smile was contagious. "Let's go."

I started running again.

"You can do this. You can do anything for twenty minutes," he said.

We stayed silent as we ran. The sound of our shoes on the dirt was calming; my breathing got more measured as my body got used to pushing the breath in and out at the right speed for running. My mind wandered to my parents' argument, addiction, French Jacqueline, Scott's face when he asked if I wanted to hang out. And then my mind stopped wandering and it was just clear and relaxed. I barely noticed Sebastian next to me. At one point, he touched my elbow and gestured to turn back, but I shook my head. I wanted to keep going. We ran the entire loop around the reservoir. My legs and my whole body felt free. My mind was focused, not on anything particular, but just a general sense of clarity. And then I saw the parking lot.

"Just slow to a walk now," he said. "Get our heart rates down before stopping."

I felt my breathing slow, my heart slow, and my body relax.

"Wow," he said, looking at me with what I can only describe as admiration. "That was four miles."

"Seriously?"

"Yeah," he said. "Forty-seven minutes."

"Forty-seven minutes? Are you kidding? It felt like fifteen or twenty."

He smiled. "You were in the zone, weren't you?"

"I guess I was." I was in the zone.

"Adrenaline," he said. "It's addictive, but not illegal."

We laughed. I felt different, like something in me had irreversibly changed. Like from this moment on, I would be different somehow. A switch had been flipped.

"Didn't you say something about a cheeseburger?" he asked.

"Totally. I'm starving. Diner?"

I retrieved my keys from the tire. Miraculously, no one had stolen them.

CHAPTER NINETEEN

We got in the car, our bodies hot and sweaty. Even sitting, sweat still trickled down my face.

"You think it's okay to go to the diner like this?" I asked.

"Sure. If it's okay with you. I don't mind waiting if you want to shower, though."

"No. I don't care if you don't," I said. I'd rather Mom not see me all sweaty and invigorated. It would be too triumphant for her.

My phone rang. Chris. I pressed ignore.

Sebastian pretended not to notice, even though there was no way he hadn't seen the giant Chris lit up on the screen.

When we got to the diner, Sebastian got us a table while I went to the bathroom. I listened to Chris's message.

"Hi," he said. I could hear cheering in the background. "Still at the game. My mom asked if you can come for dinner tonight. Can you come?"

I texted him.

ME: Yes, c u tonite.

When I looked in the mirror, I was surprised by the person looking back at me. My face was flushed pink, my eyes were bright, my lips full. I looked different. Feminine. Sweet. Pretty. Borderline happy, even. I smiled a big toothy smile to see what I would look like as a happy, pure person, and then it struck me hard, like a punch in the gut. With my fake smile and my flushed cheeks, I looked like Mom. I quickly splashed water on my face, trying to clean off the sweat and the similarities to Mom. I dried my face with rough paper towels and headed back to Sebastian.

I slid into the booth across from him, my legs sticking to the red vinyl. He'd already downed the water in his glass and was working on mine.

"Hey," I said. "That's my water!"

"Thirsty. Can't get enough. Can you see the guy? Will you get him over here? I've never been more thirsty in my life." He was letting the water run down his chin and dribble all over his lap.

I laughed. "Stop it," I said. "You're being an idiot."

"Idiot?" He said, now patting his lips and chin with a napkin. "Want to see my report card?"

"No thanks, smartass," I said, waving to the waiter.

"Not into goofy, huh?"

"I dig goofy," I said. "Come on, I have a fourteen-year-old geek brother. It was just surprising from you."

"Ah, the surprise attack," he said. "It works every time."

He raised his eyebrows at me flirtatiously as the waiter poured more water into our glasses. I pictured the water dribbling down his chin again, his fake-innocent face pretending he didn't notice, and I laughed again.

"You have a nice laugh," he said.

"Stop it," I said.

"Stop what?"

"Being all charming and stuff. Don't do that."

He smiled slyly. "Can't help it. You bring it out."

"Didn't you say that—"

"Yes," he said. "I did. We did. We said there would be none of this." He gestured back and forth between us and then opened his menu. "What are you getting?"

"Cheeseburger," I said, swallowing the lump in my throat. His words felt a whole hell of a lot like rejection.

"Me too," he said. "With bacon."

While we waited for the waiter to come back, we were quiet, staring at each other. There was electricity between us, just traveling back and forth. *Crackle crackle crackle.* It wasn't stopping, and I was convinced there was no way I'd make it out of this relationship, or whatever it was, alive.

When the waiter came, we ordered. I played with the sugar packets; he spun the salt shaker around and around.

"Everyone has their shit," Sebastian said. "Little secrets, big secrets, baggage. Everyone."

"Where did that come from?" I asked.

He shrugged.

"I just wish I knew," he said.

"Knew what?"

"What's under there," he said.

"Under where?"

"Ha! Made you say it," he said, with a giant smile.

"Oh my god. Second grade much?"

I remembered Scott playing that joke on me when I was little. I'd thought it was the funniest thing I'd ever heard.

Sebastian's smile slowly faded.

"Really, though. I want to know everything about you," he said, his voice catching on the "you."

My pulse raced, and I wondered if he could see it throbbing in my neck.

"Stop," I said. "Please."

He nodded, but his eyes still pleaded with me.

"Sorry," I said. "I just can't."

I changed the subject back to him.

"So, are things better at home?"

He nodded. "My mom and stepfather are totally dealing. I mean, I'm definitely being watched big time—I can't pick my nose without asking first—and they're walking around on eggshells, but yeah, they're there for me."

I felt a pang in my chest. Were my parents there for me? As much as I wanted to think they were, they weren't. Not really.

"Look," I said. "I know this is hard for you to appreciate from the inside, but it's amazing that they noticed something was going on with you. And even though it sucks that your mom put you in that place, she did it to make you better. And she's watching you now because she knows this is the hard part—being home—and she doesn't want you to go back to that place. She doesn't want to lose you."

"Is she paying you?"

I'd surprised even myself. I had no idea that I'd felt that way about his mom. Something made me feel a kinship toward her, a special love even, for wanting so badly to save Sebastian.

"I just mean, there must be a part of you that knows how lucky you are to have a mom who really sees you and can deal with who you are."

"You don't have that?" he asked.

"I didn't mean that. I just . . . I don't know."

"You don't have that?" he asked again.

"No, I guess I don't." Dammit, how did he do that? He made me talk. Whatever feelings were coming up, I didn't want them. I wanted to push them back down.

"Tell me. I want to know," he said.

The waiter came with our cheeseburgers. I ate a french fry before the plate even touched the table. Steam rose in swirls. We both took a moment to dress up our burgers, passing the ketchup back and forth. And then we took a bite at the same time, the taste of the warm burger making me realize just how hungry I was after running.

"Tell me," he said again.

"No, it's nothing. It's just, what the hell am *I* complaining about? Like you said, my mom's not so bad, even if we don't get along that well, and my dad is great and works really hard to give us everything."

"But they don't pay attention," he said.

"I'm not in one of your group sessions, Sebastian. This was about you. I was just trying to say that from an outsider's perspective, I can see that your mom sent you there because she knew you were hurting yourself and she wanted to make you better. That's what parents are supposed to do."

"But that's not what your parents do," he said.

"Seriously? You're turning this back on me again?"

"Well," he said. "I think we've already determined that my parents are saints, right?"

"Fine," I said. "No. I think that if my mom suspected I was on drugs or unhappy—even if she knew it for a fact— she would just put her head in the sand and convince herself

211

it wasn't true so she wouldn't have to do something hard like put me in a hospital and risk all her friends knowing that her daughter was a fuck-up."

He raised an eyebrow.

"I'm sorry," I said. "I shouldn't have said that. I'm sure your mom's not embarrassed like mine would be."

"It's okay," he said. "I know it's hard for my mom. Especially since she's a nurse. I think it *must* be embarrassing for her, but she did it anyway. To save me, as you say. I never quite thought of her as a hero, but maybe I will now." He tried to laugh but it came out as a snort. "Do you really think your mom wouldn't do anything?"

"Yes, I know it."

He reached across the table and took my hand. I pulled it away and looked around, suddenly very aware that Sebastian and I were in public.

"Sorry," he said. "I couldn't help it."

"It's just, if someone saw."

"I know. I get it," he said. But there was nothing I wanted more than to have Sebastian's hand on mine. In fact, I looked at his lips and ached to kiss them. I put my head in my hands, so I wouldn't have to look at him, to want him. I wondered if he'd thought about kissing me too.

After we finished eating, he spoke quietly. "I know we haven't known each other that long, but I've noticed."

"You've noticed what?" I asked.

"I've noticed you. I've noticed that there's something that hurts you. Even if your mom and dad haven't, I have."

I swallowed hard. Sebastian saw something in me that no one else did, and it was the real me. I felt like he was looking right through me, and I loved it and hated it at the same time. I felt the sting of tears coming and took a few breaths to try to stop them.

Sebastian got up, came around to my side of the table, and sat next to me in the booth.

"I didn't mean to make you sad." He took my hand in his. His proximity made me feel warm all over, and I didn't care anymore who saw us together.

"It's okay," I said, clearing my throat. "I'm not sad. I'm just . . . I don't know, confused I guess. I don't usually think about stuff like this. I'm really good at not thinking about it. And you're making me think, so I don't know if that makes me like you or hate you."

He laughed and then just looked at me for a minute. "Are you busy tonight?"

"Actually, I am," I said, but I was so torn, wanting never to leave him.

He was still smiling, but now it looked forced. He scooted out of the booth and went back to his side.

"That's cool," he said. "I was just thinking about a movie, maybe."

"I would love to. But I have to go to dinner."

"With Chris?" he asked, putting his elbows on the table.

"With his family."

He rubbed his forehead. "Trying to erase the image," he said, smiling sadly.

I felt a moment of exhilaration now that I knew for sure he wanted to be with me, and then an immediate crash when the hopeless reality of our situation hit me.

"Sebastian . . ." I said.

"I know," he said. "Let's not talk about it."

"Maybe we should, though."

He shook his head. He looked at the check, started pulling money out of his pocket, so I did the same.

After we paid, we went outside.

"Thanks for that," I said. "The run, everything."

"Sure." I could feel the distance building.

He stopped as we got closer to my car. I took a few more steps, but he stayed put.

"I'll drive you home," I said.

"I'll walk."

He turned away and pulled earbuds out of his shorts pocket.

"What's going on here?" I asked.

"Huh?" He turned slightly but didn't look at me.

I didn't feel like playing games. From the minute Sebastian and I started talking that night at Rebecca's, everything between us had been so honest. This wasn't going to work for me.

"I mean, what's going on? Chris came up, and now you're like this. I'm not the only one who's got something making this not happen," I said, gesturing back and forth between us.

"In your case, you mean some*one*," he said. He flicked his eyes up to mine for a second and then back down to the earbuds, which he was slowly untangling.

I shook my head back and forth. Was he expecting me to break up with my boyfriend for him when he wasn't willing to be with me anyway? Screw that.

"See ya," I said. I got in my car.

"Hold on," he said as I slammed my door closed, but I pretended not to hear him. I started the car and put it in drive.

As I pulled out of the parking spot, I watched him walk the other way, shoulders sloping. I drove toward home.

My phone buzzed and for a second I thought it might be him. But it was Rebecca.

REBECCA: Where r u?

I irresponsibly texted back while driving.

ME: Driving home.

One second later, my phone rang. It was her.
"Hi," I said.
"Hi. What are you up to?"
"I was hanging out with Sebastian."
Silence.
"What?" I asked.
"I just don't get it."
She wasn't helping with my mood.
"Why do you want to get involved with him? He's messed up, Macy. Serious baggage. And what about Chris?"
I sighed, annoyed. "It's not like that. It has nothing to do with Chris. And he's not messed up. He's out of the hospital now."
"And?"
"We just have this connection. As *friends*."

If Rebecca weren't so against the idea of my hanging out with Sebastian, I might have told her what had just happened, asked for her interpretation—whether I screwed up by calling him out on the way he'd acted. But it would just add to her case against him.

"Okay," she said. "I just don't want you to get dragged down. You have enough anger in you. You don't need someone else's shit. Plus, I think Chris is wigging out," she said.

"What?"

"Cody asked me about Sebastian last night. Wanted to know if you guys were friends and what the deal was. It felt like research."

"Oh."

"Yeah," she said.

"What did you say?"

"Nothing, whatever. That maybe you felt sorry for him or something. Just be careful."

I'd have to mention to Chris that I'd hung out with Sebastian today—make sure he didn't hear it from someone else. I didn't want him getting suspicious or jealous. And then I had some serious thinking to do. How could I stay with Chris if I was feeling this way about Sebastian, even if Sebastian couldn't be with me? But the thought of losing Chris, his friendship, and his family made me feel horrible.

"Anyway, back to me now," Rebecca said. "Cody's dicking me around."

"I thought things were going well," I said.

Cody had been a good boy—calling, e-mailing, texting.

"They were. But now not."

I groaned.

"I'm sorry," she said. "Are my little problems too annoying for you?"

"You've got to be kidding," I said. "Where's the bitch-fest coming from? I'm just pissed at Cody for screwing with you again."

"Sorry. I'm feeling a little sensitive."

"A *little*?"

"Can you come over?" she asked, pathetically.

I looked at the clock. 4:32 p.m.

"For a few minutes," I said. "I have to get home and shower, though."

Since I'd passed her street already, I took a U-turn and headed back toward her house. I parked and ran up the porch steps, two at a time, and pushed open the never-locked door. She was lying on the couch watching *Scooby Doo*.

"Seriously?" I grabbed the remote from the table and turned off the TV.

"It's the one with the Miner 49er ghost. It's a classic."

I sat down next to her and she gasped as she took in my attempt at running-wear, the *Star Wars* baseball cap.

"What the hell?" she asked.

"We went running. Did you know he was on the cross-country team?"

"Sebastian?"

I nodded.

"No, I didn't know. But did you go to Salvation Army first for an outfit?"

I plopped down on the couch next to her.

"You couldn't find something better than that? You couldn't go in your mom's closet for something? Well, at least

I don't have to worry about Sebastian wanting to get in your pants, because you look like a freak."

"Is there a reason I came over here? Because the verbal abuse I'm getting isn't really much of a draw," I said.

"Wait, running?"

"Yes, running," I said. "And actually, I kind of liked it."

Rebecca stared at me. "Who are you? Where's Macy?"

"What's the deal with Cody?"

"You're different. Are you in *love*?" She said love with like, ten syllables.

"No. I went running with him, and I liked it. It was a good feeling. You should try it sometime," I said.

She stared at me again and shook her head.

"Anyhoo," she said. "I haven't heard from Cody since last night."

"It's only four forty-five," I said.

"But usually when we're on, we're on, you know?"

"Did you call him?"

"No," she said quickly. "Well, maybe once, and maybe a text or two."

I didn't say anything.

"What?" she said. "I'm sorry I can't be all cool, *I don't give a shit about anyone or whether they like me*, like you."

"Have you moved at all from this couch?"

"I went to the freezer," she said, pointing at a pint of mint chocolate chip on the coffee table.

"Hmmm," I said, taking her spoon and digging out some melty bright green ice cream. The combination of the cold and mint burned my tongue. "It's so lame that he's screwing with you."

"Will you ask Chris where he is?" she asked.

"We're not in seventh grade, Beck. You ask him if you want."

She sneered at me but immediately started texting. We waited. Her phone dinged.

"So?" I said. "What did Chris say?"

"He doesn't know."

Then her phone rang. She looked at it and her eyes lit up like a Christmas tree in a lightning storm.

"Cody?" I asked.

She nodded and answered.

"Hi," she said, then smiled and giggled as she listened. He was obviously on one of his funny drama rants, and she was eating it all up. Next she would invite him over and all would be well in Rebecca-Cody land.

She gave me a thumbs up.

I raced to the door. I'd have to rush my shower to get to Chris's on time.

Dinner at Chris's was like always—easy, comfortable—opposite of my house. Chris's parents asked us questions, talked about the news, and listened to what we had to say. There was no wine for us, no fancy china. Just dinner and conversation. Afterward, we watched a movie. Chris, his twelve-year-old brother, Joseph, and I all squeezed on the couch while his parents sat on armchairs. His dad read the paper while we all watched the movie. Lady lay in front of the couch, flapping her tail, and Peaceboy curled up on Theresa's lap like a cat. It was all so normal. So . . . pure. There was no way I could let this go. Now with Mom fighting with

Dad whenever he was home, with all the memories of Scott released, this was my only hope for goodness, for being part of a real family.

I was almost completely ensconced in my Holtz world, making believe I was really one of them, feeling the warmth of Chris's chest where my head rested. But when I felt my phone buzz, I couldn't ignore it, so I went to the bathroom to check it.

SEBASTIAN: I was such an immature asshole today. I was completely wrong and you were completely right. I'm sorry. I'd really like to apologize in person. Can we do something tomorrow?

A rush of warmth spread through me, and I smiled all by myself.

ME: Yes.

But when I went back to the couch, it was just me again. Macy sitting among the perfect family Holtz, no longer part of it.

CHAPTER TWENTY

The next night, I half-watched a James Bond movie while I devoured the last of Darren and Kevin's roast chicken from their dinner party the night before. Everything had gone smoothly with Ben and Avery's bedtime despite the limited movement of my aching legs and butt from running. My phone buzzed. I wiped my greasy fingers on a napkin and picked it up.

SEBASTIAN: Are you free to talk?

I felt a wave of relief and excitement. I hadn't heard from him since the text I'd gotten at Chris's, and I didn't want to text him first.

ME: Babysitting til 9:30. What's up?
SEBASTIAN: A little blue. I'm alone in the house.
ME: I cud come over if u want.
SEBASTIAN: Yes. I'd love that.

I'd told Rebecca and Chris I'd meet them at a party, but I wasn't that into it anyway.

ME: OK. C u soon.
SEBASTIAN: Just come inside when you get here. The door's open. I'm up in my room.

I texted Rebecca and Chris to tell them I was too tired to go to the party. I cleaned off my dishes and waited for Darren and Kevin to come home, practically jumping out of my skin with impatience.

When I got to Sebastian's, I opened the front door and walked up the stairs, which were carpeted in a dark red and blue floral pattern. A few framed photos of Sebastian and his sister lined the wall on a diagonal, going up the stairs. I ran my hand along the banister, knowing that in a minute I would be in Sebastian's room. Alone with him. How did I feel about that? All that broke through was a very pleasant sense of calm.

"Macy? Second door on the right. Well, no door, just doorway," Sebastian called out, his voice raspy. I followed his instructions, walking on the blue and red flowered carpet that continued down a short, narrow hallway to Sebastian's room. I noticed the empty hinges on the doorframe.

"Part of the program," he said. "Privacy at this point is not a luxury I'm afforded."

He was lying on his double bed, a navy blue plaid comforter bunched up under him. His room was surprisingly "boy." Dark wood, navy blue sheets. A laptop at his desk. A few academic awards and running trophies. Some clothes in a heap in the corner. I didn't know what I'd expected—everything perfect and in its place? A look that matched his thoughtfulness?

"Are you sick?" I asked. Seeing him lying on his bed was a mix of odd things—vulnerable, comfortable, sexual.

"No," he said. "But I said I was so I wouldn't have to go with them. A pool party at one of the houses my stepfather just built. I just couldn't deal—the stares and everything. Not to mention the drinks. I thought it would be better if I didn't go."

I sat down on the edge of the bed. "Isn't it late for Sofia?"

"She's a night owl. I guess European time runs in our blood."

I eased myself farther onto his bed. He grabbed an extra pillow for me, and I stretched out, letting my head sink into the soft flannel.

"I'm really sorry about the diner," he said. He grabbed my hand and squeezed. I squeezed back and smiled. He let go and stared at the ceiling.

"Am I allowed to be here?" I asked.

"Truthfully?" he said. "They'd prefer it. I may have lied a little. They didn't want to leave me alone, so I told them we'd planned to hang out tonight."

"So, you only asked me over to make yourself feel better about lying to your parents? Now I feel like an idiot."

"No, no, no," he said. "I didn't want you to see me like this. But then I decided that I'd rather that than not see you at all."

I smiled. "And what is 'like this'?"

"I don't know. Down. Slogging through the crap in my head."

"Okay," I said. "So now I'm here. Might as well make it worth it. Let's slog through it together. What's going on?"

"Today was the hardest day since I've been out of the hospital. This morning I started getting bummed out about some stuff, and I wanted to take something to make the feeling go away. It was so natural to just want that; I was seriously ready to throw everything away—all the work I've done, everything. I convinced myself that I could use and still stay in control."

"So, what did you do?" I asked hesitantly, suddenly wondering whether he was high right now. What would I do? Call his mom? The hospital? He would hate me forever.

"I went to a meeting," he said. "And after it was over, I went to another one."

"Wow."

He nodded slowly. "Still clean. One more day, as they say."

"I'm glad," I said, which was the most ridiculous understatement there ever was. "But what made you so bummed out this morning?"

He smiled shyly and tilted his head toward me. "You mean other than the fact that you were with your boyfriend last night?"

I opened my mouth, but he continued before I could say anything.

"I was thinking about my dad, how much I'm like him, and how much it scares me," he said quietly.

"You're nothing like him."

"There's more. And you might not like me after I tell you this," he said.

I could feel my jaw tighten. What could make me not like Sebastian?

"Sophomore year I had a girlfriend. I know I told you that it was bad, but in the beginning, it was good. Really good. We were in love."

I closed my eyes. Sebastian had been in love. I didn't know if I was even capable of being in love, but I was pretty sure that if I was, it would be with him. I looked up at the ceiling, where I could see the remnants of glow-in-the-dark stars that someone had unsuccessfully tried to scrape off. I willed myself to be still, to not let my body betray my—what?—feeling of betrayal? Like he cheated on me? Before he even really knew me? But I knew that wasn't fair of me. Not only was he allowed to have a past, but I had Chris.

Sebastian propped himself up on his elbow and stared down at me. "I shouldn't be telling you this, should I?"

"No, it's okay," I said, my voice cracking. "You need to."

He lay back down on his pillow.

"Okay. Jacqueline and I were way into drugs."

He'd pronounced Jacqueline with a French accent.

I sat up. "Jacqueline?"

"Do you know her?" he asked, hesitantly.

"No," I said quickly. "But if it's the same Jacqueline, I went to rescue Rebecca from a party at her house the other night."

"Rescue?"

"She thought Cody ditched her there, so she called me to pick her up."

He put his hand on his head and rubbed.

"This is weird," he said. "Jacqueline went to a different school. I never thought you'd know her."

"I don't. I never even saw her. But, well, never mind."

"What?" he asked.

"There was something about her house that made me curious about who she was," I said. "It seemed like a really warm, nice place to grow up."

Sebastian laughed bitterly.

"*Warm* and *nice* are not exactly the words I'd use to describe her or her family. But I know what you mean— the house is very inviting. It's the French country thing. Her mother is an interior designer."

"Oh," I said. The disappointment that Jacqueline wasn't who I thought she was, that her house wasn't what I thought it was, was much more acute than I thought possible. I should have been pleased that someone who seemed so perfect and had been loved by Sebastian had crappy parents, but I wasn't. I wanted there to be hope out there.

"Is this too weird?" he asked.

Even though it kind of was too weird, I shook my head. "Go on."

He continued. "Jacqueline and I mostly took pills—oxy, that kind of stuff. Some coke, pot. We were high most of the time. But then something changed, and I needed it more than she did. Our stash kept dwindling faster and faster because I needed more and more. One day, she got pissed at me for something—I don't even remember what—and she took all of our pills and flushed them down the toilet. I turned into this raving lunatic madman. I hated her. And I hated her even more because she'd made me get as angry as my father used to get."

Suddenly, the lack of air-conditioning in Sebastian's house became very noticeable. The spot where the backs of our hands touched—my left, his right—as we lay side by side, felt clammy.

"I was literally pulling out my hair trying not to hit her. I kept telling myself, 'you are not him, you are not him.' Jacqueline was freaking out. She knew I was going crazy. It was totally surreal. But it was also way too real. Finally, I gave in, and I punched her window. There was glass and blood everywhere.

"But then she attacked me. I thought she'd push me out the broken window. That's where it was headed—she was high, and she wasn't thinking clearly either. And then I lost it. I saw red, black, whatever you see when there's nothing but anger. I put my hand around her neck. The blood from my cut hand was all over her. I'll never forget the way she looked at me. The way I probably looked when my father was in one of his rages. Terrified."

He paused. His hands clenched and unclenched at his sides.

"I realized what I'd been about to do, and I let go immediately. She was so quiet and still; it was worse than if she'd screamed. Then I just fell apart. Crying. I was a mess. My hand was in bad shape, so she called her parents to come home from a dinner party and they took us to the hospital. She didn't tell them what I'd done to her. But I knew it was over for us. And I knew it was over for me, too—that I could never forgive myself. Two weeks later, she was gone. She'd never wanted to go to boarding school even though her parents were pushing her, but I guess she changed her mind after that."

I couldn't picture Sebastian hurting anyone. Calm, soft-spoken Sebastian.

I cleared my throat.

"She might have pushed you out the window," I said.

"No excuse."

"But, she was doing drugs too. She could have tried to help you."

"Maybe flushing it all down the toilet was her way of trying to help. Macy, I hurt her. Please don't make excuses for me. That's not why I told you. I just want you to know everything. That anger—like my dad's—it exists. I know how to control it pretty well with therapy and without the drugs messing with me. But it's always there. Under the surface."

He was right. Why had I been trying to excuse him for what he'd done? I made a little gasp as a realization shot into my thoughts so quickly like an injection into my blood-stream. I was used to making excuses—for Scott and now for Sebastian.

"You okay?" Sebastian asked. I realized I'd balled up my fists and pressed them against my cheeks. I released them and nodded.

"Did your mom know what happened?" I asked.

"Only that I punched the window. Not the . . . other part. She worried, like I did, that I was just like my dad. She sent me to therapy to control my temper. But I never told the therapist about the drugs. I cut down on the pills, limiting myself to just enough to get me through the day but not enough to go on any more insane rampages. And that's what I've been doing since. Until now—the hospital, therapy, working on the anger."

He sniffed, wiped his forehead with his sleeve.

"So," I said. "You haven't seen her since?"

He shook his head.

"That must be weird," I said. "If you were so into each other and then suddenly you're not together anymore?"

"Yeah. It was weird."

"I mean, no closure," I said. "Right?"

"I guess. It doesn't really matter. It was over, even without it."

I stared at the stars on the ceiling.

"I shouldn't have told you that, right?" he asked.

"You should have. We're helping each other."

I grabbed his hand and touched his scarred knuckles.

"I haven't helped you," he said. "I don't even know what hurts you."

"You're helping me figure it out."

We intertwined our fingers, stroked each other's palms. Our hands were having their own very intense conversation, and I was starting to tingle all over, wanting to kiss him, to know what his lips felt like.

He groaned softly.

"What?"

"You have no idea . . . you can't imagine how badly I want to kiss you right now," he said, staring up at the ceiling.

"Oh, yes I can," I whispered.

"But we can't," he said, half statement, half question.

"No." I pictured Chris's face and the perfection of his family that I would lose forever.

"I guess that's best. I'm afraid if we did, I wouldn't want to stop," he said.

"Same."

He turned onto his side and faced me.

"I just feel really close to you. I wish I could be closer," he said.

I turned to face him too. We were inches apart. He put his hand on my waist. It was heavy and warm on my side.

"Do you think *this* is okay?" he asked.

I nodded. I put my hand on his bony hip. He circled his arm around my back. Now our bodies were, at most, one inch apart. His lips were a millimeter from mine, his breath warm and sweet on my face. I shut my eyes. Every part of my body was alive with Sebastian's presence. And now I wanted to kiss him. But we wouldn't. Because of Chris, and because of NA, and maybe because of Jacqueline.

"If our lips just touch, it's not really kissing," I whispered, vaguely aware that it made no sense.

I parted my lips as his touched mine, overlapping, fitting perfectly. And now I knew what his lips felt like—soft, so soft. We stayed like that, our mouths together, our breath intermingling, our noses touching, our arms around each other's sides. Our breathing fell into a joint rhythm. I was completely relaxed, aware of the easy happiness I was feeling for the first time in ages. I felt myself slip into a moment of blissful sleep—aware but not—a quick dream of breeze and sun and tree branches against the sky. Then I slid back into full awareness and opened my eyes. Our lips had moved apart, but our foreheads were touching. Sebastian's eyes were closed. I stared at his long black eyelashes, a freckle on the side of his temple. I studied his face, and then I put my fingers on his cheek, feeling the faint stubble on his creamy brown skin.

He opened his eyes. He lifted his hand from my side and put it on my face, his fingertips gently inching into my hair.

"I wish we could stay like this all night," he whispered. "But I think they're coming home soon."

"Yeah, I should go." I sat up.

"Wait. I didn't mean for you to get up right this second." He pulled me back down. "I want you to stay longer."

"I shouldn't," I said, returning to reality, knowing I probably had texts from Chris on my silenced phone, guilt creeping in and crowding out the bliss.

"Yeah, you're right." We stared at each other, and we smiled, but it seemed like an effort for both of us.

"I'll walk you downstairs," he said.

I nodded, afraid I'd cry if I spoke. I'd never wanted anything more in my life than to just stay there in his bed with him, doing nothing but holding each other and drifting in and out of sleep.

When I got to the bottom of the stairs, Sebastian, one step above me, put his hands on my shoulders and pulled me to him, so my back was against his chest. He wrapped his arms around me, right at my collarbones, and leaned his head on my shoulder, his breath warm on my neck. I reached up and covered his hands with mine, closed my eyes, felt our bodies together, separate, one.

"I feel so . . ." he started, then sighed.

"Me too," I said, leaning back against him briefly, like a final kiss, and then I took the last few steps to the door. I felt him watching me as I walked to my car, got in, started it, and drove off.

CHAPTER TWENTY-ONE

The next day, Sebastian said he had a surprise for me, so after camp I picked him up. He bounced down his porch steps with his giant shoes and his dimples, a blue backpack on his shoulders.

He looked at me carefully as he got in the car. I was still wearing my Marwood shirt and shorts.

"I didn't have time to go home and change."

"I'm glad you didn't," he said, smiling. "It would have taken too long, and I couldn't wait anymore to see you. And besides, you look cute."

My chest expanded as I stared at him, taking in his beautiful dark brown eyes. My body begged me to kiss him. Instead I smiled and drove as he gave me directions.

"Take the next right," Sebastian said, after a few minutes.

"Here?" I swerved into the entrance of the park preserve. "What are we doing here?"

I'd been here before with Dad, Scott, and Gavin. We'd gone for hikes, festivals, a few overnight camping trips. Mom would almost always bow out, claiming she wanted us kids to be able to spend some quality time with Dad, but I had always suspected she just wanted time to herself.

"Picnic," Sebastian said.

"You made us lunch? That's what's in the backpack?"

"Knapsack," he said.

"It's a backpack."

"Knapsack," he said, smiling.

"Whatever. Did you make us lunch?"

On either side of the road there must have been twenty different shades of green on the trees.

"Well, I didn't so much make lunch as assemble it, but yes, I have lunch for us."

"Are you trying to charm my pants off?" I asked.

"I have to try? What beautiful girl such as yourself wouldn't want this?" He gestured from his fuzzy head all the way down to his giant unlaced sneakers and flexed his nearly nonexistent biceps. "Besides, you're wearing shorts, not pants."

I giggled. Yes, I giggled.

"Not like you're available anyway," he said.

He pointed straight, so I kept driving. But I wasn't going to let that go; this wasn't all on me.

"Not just me," I said. "You're not available either. That Jacqueline really messed you up, huh?"

I suspected he was still in love with her, and the masochistic part of me wanted to push him to admit it. At the mention of her name, he turned his face toward the window, and I wished I'd kept my mouth shut.

"So, after the bridge, you'll pull into the parking lot," he said.

We entered a part of the preserve I'd never been to. The road became a narrow wooden bridge and emptied into a dirt parking lot where there were two cars and a blue porta-john.

I parked, and we walked to a half-grassy, half-mossy clearing with a few picnic tables that faced a shallow stream trickling over rocks. A woman was walking her dog toward a path in the woods.

"This is peaceful," I said.

"My mom used to bring me here before she met my stepdad."

Sebastian spread out a red fleece blanket, and we sat by the stream. We stayed quiet for a while, watching the water, listening to the birds. The sun glinted through the leaves and danced on his fingers. We were sitting so close that I could almost feel the hair on his arm against mine. I wanted to jump him—to wrap my arms around his neck and my legs around his waist and hold on tight, press my lips against his and breathe him in. I tried to shake the image by concentrating on a squirrel chasing another up a tree.

"How's today been?" I asked.

"Better than yesterday. My meeting was good. Hopeful."

I nodded.

"Okay," he said. "Give it to me. I'm ready."

"What?"

"Tell me your stuff now."

I felt my cheeks get hot.

"You should know by now I'm not letting up," he said. "You need to talk about it; you said I was helping you figure stuff out. But what stuff? Like why you hate your mom?"

"I don't hate my mom," I said.

"Well, you told me she doesn't notice you. Look, you've seen the worst of me now, and I'm still standing."

He touched my shoulder and looked at me curiously. At the thought of telling him, my heart plunged to my stomach, like when you take a hill too fast in the car. I remembered my excitement when Scott would enter my room, my confused self-disgust when he'd leave, and everything that happened in between.

Sebastian must have seen a change in my face because he said, "What is it?"

Part of me wanted to just open my mouth and let it all spill out, but I couldn't. Instead I stood and turned toward the parking lot. I walked fast, tears stinging behind my eyes.

"Don't!" he called after me. "Macy!"

Suddenly he was right behind me, but I just kept walking as fast as I could.

"Why won't you just leave it alone?" I said.

I wouldn't look at him but I could hear him breathing. He was staying a slight distance behind me.

I got into my car. I had no plan to leave. I didn't know why I was being like this.

Sebastian grabbed the door before I could close it. I glared at him, but he just stood there.

"Let go," I demanded.

"No." He was calm. Solid.

"Goddammit," I said, trying to pull the door closed, but it wouldn't budge with him holding onto it. "I don't want this. I don't want to talk to you." But I also wanted nothing more than to talk to him.

He let go of the door and I slammed it shut. But then he walked around to the passenger door, opened it, and folded himself into the seat. I tried to take a deep breath, but it caught in my throat and made a small choking sound. Sebastian closed his eyes. He waited. I breathed. He waited some more.

"You don't have to talk, but I'm not going anywhere," he said.

He didn't open his eyes, but he reached for my hand and found it. Instinctively, I grasped his hand tight, relieved that he really wouldn't leave.

That night at Rebecca's had launched a sea change in me. I'd begun to look at my life through fresh eyes, through Sebastian's eyes. It was like he *knew*, like he'd always known, and was trying to get me to tell him so he could help me see that it was wrong. So long ago, I'd stuffed my dusty memories and feelings into a neat little lockbox in my gut, coated it with numbing anesthesia, added a touch of self-deceit, and thrown away the key. The result was denial . . . and emptiness. Whenever I thought about what happened with Scott, that lockbox swallowed the truth and spat out lies, making me believe that it all was no big deal, that it was normal. But now, it was like Sebastian had taken a sledgehammer to that package. And I knew it was time to tell someone. To tell *him*.

"I've never told anyone," I said quietly. "But since that night at Rebecca's, I haven't been able to fake myself out as well as I used to. I know that things I've always tried to pretend were nothing, were actually something."

He squeezed my hand gently and stayed quiet.

"My cousin Scott, you know, the asshole-slash-not-asshole."

"Mmmhmm?"

My heart beat faster than it had when we'd gone running. Was I really going to do this?

I took a shaky breath and tried to find the words.

"Macy, I was in the psych ward. I heard a lot of shit. Nothing you say will shock me."

I couldn't say it. I didn't even know *how* to say it.

"Is it what I think it is?" he asked quietly.

"Probably."

He said "shit" under his breath. He let go of my hand, grabbed the back of his head, and rubbed. Then he put his face right in front of mine and made me look at him. His eyes were wild, frantic, trying to get into mine.

"He sexually abused you?"

The way he said it so clinically, like it was a diagnosis, made me feel sick to my stomach.

"It wasn't *abuse*," I said.

"What was it then?"

"I don't know."

He stared at me.

"I don't know," I said again. "I thought it wasn't a big deal. I wanted to be with him. I thought that maybe something was wrong with *me*, but not him. But now, since I met you, since visiting you there and stuff, seeing these little kids at camp, it seems to matter more. I think I'm confused."

"Let's get out of the car," he said gently. "Come on."

He came around to my side and opened my door. We walked back to the blanket.

I could feel my eyes burning like they wanted to cry, but nothing was coming out. We sat on the blanket, keeping about a foot between us. For a second, I worried that he was keeping his distance because he was disgusted by what I'd said. But I knew he was probably just trying to give me space.

"Tell me about it," he said. "Tell me what happened."

I didn't even know if my voice would work.

"Tell me how it started," he said quietly.

I thought of the day Scott taught me about football when I was seven. How he had me sit on his lap, then moved his legs up and down faster and faster, and I figured he was just excited about the football game. Deep down, I'd known there was something else happening that I couldn't quite figure out.

"I'll tell you about the day it ended," I said. "I almost drowned. It's why I don't swim anymore."

I stared at a tree branch waving delicately in the breeze. It reminded me of my oak tree and I felt calmer.

"I was twelve, so Scott was nineteen. He always treated me like I was more grown up than I was. He told me I was so mature and that I really understood him. He said he wished there were more girls like me his age.

"This one day he wanted to hang out—that's what he always called it—'hanging out.' I was in the pool and he got out and sat on the edge so I could, um—"

My face suddenly felt hot. I didn't want to go on. The shame rose up in me—I was disgusting, a girl willing to give her own cousin a hand job without even questioning it. I was the only girl I knew who did that. Anyone else would have had more respect for herself, would have known to keep her innocence. Anyone else would have said no. So why didn't I?

"Go on," Sebastian said. "It's okay."

The soothing tone in his voice made me keep talking.

"Then I felt a shadow, and I looked up and saw my dad standing there, blocking the sun. I remember thinking he looked like a giant. But I could see his face and it was filled with disgust. He yelled something, but everything was a blur. All I could see was his revulsion. And then thoughts started crowding my head. That we got caught. That I was a horrible person. That I was the biggest disappointment. That my dad was repulsed by me.

"I hated knowing that, and I didn't know what to do. I don't know what happened next because my mind went blank. I was in the deep end of the pool, and I couldn't keep my head above the water anymore. I went under and breathed in, and the water filled my mouth and nose. I sank. But then I guess I understood what was happening and I started pushing myself up, choking and freaking out. And then I blacked out."

Sebastian stayed quiet.

"When I woke up, I realized Scott had pulled me out of the pool."

I could still smell the chlorinated water in my nose, the way my throat burned from the choking and coughing.

I turned toward Sebastian. I watched his long eyelashes moving up and down as he blinked.

"No wonder you don't swim anymore," he said.

I nodded, but I realized that I wasn't afraid of drowning like I'd always thought; I was afraid I might *want* to drown. I didn't want him to see my face. I was afraid he'd know what I'd just figured out.

"My dad cried and kept hugging me," I continued. "It was terrible to see him cry. He asked me a thousand times if I was okay, and I just kept saying yes. It wasn't a lie, I guess, because I was alive. Later that day when my mom got home, she got all dramatic. She blamed herself for not being home. She wanted to fill in the pool. She promised to always protect me, blah, blah, blah."

"Your mom knows," Sebastian said. "That's good."

"Yeah, but it doesn't make a difference. I mean, Scott never touched me again. But nobody ever mentioned it again either."

"What? They never did anything or talked about it?"

"Nothing. Never."

"Well, what did your mom say when you told her about what had been going on?" he asked.

"I didn't want to tell her what happened. I was so embarrassed, and she just always doted on Scott, you know? I thought she would blame me because he was so perfect. But my dad said she had to know, so he said he would tell her himself when she got home. And then, I guess because I knew she knew, I just kept waiting for her to say something and like, act like a mom, but she never did. I think she was so disgusted with me, she just wanted it to go away."

Sebastian looked at me for a long time, his eyes sad.

"I'm sorry, Macy."

I'd always felt that I may as well have drowned that day—because no one heard, no one cared. And if everyone acted like what happened wasn't a big deal, then I just had to believe them. I was twelve; what the hell did I know? Since then, I'd always thought I was okay, that I was tough, that I could swim my way through life. But maybe I had just been surviving. Just floating. Not swimming.

"And you know what the thing is?" I said.

"Hmmm?"

"She still worships Scott."

"It's so wrong," he said.

"I never did anything about it, though. I almost looked forward to our time together. Isn't that disgusting and pathetic?"

After all I'd told him, this was almost the worst. I'd wanted Scott to want me, to love me.

Sebastian squinted at me in the sun.

"He took advantage of you. He took your innocence."

"I wanted it too." I choked a little on the last word.

"You were too young to get it," he said. "And he was old enough to know better."

My eyes burned.

"And your parents never even dealt with it. Really, not a word?"

"No, my mom's never said anything other than 'that day' references, and stuff about my pool phobia. My dad always asked me if I was okay, big sympathetic hugs, that kind of thing, and he and Scott never really got along well afterward, but he's never actually mentioned it. I think it's his way of pretending that he didn't see what he saw. I mean, no father should see his daughter doing that."

"I'm so sorry," Sebastian said.

I felt the tears wanting to come again. But I'd let it all out and now I was done.

"It's okay," I said. "I'm fine now. Ancient history. As far as I'm concerned, it was some other girl."

"But it wasn't some other girl, Macy. It was *you*."

Now I was ready to shut this thing down.

"I'm done talking about it now," I said, my voice cold. Sebastian looked stunned, but he recovered quickly and played along.

"Okay. I get it."

He lay down on his back and looked up at the sky.

"There's an elephant." He pointed at a cloud that definitely had a trunk-looking thing.

I lay down next to him. I rubbed my eyes.

"Tulip," I said, pointing to another cloud.

Sebastian reached up and took my hand, interlaced his fingers in mine, and then put our joined hands down between us on the blanket.

I leaned my head right up against him, his shoulder touching my eyebrow. I closed my eyes and drifted into a perfect dreamless nap.

CHAPTER TWENTY-TWO

Six hours later, I stood in front of the mirror trying to apply black eyeliner.

"Shit, shit, shit," I said under my breath. The simple task of putting on eyeliner seemed impossible—it was going all over the place. I'd thought telling Sebastian would make the memories stop haunting me. But it was the opposite—my secrets, memories, feelings—were all out, roaming free, swirling all around. After being pushed aside for years, they'd taken center stage.

Through my open door, I could hear the water running in Gavin's bathroom while he shaved. *Tap tap tap.* I kicked my door shut, but I could still hear the sound in my head.

Tap tap tap. Scott brought the razor to his face and slid it down his white foam-covered cheek, making a clean line like a plowed row in a field.

"So, what'cha reading?" he asked.

"Oh, um, it's about surviving a nuclear bomb." I showed him the book in my hand—an ominous mushroom cloud on the cover.

"Sounds uplifting," he said.

Scott never invited me into his room. I waited patiently to see what he wanted from me, but so far, nothing. Maybe I was getting old enough and interesting enough that he really just wanted to talk.

"Where are you going?" I asked.

"To the city with some of the guys from school. Try to get into some clubs." He was home for the weekend from boarding school. He went there after he got kicked out of public school for smoking pot in the bathroom.

"So, how's fourth grade going?"

"Fifth," I said.

"You got a boyfriend?" He finished shaving and then wiped his face with a towel.

"No."

"What about that kid you're always with," he said. "The chubster down the street."

"Chris. He's my friend." It normally infuriated me when people made fun of Chris's weight, but I didn't bother calling Scott on it.

"Yeah, right," Scott said and winked at me. He went into his room then and pulled jeans and two shirts out of his closet.

"Which one?" He held up a black T-shirt and a yellow and green striped polo.

"That one," I said, pointing at the yellow and green.

"Hmmm. I think the black one's cooler." He threw the yellow one on the bed. He let the towel drop from around his waist and stood naked. I turned away. He got dressed, brushed his hair.

"Have fun," I said and started to leave his room.

"Wait. Let's hang out a little."

I stepped back in and he closed the door. He walked into the bathroom, so I followed him.

"Come in here. I want to try out something new."

"Okay."

Scott locked the door even though no one was home.

"Take those off," he said, meaning my pants and underwear, so I did, covering myself with my hands.

"Lie down and close your eyes," he said. I obeyed.

I wriggled a little to get more comfortable, which was hard to do on the bathroom floor, and the top of my head pressed against the base of the toilet.

"Move down," he said, so I did. The bathroom rug was soft under my naked butt. But my feet were cold where they rested on the tile floor.

"Okay, ready?" he asked.

"Uh-huh." But I had no idea what I was ready for. All I knew was that I was naked from the waist down, and I felt silly lying there. He knelt on the floor.

"Close your eyes now," he said.

"They're closed."

And then he moved my hands away, and I felt the most amazing thing I'd ever felt in my entire life. Who knew that anything could feel this good? What was he doing? I opened my eyes. His head was between my legs. There had to be something wrong about that. Right? But it felt so good. I closed my eyes again. And I let him do it some more, even though I was pretty sure it was wrong. After a few minutes, he stopped.

"Did you like that?" he asked.

"It was okay." I didn't want him to know how good it felt. Maybe that would mean something was wrong with me. Or if I told him I liked it, maybe he wouldn't do it again.

Just then, we heard the garage door opening. He got up quickly.

"See you later," he said, grabbing his wallet from the dresser and shoving it in his back pocket.

I lay there for a second, my legs still open, my feet on the cold floor.

"Deb?" I heard him say when he got to the bottom of the stairs. "Can you give me a ride to the train station?"

"Sure, sweetheart," Mom said. "Where's Macy?"

"I think she's in her room."

"Macy?" Mom called up the stairs. "I'll be right back. I'm just taking Scotty to the station!"

I heard the mudroom door slam, the garage door open again, and Mom's car drive away.

I got up slowly and put on my underwear and pants. I wanted him to do it again. There had to be something wrong with me.

I wiped the eyeliner off, climbed into bed fully clothed, and shut my eyes as tight as I could, watching the glowing circles move around underneath my eyelids. And then, for the first time since I was a little girl, I put my thumb in my mouth, trying to forget.

A few minutes later, my phone buzzed.

REBECCA: R u coming??

I was already fifteen minutes late to pick her up.

ME: Leaving now.

I got up and put on giant hoop earrings. Despite everything, I looked halfway decent in my tasseled vest and black tank top. And my hair was getting even more dread-y. I put the front up in a clip. I reapplied the black eyeliner successfully, and it made my eyes look big and intense—in a good way.

Gavin had finished shaving and was watching *Minority Report* in the family room. His gangly body was draped on the couch, remote in hand. He clicked. *Teen Mom*. He clicked again. A documentary on surfing.

"Hey," he said. "Where you going?"

"A party."

"Where?"

"A guy who graduated a few years ago," I said. "Where's Mom?"

"She went to the city. Meeting Scott at Tarantula for some event."

I rolled my eyes. "Was she all decked out?"

"Is there sand at the beach?"

"Gav," I said. "Get off the couch. *Do* something."

"Okay." He clicked the remote again. Comedy Central. He was blowing me off.

"See ya," I said.

"Later."

When I pulled up in front of her house, Rebecca was on the porch swing—the same one where Sebastian and I had talked that night almost a month earlier.

Rebecca ran down the porch steps, her melon-boobs bouncing in a cleavage-revealing purple tank, her white blond hair spiky, and a flippy skirt to go with the top.

"You look smokin'," I said as she got into the car.

"Thanks. I do what I can with what I've got." She lifted up her boobs.

"Yeah you do," I said.

"Cody better like it, or I'm gonna go for Russ."

"Uh-huh," I said, my mind back on Sebastian. The feeling of his hand on mine as I bared my soul to him.

"Uh-huh, what? You don't think he'll like it or you don't think I can get Russ?"

"Of course he'll like it," I said. "And you can get anyone you want. It has nothing to do with that. I'm just really distracted tonight."

"What's going on?" she asked. Rebecca knew my quirks, my need to clutch Fozzie Bear as I fell asleep—she knew it all. But she didn't know this. And now Sebastian did. I felt like I'd betrayed Rebecca by telling him first, but I couldn't tell her now. Especially now when she was all vamped up to get action.

"Nothing new," I lied. "The usual crap with my mom."

When we got to the party, the long circular driveway was already filled with cars, so I had to park on the road.

I turned off the engine and pulled the rearview mirror toward me to check out my mascara.

"What's going on with you?" she asked again.

"Nothing, I'm fine."

"There's something different about you," she said. "You're less, I don't know, something. Less . . . cynical?"

"I have no idea what you're talking about," I said. "I'm not cynical."

"Yes, you are. It's part of what makes you *you*. So, what's different?"

"Nothing!"

"Is it Sebastian?"

"Rebecca, stop. There's nothing different. I'm distracted. I've got shit on my mind."

"Yeah, shit like how you're in love with Sebastian," she said, folding her arms across her chest.

"No, I'm not. Where are you getting this? Why am I on the firing line?"

"Listen," she said. "I know I'm being repetitive, but I just don't get it. And I feel bad for Chris. Whatever it is you're doing, it's not fair to him. I'm totally on your side, no matter what. I just wanted to get that out there."

I fought the urge to tell her to mind her own fucking business. I knew that we'd be treading on thin ice if I did that, though, and I wasn't willing to lose Rebecca. Especially right now when I was on the edge of losing myself—or finding myself—or whatever it was I was doing. So, I took a deep breath and tried to stay calm.

"There's nothing going on with Sebastian. We're friends now, real friends. And I know he has a lot of baggage, but I *am* willing to take it on. . . . And everything is fine with Chris."

"See? You *are* different. The old you would have told me to mind my own fucking business. Who are you, and what have you done with Macy?"

"Maybe I'm maturing," I said. "The old me sounds like a real bitch."

"Yeah, but I love her," she said.

"It's me. I haven't gone anywhere." I opened the car door. "Now get the fuck out of my car and make Cody and Russ duke it out for your tail."

"There's my girl."

We made our way toward the music on the patio out back. There were about thirty people sitting or standing and a few guys by the grill flipping hamburgers and hot dogs. This was what college boys did? Seemed more like thirty-somethings, but I wasn't complaining. If someone was making burgers, I'd eat them. Suddenly, I realized I was starving. Sebastian and I had never quite gotten around to eating the lunch in his backpack—knapsack—whatever it was. As if on cue, my stomach growled.

"Jesus," Rebecca said. "I *heard* that."

I went to the table on the patio and grabbed some potato chips while Rebecca greeted everyone. I smiled through mouthfuls as she re-introduced me to people. I recognized most of them—some were in drama club with Rebecca and Chris; some were people I'd seen around the halls and at parties. Cody stood off in the shadow of a tree with a tall brunette I recognized as the girl who'd played Maria in *West Side Story* when we were sophomores. Rebecca, who was now catching up with the guys at the grill, hadn't noticed Cody yet. I stared at him until he finally looked at me. Immediately Cody straightened, looked around, and excused himself from the girl. He nodded as he walked past me toward Rebecca. Good boy. Crisis averted.

My phone buzzed.

SEBASTIAN: Are you okay? I haven't stopped thinking about today.
ME: I'm ok.
SEBASTIAN: I was right. You are so brave and so strong and so sweet, Macy Lyons. Just like a lion.

A thrilling chill went up my spine. I held my phone to my chest, and suddenly I couldn't be at this party, around these random people.

I told Rebecca that something I ate hadn't agreed with me, and I went to my car and drove home. I ran up the stairs, grateful that both Mom's and Gavin's doors were closed. I found Sebastian's lion drawing in my drawer and brought it into bed with me. I fell asleep holding it, the warmth spreading through me.

CHAPTER TWENTY-THREE

"So? Who's this guy Sebastian?" Mom asked. She was clearly trying to sound innocent, but it wasn't working.

"No one," I said.

"No one," she said bitterly. "That's funny. I met a guy named Sebastian the other day right here in this kitchen. He didn't seem like no one. He had a voice, a face, hair, you know, all the stuff that *someone* would have."

I slammed the bread drawer closed and put a piece of thick, nutty zillion-grain bread—white flour was verboten in our house—in the toaster.

"So, does Chris know this no one?" Mom continued.

I sighed loudly. "He's just a friend."

"Okay." She seemed grateful that I'd answered her.

My toast popped up. I buttered it then waited for it to cool.

"You know," Mom said. "It's totally understandable that you'd want to play the field. You and Chris—you've just known each other so long."

While Mom always claimed that there was nothing *wrong* with Chris, I knew from her not-so-subtle comments that she didn't want me to end up with him. That was one of the reasons why I ended up with him.

"Sebastian seems smart. Sophisticated," she said. "There's something about him that struck me. He has an old soul. I like him."

No. Mom could not like Sebastian. I refused to allow her to taint him with her approval.

"I think he would be good for you."

There we go. That was it. I snapped.

"Since when do you care what's good for me?" I asked, gritting my teeth.

Mom stepped back in surprise.

"Of course I do. I'm your mother."

"Hardly," I said. I grabbed my half-eaten toast and started upstairs to my room. Just let her try to tell me not to eat upstairs. I'd said it. Would she even know what I meant? What kind of mother turns her back on her daughter when she most needs her—and then tries to assert her "motherness" when it's convenient for her? How could she "see" something in Sebastian, but not even notice her own daughter?

Plus, Mom didn't know the whole story. If she knew about Sebastian's violent past, she wouldn't say he was good for me. She would do everything in her power to keep him away from me. Ironic, considering she did nothing to keep Scott away from me.

I fumed. I looked in the mirror while I covered my head with a green bandana and tied it underneath my hair, letting the thicker dreads hang out the back and pulling some smaller ones out of the front. My face was set in anger. I looked more closely, and I could see it in my eyes. I was tired of being angry. I wanted to be released.

I took off my robe and put on shorts, my Marwood counselor T-shirt, and socks with giant yellow smiley faces on them. The irony made me laugh a little.

"What's funny?" Gavin said, making me jump.

"Jesus. You scared the shit out of me," I said.

"Your door was open."

"Why are you up so early?" I asked.

"No reason."

"Just come with me to Marwood. Bring your laptop and sit by the pool," I said.

"Fine." He sighed like it was some great hardship when I could tell he'd wanted me to ask him to come.

We went downstairs.

"Morning," Mom said as she poured herself another cup of coffee. Her exercise outfit today had a cutout daisy on her left hip and you could see her bare skin through it. If all the women weren't wearing the same thing, I'd say she looked like a midlife housewife slut. But then again, just because they were all wearing it didn't mean they weren't all sluts.

"Hi," Gavin said, heading for the garage door. "I'm going to Marwood with Macy."

"That's nice, sweetie. I'll see you there," she said, turning back to the newspaper on the counter. Mom always stood in that exact spot at the kitchen counter. She never sat down to drink her coffee and read the paper.

"Wait!" she said, just as we reached the door. "Gavin, you have to eat something."

"I'm not hungry, Mom. I'll eat something at the Club later." She grabbed a banana from the fruit basket and tossed it to him. It hit him on the knee and fell on the floor.

"Ouch?" Gavin said. He picked up the banana and put it in his pocket.

"Keep that in there so the boobsie twins see it and wonder," I whispered to Gavin. He laughed out loud. Mom looked hurt, like I'd been whispering about her, and I decided to let her think that.

I pushed Gavin out the door toward my car.

"What was all the yelling before?" Gavin asked when we were in the car.

"The usual. Mom likes to tell me who my friends and boyfriends should be. And I don't like Mom to tell me who my friends and boyfriends should be."

"She's giving you shit about Chris again?"

"Sort of. I don't know. None of it's any of her business," I said.

"So . . ." he said, hesitantly.

"So, what?"

"So this guy Maynard told Eliza he saw you with some guy who wasn't Chris. At the diner. Who was it?"

"Who the hell is Maynard and why does he know me? And who the fuck names their kid Maynard?"

Shit. Would Chris care if he heard?

"I don't know," he said. "Another dork in my grade."

"You are not a dork. And even if you were, there's nothing wrong with that. Maynard, on the other hand, well, he just deserves to be a dork, doesn't he? With a name like that."

"Seriously, Macy. Are you cheating on Chris?" He pouted as though I were cheating on *him*.

"No! Not that it's any of your business, but no. I was at the diner with a friend. I went running with him."

"Okay," he said. "Now I know you're lying. Just don't try to tell Chris that when he finds out. It will totally blow your cover."

"I swear. We went jogging by the reservoir. And I actually liked it. If you tell Mom, I will tell her about certain blogs you frequent." His neck turned ruby red. "Do a better job of clearing your history, dude. And sorry about your hat."

"Wait a second. That was your sweat? I thought Mom washed it and left it in my room to dry. That is revolting, you know that?"

I stifled a laugh. "Sorry."

"Who is he?" His tone was accusatory.

"Sebastian Ruiz. We've gotten to be friends."

"Why?"

"What do you mean, why?"

"Why are you hanging out alone with a guy who's not Chris?"

"Gavin," I said, slowing for a red light. "What is your problem? You hang out with Eliza all the time and she's not your girlfriend."

"But I want her to be," he said quietly. Suddenly I felt horrible. I was guilty as charged.

"I don't know," I said. "But for some reason, I am compelled to hang out with him, okay?"

"It's green," he said. We drove the rest of the way in silence. When I pulled into a parking spot at Marwood, I turned to him.

"Gavin, he's just a friend."

"I don't believe you."

"Do you realize how ridiculous this conversation is? Chris knows that Sebastian and I are friends, and you sound like a jealous boyfriend."

"Well, I think you're taking advantage of Chris."

"Whoa," I said, leaning back in my seat. "Them's fightin' words."

"Screw you," he said, getting out of the car. "I'll get Mom to take me home." And he stormed off. I gritted my teeth, tried to push it down. The only thing that made me feel better was the thought of seeing Sebastian.

I pulled out my phone and texted him.

ME: Just startng work. What r u up to today?

I walked slowly toward the Club, waiting for him to text back. He was probably asleep. When I saw Darren with Avery, I put my phone on silent and slipped it into my back pocket. Counselors were not allowed to use phones during camp hours.

Avery ran to me.

"Macy, I like the green thing on your hair. It's pretty. Papa said when I'm six I can get a snake!"

"That's awesome!" I said, rubbing the top of her head.

Darren scrunched up his nose. "Yes, well, Papa said that without asking Daddy if he agreed. Luckily he gave me two years to pray she forgets."

"Come on," I said to him. "Who wouldn't want a mouse-eating slimy reptile in their living room?"

I shuffled the kids toward the indoor tennis court, where I met up with Rebecca.

"So, how was everything with Cody?" I asked.

"Good, I think. I don't know. I saw him checking out Melinda Hayes a lot. Remember her? She played Maria in *West Side Story* when we were sophomores?"

"But you were with him all night, right?"

"Yeah. But even when we're together, sometimes I feel like he's not with me."

I wondered if Chris ever felt that way with me.

I put my hand on her knee and squeezed it.

"Chris was looking for you," she said.

"When?"

"He showed up after you left."

"I thought he was staying in the city with his dad. He didn't tell me—"

"He got home early and figured you'd be at the party. Didn't he call?" she asked.

"I don't think so." I pulled my phone out of my pocket to check my texts.

SEBASTIAN: Hi. I'm taking care of Sofia until 1. We may go to lunch and a playground.

I scrolled down. There was one from Chris from the night before.

CHRIS: Hey u ok? Ur sick? Call me in the am.

I'd have to wait until camp was over to write back.

"Anything?" Rebecca asked.

"Yeah. I guess I missed it somehow."

Just then, Darren walked in, and he made a beeline for me.

"Macy, I need you for a minute," Darren said. His voice was serious. I never should have taken out my phone. Maybe this wasn't exactly what I'd wanted to do this summer, but it was a good job. I didn't want to lose it, and I didn't want to disappoint him. He led me off the tennis court.

"Listen," he said. "Kevin's in the hospital."

"What?" I said loudly.

"He's fine, but his foot may be broken. My mother's coming to get Avery, but she can't get here until one. Can you stay with her at the playground?"

"No problem," I said. "Poor Kevin."

"Thanks, sweetie. I'll give him your love."

Before returning to the court, I texted Sebastian.

ME: Babysttng Avery from 12 to 1. Meet us @ Marwood playgrnd? I'll give ur name to front desk.

SEBASTIAN: It's a date.

CHAPTER TWENTY-FOUR

After the rest of the campers had been picked up, I told Avery about her papa's hurt foot and the new plan, and we headed to the playground. Sebastian was already there, pushing Sofia in a swing. He wore a faded mustard yellow T-shirt with brown trim around the neck and a random math equation on the front. His skinny body made his clothes look like they were hanging rather than being worn, and it emphasized the hugeness of his orange and white sneakers. He laughed at something Sofia said. He looked happy.

He saw me and held his hand up to wave. Suddenly I was aware of how *I* looked. All camp-counselored-out, sweaty and dirty from the day. Definitely not hot. But his look made me feel like I was.

"Hey, guys," I said. "This is Avery." I led her onto the playground, and she immediately jumped on the swing next to Sofia.

"And this," he said. "Is Sofia."

Sofia continued pumping her legs up and down.

"I can touch that." She pointed her toes toward the top of a tree. Her eyes were the same as Sebastian's—big and dark brown with long eyelashes that curled at the ends.

I started pushing Avery on the swing.

"I'll bet you can," I said.

"I can touch that one," Avery said.

Sebastian turned to me. "You okay?"

"Yeah."

He raised his eyebrows like he didn't believe me.

"Higher, Sebastian!" Sofia shouted. He turned away from me to push her.

"Hey," Sebastian said to someone, nodding. I looked up.

"Gavin!" I said. "What are you doing here?"

"You brought me here, remember?"

"I thought you were going home with Mom."

"She's got a tennis match," he said. "Are you leaving soon?"

"I'm here until one if you want to wait."

"Cool." He sat on a bench next to the sandbox.

"This is Sebastian," I said. After this morning, there was no way Gavin was going to be friendly. "Sebastian, this is my brother, Gavin."

They both said hey at the same time.

Gavin opened his laptop and began typing furiously. Sebastian looked at me and I shrugged. How to convey Gavin's immediate and undeserved hostility toward him? I couldn't.

"Are you a writer?" Sebastian asked Gavin.

Gavin looked up. "Why?"

"Not many people sit at a playground typing in the summer unless they really have something to say."

"I'm writing a novel," Gavin said.

"Wow. That's a major undertaking."

"He's really good," I offered. I knew Gavin wouldn't brag, so I'd have to. "Half-robot, half-boy trying to save the world and figure out who he is. It's amazing."

"Cool premise," Sebastian said. "Do you work from an outline or just see where your writing takes you?"

Gavin's face changed visibly. Very few people were interested enough to talk about the actual writing of the book, including me, and I suddenly felt like a jerk for never asking more about it.

"Um," Gavin said, clearly wanting to keep up his angry act but also seduced by Sebastian's interest. "I started with an outline, but I always stray from it, which is bad. It's a really plot-driven book. I kind of need to get back on track."

"I hear you," Sebastian said. "There must be so much to keep track of—like a giant puzzle."

"You write?" Gavin asked.

"No, mostly I draw. I have some ideas for novels, but I definitely couldn't actually write one," Sebastian said.

Gavin couldn't help himself—he was won over. And I knew that Sebastian wasn't even trying to be charming. He really meant all the things he was saying.

Avery and Sofia jumped off the swings and chased each other to the jungle gym.

I watched Avery climb to the top of the structure. I wasn't sure if she was big enough to try the monkey bars so I scooted under her just in case.

"Mom said the tennis ladder is heating up. I'm sure she's going to screw me on the sci-fi convention tonight, and I can't get in unless I'm with someone over sixteen."

"I can go with you," I said.

Avery hesitantly put a hand on one of the monkey bars. Sofia was going down the slide, and Sebastian waited at the bottom to catch her.

"So then you're not leaving for Cape Cod until late?" he asked.

Cape Cod? Oh my god! I was going away with Chris's family for the weekend, and I'd completely forgotten. I hadn't even packed. Gavin stared at me like I was a zombie with eight legs.

"Seriously? You forgot you were going to Cape Cod with your *boyfriend? Today?*" Clearly, Sebastian's charm had worn off.

Sebastian seemed to be concentrating hard on Sofia's climb back up the slide.

"We may go tomorrow," I lied. Even though it was obvious I'd forgotten the trip, I wasn't going to own up to it.

I was the worst girlfriend. I pulled out my phone, which was still on silent. Chris had texted an hour before.

CHRIS: U out of camp yet?

I typed quickly, hoping to make up for my reprehensible behavior.

ME: Sorry! Fone silent. Babysitting. What time r we leaving?
CHRIS: 3 ok? Psyched!
ME: 3:30 is better. Me too.

When I'd agreed to go to Cape Cod with Chris's family, things had been different. I'd wanted to get away from the complications of everything. I'd wanted so desperately to be part of the Holtz world. But now, I didn't want to go. I wanted to stay here with Sebastian. Now that my secret was released, I wasn't sure I could shove it back down. I could feel the power I'd once had—the power to pretend—draining out of me, drop by drop.

"Daddy!" Avery cried out and ran to Darren, who was approaching the playground.

"I'm sorry it took so long," Darren said to me. "My mom got stuck in traffic, so I figured I'd just come get Ave."

"How's Kevin?" I asked as he swooped Avery up into his arms.

"His foot's not broken, just sprained."

"Oh, that's good," I said.

"Yeah, but it's the worst timing. We're having a party at our house on the Cape tomorrow, and it's too late to cancel. He'll be completely useless to me. I'll have to prep for the party myself *and* take care of the kids. Oh my god, I'm so self-ish. My husband is in pain and all I can think is how much more work I'll have to do."

I twirled a dreadlock as an idea took shape.

"Maybe I could help with the kids while you're getting ready for your party," I said.

He looked at me like I was crazy and then smiled.

"You want to come to the Cape with us?" he asked.

"Well," I said. "Coincidentally, I'll be on the Cape this weekend with the Holtzes. And Theresa told me that your house is nearby."

"Yes! Yes, yes, yes," he said. "That would work. If you're sure you want to, it would be lovely."

Somehow the word *lovely* worked for Darren even though it hadn't for Rebecca.

I breathed a sigh of relief. Having Darren's house to escape to would help. Because at this point, I wasn't sure how I was going to spend an entire weekend faking it with Chris.

"Just text me when you get there. We'll work out all the details then," Darren said.

I nodded.

"Come on, sweetie," he said to Avery. "Let's go see Papa."

"Bye, Macy!" Avery shouted as Darren lifted her onto his shoulders.

I turned back to Sebastian, who had pulled pretzels out of his backpack and given them to Sofia.

"I guess we'll head out," he said. I tried to hide my disappointment. If Gavin hadn't been here, I could have talked to him. I could have said something. But I wasn't even sure what. There wasn't anything to say. We weren't—and wouldn't be—together.

"I'll talk to you later?" I said to Sebastian.

"Yeah, sure," he said, and he led Sofia toward the guest parking lot.

Gavin slid his laptop into his backpack and waited by the gate.

When we got to my car, he opened his mouth to speak.

"Don't say a word," I said first.

We drove in silence the rest of the way home. I had enough to worry about without Gavin's disapproval right now.

CHAPTER TWENTY-FIVE

"You okay?" Chris asked, turning down the music. I didn't move my eyes from the blur of trees, signs, and the bridge that would take us over to Cape Cod.

"Yeah." I turned the music back up. I pressed my head against the window. Mom and I had a huge blowout right before Chris came to get me. I'd overheard Mom talking on the phone to Scott. She told him that Dad was always working, traveling, having dinner with clients—just never around. She said she felt like he was neglecting the family, and she wasn't sure how much more she was willing to take.

After Mom said, "Thanks for listening, Scotty," I waited until she hung up, and then I lost it.

"You're having issues with Dad, and you're spilling your guts to *Scott*?" I yelled. "*Scott? That's* who you've chosen to depend on?"

"I'm so tired of your judgments and anger toward him, Macy. Just get over it."

"How can you say that to me, Mom? Believe me, I've tried to get over it. Maybe you were able to forget it all, but I can't. I *wish* I could forget. You just let him get away with it. You really just don't care." And I stormed out to Chris's car. I don't even think she tried to yell after me.

"Are *we* okay?" Chris asked, turning the music off now. He took his right hand off the steering wheel and put it on top of mine. I flinched. He held on tighter and rubbed the back of my hand with his thumb. Normally, I'd pull away and give him some shit about the pointlessness of hand-holding or his terrible driving. But now, if I pulled away, it would mean something. It *did* mean something. So I just let him do it.

"Macy? Are we okay?" Chris asked again.

"I don't know." It was the truth. I'd lied about me being okay. I knew *I* wasn't okay. But at least I could tell him the truth about our relationship.

He took his hand away and ran his fingers through his thick blond hair.

I looked at him and I ached. I ached for what he represented—the best part of my messed-up childhood, someone who loved me and who didn't ask for anything in return. I wished I could be satisfied with that.

Chris sulked next to me.

"Is there something going on with that guy Sebastian?" he asked. Hearing Chris say his name made me feel nauseous.

"No," I said. "I mean, I do care about him, but nothing's going on." This was basically the truth.

"Are you sure? I know you've been hanging out with him. I'm not jealous usually, but you've been acting different."

"I have?"

"Yeah," he said. "You have."

"I've been thinking about a lot of shit lately. I've been preoccupied, I guess."

"I knew this would happen at some point," he said sadly.

"What would?"

"You'd break up with me."

"Why? Why would you think that?"

"I'm not blind," he said. "You've just been going along with this. It's always been one-sided. I wanted to try to change that, but . . ."

"What are you talking about—one-sided?"

"I could always count on you, you know, to defend me when I was getting my fat, zitty, stupid ass kicked in middle school, to watch the dumb school plays, listen to me whine about the stage stuff, the guys, all that. But *you've* never really needed *me*," he said.

He wrinkled his forehead, the same way he had when he was nine and trying not to cry.

"That's not true. I do need you," I said.

"No you don't. What's the stuff you've been thinking about that's so preoccupying? Why haven't you turned to me, your boyfriend, to help you?"

I hesitated. "It's complicated."

"Too complicated for me, obviously. Does it take someone smarter? Like Sebastian?"

I didn't answer.

He stared at the highway, his fingers tight on the steering wheel.

"Let's just get through this weekend," he said and turned the music back on.

When we got to the Holtz's beach house, I wished everything had been different. I wished that this could really be my life—Chris's girlfriend, an easy weekend with a fun-loving family at a beautiful beach house by the bay. But it wasn't really my life. It was becoming harder to figure out who I was and what I wanted and where I belonged. Or as Chris put it, what I needed.

My phone buzzed with my third text from Mom.

MOM: Please call me.

I unpacked my things in the guest room. Theresa would have been okay if Chris and I stayed together in the same room, but we never had. And now, we never would. I leaned against the white dresser painted with pastel seashells and stared into the matching mirror. Same face as always. I'd been Chris's girlfriend for almost seven months. Would I look different if I wasn't anymore?

In the kitchen, I found Theresa.

"Chris took Joseph to the market to get the lobsters," she said. If it had been the weekend it was supposed to be, Chris would have come into my room, we would have fooled around, and then he would have asked me to come with them to the market. But now we were operating under different rules. I wondered if Theresa sensed it.

"Jim and I are going down to the bay. Do you want to come?" she asked.

"Thanks, I think I'll just read on the deck."

"We'll be down there if you change your mind," she said and went out the back door to the beach stairs.

I checked my phone—a voice mail and two more texts from Mom, a text from Rebecca, and nothing from Sebastian. The disappointment created a tiny hole in my chest that I knew would only get bigger, so I decided to text him.

ME: Hi. Hope ur ok. Thinkin of u.

It was dumb, but it was something.

After Chris and Joseph got back and we had our dinner of lobsters and steamers, Chris and I walked down to the beach with a couple of beers he'd swiped from the fridge when Theresa wasn't looking. When Joseph made a move to come with us, Chris gave him a look, and Joseph did the "Oh, I forgot I have to do something . . ." fake-out.

We sat on the rough stairs, watching the finishing touches the sunset was painting on the sky. Purples, pinks, wisps of gray replaced the bright blue sky and sun from earlier in the day.

"So, are we breaking up then?" Chris asked.

I took a sip of my beer.

"I think we are maybe," I said.

"That sucks," he said.

"Sure does."

"Is it because of Sebastian?"

I hesitated. "It's not *because* of, but . . ."

I could barely see the blue of his eyes in the darkening sky.

He stood and turned his back to me.

"I'm going to need some time," he said, his voice shaking. "I can't just go right from this to friends."

"I know. Me too."

"I can't believe I'm never going to kiss you again," he said.

"Never say never." I tugged at a blade of dune grass.

He looked at me. "Do you mean that?"

"Yeah," I said. Even though I felt that right now everything I had in me was for Sebastian, I would always love Chris, my best friend, and there would always be a piece of me that would hold out hope for us, for me. That maybe someday a less complicated, easy version of myself could be right with Chris.

"Maybe we'll do our own thing," he said. "We'll lose touch, and then after college we'll run into each other on our lunch break at a deli on Broadway or something. And we'll be like, 'Hey, I used to love you once. Let's try that again.' And it will be all good."

"Totally," I said, laughing. "Except you'll be a famous set-designer for shows *on* Broadway, and we'll never lose touch. Ever."

I stood and leaned my head against his shoulder. We drank our beers until they were gone.

"Do you want me to take a bus home tomorrow?" I asked.

"No. Stay. We don't have to tell my family yet. They don't need to be in our business."

When I got back into the guest room, there was a text from Sebastian.

SEBASTIAN: Fine here.

Sebastian was giving me the cold shoulder, and now I had to spend the rest of the weekend hanging out with my ex-boyfriend and his perfect family, pretending, always pretending.

I curled up on the bed and fell asleep listening to the waves.

Saturday afternoon, I left the beach early to get ready for babysitting. I'd been reading all day, and Chris had been playing a lot of Frisbee with Joseph. We tried to make things as normal as possible without having to touch each other or talk much.

Darren had said he might want me to take Avery down to the beach while he and Kevin got ready for their party, so I kept my bikini on. It was orange like the one I wore when I first met Sebastian—when I'd left him to go swimming with Scott. The orange no longer made me feel brave like a lifeguard, though. I threw a beach dress on over the suit and went outside to wait for Darren.

When he drove up, I had just closed my eyes to the sun, allowing the smell of the pine trees to lull me into a false sense of okay. I got in the car.

"You having a good time?" Darren asked as I buckled my seatbelt.

I nodded.

"Liar," he said.

"Chris and I broke up."

"Sorry," he said. "That's rough."

"He's my best friend."

Darren nodded. "I know how that goes."

When we got to his house, my jaw dropped. The house was amazing and completely original. It rose out of the dune like a rocket, almost cylindrical. Inside the house, I twirled around like a little girl in a chocolate factory, taking in the curved walls, the painted pale gray floors, the living room and kitchen that seemed to be one giant window looking out onto the bay.

"Wow," I said, because words had abandoned me.

"Thanks," Darren said. "We still have a bit of a punch list, but for the most part, it's finally done. I'll give you a tour in a bit."

Kevin lay on the couch, his foot covered in a soft cast, resting on a pillow. He had a large hardcover book opened on his chest. Avery was kneeling at the coffee table in front of him, concentrating on coloring.

"Hi there," Kevin said to me.

Avery didn't look up.

Kevin nudged her.

"Hi, Macy!" she said.

"How's your foot?" I asked Kevin.

"It's getting better. But I can't stand being a cripple. Right, Dar?"

Darren rolled his eyes. "More like *I* can't stand him being a cripple. He's a giant child. Like it isn't hard enough having two."

"Well," Kevin said, pulling himself up so that he was sitting. "At least I was able to get the hors d'oeuvres done."

I sat on the floor next to Avery, watching her draw a person. She was very precise about it, choosing her colors carefully.

Darren turned to me. "The guy who designed the house is one of Kevin's best friends from Berkeley, so we're hosting this shindig. Maybe drum up some business for him."

My ears perked up. Berkeley? As in UC Berkeley?

Kevin held up the book on his lap. "This was my student directory at Berkeley. We called it The Facebook. Isn't that funny? Before the dawn of all things social media, Facebook used to actually mean *this*!"

"So, you went . . ." my voice cracked a little, so I cleared my throat, "to Berkeley?"

Kevin looked at me curiously. "Mmmhmm. Are you applying there?"

"It's my reach school," I said, probably beet red. "The architecture school, actually."

Kevin lit up like a firecracker.

"My goodness. That is what I call kismet. Seth Peters, as you can see here, is an architect of the genius variety. And, as it happens, he was my roommate at Berkeley. And I'm going to talk to him about you, and I'm going to help you with your essays, and we are going to do this thing. Oh, thank god, I needed a project this summer. And pretty girl, you are it."

Darren shook his head. "I think we can let Macy decide if she wants to be your project."

"I can use all the help I can get," I said. "I've got decent grades and test scores, but no experience."

"I'll let you know how tonight goes," Kevin said, getting up and hobbling to the kitchen. "Darren, you've been dying for a swim. Take Macy down with you. I've got Ave—she's so busy. And Ben'll sleep another hour. Sorry we brought you over here for nothing really, Macy. We thought we'd have so much more cooking to do, but we got most of it done already."

"No problem," I said. "Are you sure you don't want to go down? I can stay with the kids."

"Not with this thing," Kevin said, pointing at his foot. "Besides, Avery's drawing me, and the model can't really just leave!" He hobbled back to the couch and gave Avery a kiss on the top of her head.

"Okay, then," Darren said. "Let's go."

We walked down the steep stairs to the beach.

"Do you think Kevin can really help with Berkeley?" I asked. I didn't want to get my hopes up, but I could feel them rising, my chest expanding with possibility.

"Kevin gets pretty much anything he sets his mind to." Darren winked at me. "Don't let him bully you into anything, but if you really want it, he'll make it his life's mission. Just be prepared—he'll work you like a dog. You'll rewrite your essays a thousand times until he's happy with them. If he thinks you can do better on your SATs, he'll tell you to take them again."

"That's good. I think I might need that."

I'd been studying the Berkeley brochure, but I hadn't even thought about what it would take to actually put the application together. I needed this.

We stepped onto the sand, which felt so soft and warm on my feet.

"Every time I come here, I can't get over it," Darren said. "Like how can the sky really be that blue? Is it that blue at home? I don't think it is."

"It definitely seems brighter here."

"I love it. It feels like vacation. Everything just washes away." He swept his hands down his body like a squeegee, wiping the dirt away from a window.

I tried to make everything wash away, but my dirt was stubborn, ground in until it had become a stain. *Out, out, damn-spot.*

I stood at the water's edge while Darren ran in and dove—carefree, childlike.

The water lapped at my feet, teasing my toes, making my feet sink deeper into the sand. I wanted to go in, to glide in the smooth bay water. I wanted to get my hair wet, hold my arms up to the sun and let it dry them off. I reached down to scoop up some of the cool water and sprinkled it on my arms. I took a few more steps into the water so that my ankles were covered and the little waves brought salty drops nearly up to my mid-calf.

"It's soooo refreshing," Darren said, floating on his back, letting his toes bob out of the water. He turned over, swam a few strokes, and then started walking toward the shore, the sandy bottom of the bay exaggerating his footsteps. He stood next to me.

"You seem sad," he said. Something about the way he said it took my breath away. Yes, sad. I'd thought I was anxious, overwhelmed, even angry. But I *was* sad. I nodded.

"Anything you want to talk about?" he asked gently.

"I don't know. I guess college applications and stuff," I lied. "Talking to Kevin got me thinking about how much I have to do. Overwhelming, you know?"

"And breaking up with Chris?"

"Yeah, of course. Chris. It sucks."

Darren sat down in the sand. I sat next to him.

"Is there anything else?" he asked. Again, gently, innocently, but like Sebastian, it felt like he *knew*.

He put his hand on my arm.

"Believe me," he said. "I won first place at pretending A-okay. You know how long it took me to come out to my parents? I see that look in you that I had, the covering up. But you can tell me anything. I'm listening."

That was it. My eyes stung; the tears were coming. I looked down.

"Something happened," I said, breathing rapidly. "I didn't think it was a big deal, but lately it's been bugging me out, and I can't stop thinking about it. But I don't think I should say anything."

"Sweetheart, I've known you a long time. Anything you tell me stays right here."

If I told him, he'd know. The idea was both a relief and completely frightening. I'd already told Sebastian, but maybe I needed an adult to know. Maybe I needed to see if he agreed with Mom and Dad—that it could just be forgotten like it was nothing—or if he thought it was really something.

"Um," I said. How was I going to say it? "Scott and I used to do stuff together. Sexual stuff. I didn't think it was a big deal, but I guess it kind of was."

Darren drew his breath in quickly. "Scott molested you, Macy?" He said it harshly, clinically, like Sebastian had. And again, it didn't fit right.

"I . . . um, I don't know if I'd say *that*. I mean, he didn't rape me or anything. I never said no."

Darren's eyes were serious. Gray, like the stones at the edge of the water.

"He's what? Seven, eight years older than you? It doesn't matter what you said or didn't say. Whether it was violent or not."

"I know but—"

"When did this start?"

"I was seven," I said, quietly.

"Seven? Oh god," he said, putting his head in his hands and then looked at me. His jaw was clenched tight. I picked up a shell and made circles in the sand next to me. I concentrated on the circles, making them smaller and smaller.

"I guess it made me feel grown-up. He usually ignored me, but when we were doing stuff, he was paying attention to me. I liked that. And," I looked down at my feet in the sand, embarrassed, "the stuff he did felt good."

Darren nodded. "Yes, but you were too young to understand those physical feelings."

He stayed quiet, so I kept talking to fill the silence, to let the information belong to someone else.

"I remember not wanting to do it sometimes, but doing it anyway. It wasn't really that I thought it was wrong; it was more like, if I was reading and he came into my room, I was kind of annoyed. And sometimes I felt like I wasn't doing it right. I was worried I was disappointing him."

Darren shook his head now. "Sitting duck," he mumbled.

"What?"

"You were a sitting duck in your own home. He could come to you anytime anywhere and you'd have to do what he wanted, even if you were busy. Right?"

"Well, I was just a kid. How busy could I be?"

"Yes, that's the point. You were just a kid. You were a kid who was reading, playing, doing age-appropriate stuff. And he took you away from that. At his will."

"But Chris and I checked each other out and stuff around then too," I said, blushing.

"That's different. Kids the same age. Curiosity. I think you know that," he said. "But Scott was what? Fourteen? Yes, he knew better than to touch a seven-year-old girl. Even if you think you were a willing participant, you were not old enough to agree to any of it. He had all the power, and you had none. You really had no choice to make."

I understood what he was saying, but I still couldn't feel it.

"Listen, Macy, I've been working with kids for a long time. *And* I'm a father. And I love the shit out of you. You did nothing wrong. Everything that happened was because Scott forced you to do it. I know you don't think you were forced. But you were. I knew you when you were seven. You were playing catch and watching cartoons. You knew nothing about sex and you shouldn't have—not for a long, long time. You loved him, and you wanted to make him happy. Those feelings are all normal. But what you had to do to get attention from him was not normal at all. He took advantage of you. You may love him in many ways and you may feel like you want to protect him, but what he did was plain wrong. He *harmed* you. In fact, if it continued after he was eighteen, it's a felony. He could go to jail. Do you understand?" He looked fierce now.

I nodded. But, holy shit. He was my cousin, not some random child molester who should be in prison. I shook my head back and forth.

"Mace, honey," he said, more quietly now. "I'm not saying you have to press charges against him. Even though he was old enough to know better, he may not have been aware of the effect it would have on you. I'm just saying you have a chance to make things right now. With your family and with yourself."

It all seemed like too much work. Fixing things with my family sounded impossible and exhausting. I didn't even know who my family was anymore.

"I will never forgive myself," he continued. "I should've known. I knew something was going on with you. How could I not have seen it?"

"What do you mean?"

"At camp. Some days you were happy and open, and some days you wouldn't say a word. You'd sit in a corner and just watch everyone with these eyes. And some days the counselors would tell me you didn't eat anything at lunch. Or you were overly flirtatious with the boy counselors. Or sometimes you were, I don't know, just different. You were so erratic, but I thought—I didn't know what to think. I was an idiot in those days. But now I have a daughter. Everything is different."

He ran his hands through his damp hair.

"But, Scott!" he said. "I definitely knew something was wrong with Scott. He had this attitude. He didn't care whose feelings he hurt, what rules he broke. There was no disciplining him. I told your mom. She got defensive. That's when things started going bad with our friendship. Dammit, I should've known."

I stared at a seagull with beady eyes perched on a rock. A few moments passed.

"I'm glad you told me," he said.

"I don't know why I've been thinking about it so much lately," I said, scraping all my circles clear with the shell, like I was erasing a chalkboard. "I guess just watching these kids at camp, seeing how young they are. It made me realize how young I was. And I get really pissed. But on the other hand, he was never forceful."

"He seduced you. He manipulated you."

"But he's not an evil person," I said. Why was I defending him? Just like with Rebecca.

"What I know is that *you* are not a bad person, Macy. And I know that a good person *can* be tempted to do something horribly wrong like hurt an innocent child, but he or she resists doing it."

"But I'm sort of okay, you know? I'm not like a total screwup. I do okay in school, I have friends, I have a boyfriend—or I did, anyway. I'm not like whoring myself out on the street for my next fix."

Darren sighed.

"All *despite* what happened to you," he said. He wasn't letting up. Did I want him to?

"I can't help it. I mean, I *know* what you're saying is true. But sometimes it feels like it's not that big a deal. It's Scott. It wasn't my dad or dirty old uncle. And we didn't really have sex. Maybe it was just experimentation too."

He sighed again. He was getting frustrated with me.

"You've trained yourself to think that as a defense mechanism. If you realized how horrible what he did was, you wouldn't have survived as well as you did. And because he's young and handsome and charming, it's easier to believe that it was nothing. That's why he's gotten away with it. But I'm telling you that it is *not* okay. It never was. Okay?"

"Okay," I said, putting my chin on my knees.

"You know you have to tell your parents," he said. "I can be with you when you do, if you want. I know your mom.

When she finds out this went down in her house, watch out. She's a mama bear if I ever saw one. She'll make it right."

Clearly Darren knew a different Deb Lyons than the one I knew. He assumed Mom and Dad didn't already know. I considered whether to tell him that they did, and just didn't do anything. But, despite everything, I couldn't sell them out like that.

I stayed quiet, digesting what Darren had said, watching the water sparkle like tiny stars.

"I haven't been in the water since I was twelve," I said suddenly.

"I know."

"Will you come in with me?" I asked, surprising myself.

"Of course," he said, standing up.

I stood, took off my cover-up and threw it behind me.

We walked into the bay. Darren waited patiently as I got used to the water—my thighs, my hips, my stomach, my chest. My breathing became shallow. I tried to block out the memories of water pouring into my lungs, losing consciousness, knowing that everything had changed forever. I took one breath and dunked my head under the water, jumping back up and shaking my wet dreads everywhere.

Darren, his face dotted with droplets from my hair, laughed. "Good god, you're worse than a goddamned dog!" And then he hugged me so tight I thought he might squeeze the shame right out of me.

CHAPTER TWENTY-SIX

Chris drove me back on Sunday. Joseph was in the back-seat, reciting lines from his favorite movies, so we didn't talk much. It was probably for the best. We'd said everything we needed to say for now.

Thankfully, no one was home when I arrived, so I dropped off my bag and got right in my car. I was dying to see Sebastian. The urge to tell him my feelings was overwhelming, and I wanted to get to him before I lost my nerve.

I drove straight to Sebastian's house as fast as I could without risking a ticket. I pulled up in front of his house and ran up the steps. I pounded a little too hard on the door. After what felt like forever, but was probably thirty seconds, his mom opened the door.

"Hi, Mrs. Ruiz," I said, breathing heavily. "Is Sebastian here?"

She smiled. "Sebastian is not here. He's gone to the diner. I'll tell him you came."

"Thanks." I ran back to the car.

There weren't any parking spots in the diner lot, so I circled around the block until I found one on the street. I was a mess—my hair was all over the place and I still had sand in my toes. I opened the door to the diner and there he was, sitting at the same table where we'd had lunch. He was reading a book. I was dying to run to him, but I didn't want to cause a scene, so I walked as calmly as I could.

"Hi," I said. I was actually panting. He looked up from his book and smiled. He stood and hugged me, and I felt every nerve ending come alive with his touch.

"You're back," he said.

"I'm back. I have so much to tell you."

"Wait—"

"I broke up with Chris. I know this isn't the right time for you, but I'll wait for you to be ready. I want to be with you. We should be together. But I can wait." I couldn't believe I was saying these things to him. Out loud. He didn't say anything but he looked concerned, and then he saw something behind me, and his face changed.

"Macy, this isn't a good time," he said.

"But—"

He grabbed my elbow. "Please stop," he said.

Just then a girl came up beside me. Long, dark red hair, a black streak down the front. She wore jewelry, lipstick, a big fashionable handbag, and expensive shoes.

"Hi," she said. "Sorry I'm late." She looked at me curiously.

Sebastian stood perfectly still, staring at her.

"Macy, this is Jacqueline. Jacqueline, Macy."

Jacqueline. Beautiful French Jacqueline. The love of Sebastian's life. Jacqueline was standing in front of me now, interrupting my love confession to the love of *her* life. And Sebastian was staring at her, mesmerized by her beauty, probably remembering how much he loved her. I stood there, frozen. And then I turned and ran all the way around the block to my car, the tears streaming down my face.

It felt like a large, strong hand had reached into my chest and was squeezing my heart over and over. Literally, physically. I felt the pain so thoroughly and completely, like someone was pushing a finger in deeper and deeper.

I started my car and drove. After a few blocks, I had to pull over. It wasn't safe to drive while my body convulsed with sobs, and tears blinded me. The tears were so fast and hot, they were all over the place—on my face, my neck, the steering wheel. I let go. I cried. I wailed. I sobbed. I hurt.

Nothing I'd been through had ever felt this bad. At least, I'd never allowed myself to feel this bad. Sebastian, the person who had made me feel better than anyone else had ever been able to, had also made me feel the worst.

Finally, my sobbing slowed down, and I breathed. Every bone, every muscle in my body was spent.

I picked up my phone, hoping, praying, expecting a text from Sebastian. But there was nothing. Another wave of sobs. This is what it meant to have your heart break. Whoever came up with that saying was good. It did feel like it was breaking. Or ripping apart. A messy, jagged tear.

I started driving again. My car was bringing me to Rebecca's house. I needed her now. Even if I didn't tell her about Sebastian, about Scott, about Mom and Dad standing by and doing nothing, at least I could tell her more about my breakup with Chris. I could start with that. I pulled up in front of her house and went slowly up the porch steps. I knocked lightly on the door and then pushed it open. It was never locked.

"Beck?" a male voice called from inside. I walked through the hall into the TV room and there was Rebecca's brother Charlie sitting on the couch watching TV, a beer in his hand.

"Oh, hey," he said.

"What are you doing here?" I asked.

"Um, this is my house? I'm home for a few days. Are you crying?"

"No," I said, sniffling. "Where's Beck?"

"I don't know."

I pulled my phone out and texted her.

"You look like you could use a beer," he said. He went to the kitchen and pulled one out of the refrigerator. A beer would be good. It would calm my nerves while I waited for Rebecca to text me back—to let her make me laugh.

I sat down and put the bottle to my lips, taking a long gulp. It was cold and bubbly and it tasted good. Within minutes, I needed another.

"Wow," Charlie said, going to the refrigerator again. "You're thirsty."

I accepted the beer he gave me.

"So," he said. "What have you been up to this summer?"

Yes, this was good. If I couldn't have Rebecca, I'd talk to Charlie. He'd always been such a good guy. Even after I lost my virginity to him, he'd never changed. He'd just gone back to being Rebecca's brother.

A tear made its way out of my eye. I swiped at it.

"Did I say something wrong?" he said. "I think I used all the right grammar. What-have-you-been-up-to-this-summer? Yes. I'm pretty sure I said it right."

I smiled.

"That's better," he said. "You're not really the crying type."

"What's that supposed to mean?" I asked.

"Well, you know, you're not all girlie-girlie. You're tough. I've always liked that about you."

"But now you don't like me because I'm crying? Now I'm girlie-girlie?"

"Oh boy, yeah, I can't say anything right. I'm gonna shut up now. I know you need my sister—I'm sure she'll be here soon."

He started flipping channels.

I went to the kitchen to get a napkin and wiped my eyes and my nose.

"My life is falling apart," I said, sitting back down on the couch.

He looked at me. He mimed buttoning his lips.

"You can talk," I said. "Just don't say anything wrong."

"I'll try. But your bar is sky high. Man."

I smiled sarcastically.

"You can talk to me until Beck gets here if you want. Just think of me as her. Let it all out." Then he batted his eyelashes and pretended to primp his hair and adjust invisible boobs. He grinned and started chanting. "Talk, talk, talk, spill, spill, spill."

"Fine. I just broke up with my boyfriend for someone else. And I just did this whole like *Graduate* scene where I showed up to tell the other guy. And then his ex-girlfriend showed up, and the way he looked at her, he must be totally in love with her still. And she is beautiful, I mean stunningly gorgeous. She was wearing open-toe heels. In the middle of the day."

He covered a laugh with his hand. "Sorry. Are you talking about shoes? I didn't get the reference."

I punched him in the arm.

"And my mom and I just had this huge thing that I can't get into, and my dad is a total disappointment, and everything is falling apart."

I felt the tears burning behind my eyes again. He was right. This wasn't me. I didn't cry.

Charlie patted me on the shoulder, and then he got up to get me another beer, which I drank. And the next thing I knew, I was making out with Charlie, and we were stripping each other's clothes off as we moved to his bedroom, and I wasn't thinking. Except about how good it felt to be wanted and to be kissed like I was someone who deserved to be kissed. Jacqueline could have Sebastian for all I cared. I could get any guy I wanted.

Charlie reached over to his bedside drawer and pulled out a condom.

"Is this okay?" he asked as he tore the wrapper.

"Is this okay?" Scott asked, as he touched me.

Scott had asked, but there'd only ever been one right answer. I never knew there was another option, another answer to the question. I'd never really had a choice.

Suddenly, I couldn't catch my breath. I sat up quickly and pushed Charlie off me. I shook my head, trying to clear the beer out of my clouded brain.

"What?" Charlie asked. "Are you going to throw up?"

"No. I need to think. Hold on."

He sat still, staring at me. What the hell was I doing? Why was I fooling around with Charlie Maroni when I wanted to be with Sebastian? When I had just broken up with Chris?

The answer was just on the edge of my brain, like when a word is on the tip of your tongue and you can't quite reach it.

"Macy. Are you okay?"

"Shhhh," I said, waving my finger at him. I looked up at the ceiling and the pieces started to come together slowly.

Choices. I never had a choice with Scott, and since then, I hadn't even understood what it meant to have one. Fooling around with Charlie was making me feel wanted but also dirty and used. The meaningless sex I'd had with all the boys before settling down with Chris—those boys made me feel wanted, but they didn't make me feel *good*. I could have been any girl to them, just like they were any guy to me. Expendable, worthless. Even with Chris, I felt like I was never pure enough for him, but him wanting me always seemed like enough. With Sebastian, though, I didn't feel that way. With Sebastian, I was just me, totally me. And even if it didn't work out, I knew that I'd made my own choice. I'd chosen Sebastian.

I took a deep breath, proud of myself. The power of being wanted was nothing compared to the power of choice. I could ask myself the question—*is this okay?* Yes or no? Either answer is fine. Sometimes yes, sometimes no. You choose. I choose.

I turned to Charlie. He was still sitting there, looking confused.

"Sorry," I said. "No, it's not okay."

"Shit. Did I just totally take advantage of you?"

"I knew what I was doing," I said. "I just changed my mind."

Then we heard the front door of the house open and the sound of footsteps.

"God, Charlie, you're such a freakin' slob," Rebecca shouted from the living room. She must have seen the clothes strewn all over and the line of beer bottles on the table. And then her footsteps were coming down the hall to Charlie's bedroom. I scrambled to find something to cover myself with, but it was too late. Rebecca opened the door and saw me sitting naked on the edge of the bed. And Charlie sitting just as naked next to me.

Her face nearly turned purple. "Are you fucking kidding me?" She stormed out.

"Rebecca, wait!" I yelled, trying to get up and pull the sheet around me, but I kept tripping.

"She on the rag or what?" Charlie said.

"It's not funny," I yelled at him. "She was furious before when we slept together."

"She was?"

"She didn't speak to me for days. Oh, of course *you* never heard anything about it. The girl gets the blame. Whatever."

He looked sheepish. "Sorry. I didn't know."

I dragged the sheet with me as I picked up my clothes in the TV room and quickly got dressed. I went to Rebecca's bedroom and knocked on the door.

"Beck," I said. "Please let me in. I came here to see you, and we got drunk, and I'm sorry. It shouldn't have happened. Please let me in. I need you." My voice was shaky. I tried the door handle but it was locked.

Charlie came out of his room, dressed.

"I just totally made everything even worse. Let me work on her. I'll straighten this out."

I sat down on the couch with my head in my hands, listening to Charlie bang on Rebecca's door, begging her to let him in. I was alone. No Rebecca. No Sebastian. No Chris. No Mom. No Dad.

CHAPTER TWENTY-SEVEN

After Rebecca finally let Charlie into her room, I went out to the porch swing to wait and looked at my phone. Still no message from Sebastian, but two more from Mom, wondering when I'd be home so we could talk. The front door opened and Rebecca came out.

"Hi," she said.

"Hi."

Her eyes were red.

"You are so messed up, you know that?" she said.

"You don't know the half of it."

"So I hear." She sat next to me, and we started pushing the swing back and forth.

"I'm sorry about Charlie," I said. "I was only thinking about me. Actually, I wasn't thinking at all. There was pretty much no thought involved."

"There *were* a lot of beer bottles in the TV room."

"I knew how you felt about Charlie and me. I never should have let it happen again."

"He told me you were upset about something. About a guy. And that he got you drunk."

"Well, I got myself drunk," I said. "Charlie was just being nice."

"Nice like thoughtful? Or nice like sticking his wiener in you?"

"Come on!" I said. "And we didn't have sex."

"Tell me what's going on. You never get drunk like that. In your text yesterday you said you were okay about breaking up with Chris."

"I was. I am. It's about Sebastian. And my mom. And . . ." I had to tell her. She was my best friend. If I didn't tell her, there would always be this missing piece. "And Scott."

"Scott?"

I nodded.

And then I told her everything. All about Scott. How it started. How it ended. And everything in between. She stared at me while I talked, her aqua-blue eyes gigantic and wet as tears trickled down her cheeks. I told her about Dad and how he saw us. I told her how Mom never mentioned it to me, not once. I told her about Sebastian, that I loved him more than I thought it was possible to love another person and how I found him at the diner with Jacqueline, and I thought my heart would combust. When I finished, she looked straight ahead.

"Why didn't you ever tell me any of this?"

"I didn't tell anyone."

"I could have been there for you. You were all alone," she said.

"No I wasn't. I had you."

"But I didn't know."

"That didn't matter. You've been the best friend anyone could ever ask for. Especially to a pain in the ass like me."

"God," she said. "This is really huge."

"It is huge. I know that now."

"How do you get over something like this?" she asked.

"Who knows?"

"Let's go inside," she said.

"I should probably go home and have it out with my mom—and my dad, if he's on this continent. Otherwise, what's going to change?"

"Maybe you should slow down. You have more shit right now than any person can handle."

"I'm sorry I screwed up today," I said.

"Forget about me. It's dumb. I shouldn't care if you and Charlie have a thing. Even if you wanted to date him, I shouldn't care."

"I don't."

"Good." She smiled sheepishly. "I felt left out. He's my closest brother; you're my best friend."

"I get it. It's not happening."

"Anyway," she said. "Before you confront your parents we should just go inside, hang out, have a milkshake or something. Think about it. It can wait till tomorrow. You can stay with me for a night—maybe a few. Just take a break for a while."

She put her arm around me. And suddenly, I was exhausted.

"Okay," I said. It wasn't even me talking. I imagined lying on Rebecca's soft bed, and I already felt like I was asleep.

A fresh pain shot through me as the image of Sebastian taking in Jacqueline's beauty resurfaced.

"I still haven't heard from Sebastian," I said.

She nodded slowly.

"I thought what we had was so real."

I gulped back a sob as she led me back inside the house.

After we got to her room, Rebecca went to call her mom at the radio station to check in. I was spent. I had no words left, no more energy. I couldn't wait to be still. To just lie down. I pulled down all the shades. I needed to be enveloped in darkness. How dare the sun shine on a day so dark for me? I peeked out before I let the shade fall, expecting to see ominous clouds, the threat of a storm, something so that climbing into bed in the middle of the day would seem okay. But it was blue sky, sunny, eighty degrees—taunting me, teasing me, scoffing at me for snubbing it.

I stripped down to my T-shirt and underwear and climbed into Rebecca's unmade bed, pulling the pink flowered poufy comforter up to my chin. I stretched out my legs so far that I nearly gave myself a leg cramp.

There was a light knock on the door and then Rebecca came in.

"You don't have to knock, it's your room," I said.

She came in with a steaming mug.

"I know, but I want you to have your privacy," she said. "Here's some tea."

"Tea?"

"Well, it just seemed appropriate."

She sat on the bed, put the mug on the side table. It actually smelled really good—a dark, woodsy smell.

"I'm kind of lost here," she said.

"You and me both."

"I've never seen you like this. I feel like I should be doing something," she said, her eyes shy.

"This is enough. I think I just need to be here doing nothing, like you said. Like let the world stop for a minute so I can catch up and figure out what to do next. How to fix things."

"Okay," she said. "I'll be in the TV room."

When Rebecca shut the door, I closed my eyes tight. And then I fell asleep hard. I vaguely heard movement in the rest of the house every now and then but I'd turn over and fall right back to sleep.

I felt something move. The room was almost dark now.

"Hi," Rebecca said. She was sitting on the edge of the bed.

"Hi," I said.

"It's eight o'clock. You want something to eat?"

"No thanks." I couldn't keep my eyes open. I'd never been more tired in my entire life.

"You want to go back to sleep?" she asked.

"Yeah. You going out?"

"No, I'm staying with you," she said.

"You don't have to babysit me."

She hesitated. "I just want to go pick up some dinner. We have nothing in the house."

"Okay," I said, just wanting to be asleep again.

"Um . . . Charlie's here if you need anything."

I smiled half-heartedly. "You have nothing to worry about," I said. "I don't need anything. Especially that."

She groaned.

"Sorry. It was an exhausted attempt at humor," I said.

"Are you okay? I feel like I should do something."

I shook my head back and forth on the pillow, my eyes closing as she shut the door gently behind her.

I dreamed that I was in an empty room with wide shiny wood floors, high tree-trunk beams with sunlight shining through. There was no furniture in the room. I couldn't find anywhere to sit. I turned around in a circle and finally saw a single folding chair on the far side of the room. I walked over and sat in it, and I felt as if I hadn't sat in years and years—like I'd been standing, walking, never sitting—for years. But I knew something was still missing. And then, when I turned, Sebastian was on a folding chair next to me, and he held my hand.

Sometime later, I rolled over onto something soft. Fozzie Bear. Rebecca had gone to my house to get Fozzie Bear. I clutched him to my chest and fell back to sleep.

The music was loud. Insanely loud. I felt like my head was pressed up against an amp at a headbangers' ball.

It was my phone, playing a heavy metal tune I didn't recognize. Knives of sunlight sliced Rebecca's room through the cracks in the shade. I grabbed my phone from the nightstand, where the tea from last night sat, now cold. It was Gavin. He must have changed the ring tone I had for him on my phone. Very funny.

"Where are you?" he asked when I picked up. "Are you at work?"

I noticed a pink piece of paper on the bed.

I didn't want to wake you. I'll tell Darren you aren't feeling well. —R

I knew I should care, but right now I couldn't. I felt a slight tug, knowing I was letting Darren down. I'd promised him I wouldn't.

"What's up?" I said to Gavin.

"Mom's worried about you. She said you're not answering her calls and texts."

"I can't deal with Mom right now."

"How was the weekend?" he asked.

"We broke up." It felt strange to say it aloud to him.

Gavin was silent.

"Don't worry, Gav. He'll still be around; we'll still be friends."

He cleared his throat. "You should call Mom so she knows you're okay."

"You tell her, okay? I've gotta go."

I hung up and checked my texts.

DARREN: Are you ok? I'm here if you need me.
SEBASTIAN: We need to talk.

I felt a mix of relief and dread. He'd texted me—yes, a day later. He'd probably spent the night being charming for beautiful Jacqueline. I didn't write back. I didn't want to hear his explanation of how he and Jacqueline were meant to be together. I couldn't bear looking in his eyes and seeing pity because I'd been stupid enough to think he could be in love with me. I didn't want to hear him say "let's be friends."

I crashed back down on the pillow and fell asleep again.

My stomach growled. I was starving. I hadn't eaten since Chris and I left the Cape yesterday morning. All I'd had were the beers with Charlie, the thought of which made me gag. I needed to eat something, but getting out of bed would require too much energy. I let my head fall back onto the pillow.

My phone started playing my ringtone for Mom—*I'm a bitch, I'm a lover / I'm a child, I'm a mother.* I pressed DECLINE and closed my eyes. And then the phone buzzed with a text. My stomach was in my throat. Could it be Sebastian again?

MOM: Please call me.

I didn't answer.

MOM: Are you at Rebecca's still? I know you're not at Marwood, I checked.

Again, I didn't answer.

MOM: I'm coming there.
ME: No.
MOM: Too late.

I considered getting dressed or brushing my teeth. For Mom? That was insane. Besides, I was still so weak from hunger, I couldn't move.

Fifteen minutes later I heard the doorbell ring—then voices.

There was a knock at my—Rebecca's—bedroom door, and Charlie peeked in.

"Hi," he said. "Your mom's here."

I groaned.

"You want me to tell her to go away?"

The Maronis were Italian. Protectors. They stuck together. And now I was in their house, so I was one of them.

"No," I said. "It's okay."

He closed the door gently. More murmurs. Then Mom came in.

I kept my face to the wall. I felt her sit on the bed. She touched my back, and I tensed immediately.

"What do you want, Mom?"

"What's going on?" she asked quietly.

"What do you care?"

"I care about you more than anything. Please. Why won't you talk to me?" She sounded like she was going to cry.

"You really want to start talking about it now, after all these years?" I asked, turning toward her. She was wearing jeans and a T-shirt. No gym clothes, nothing fancy.

"About what? What am I missing?"

"Fine, then." I sat up forcefully, despite how weak I felt. "How could you never do anything about it? Never talk to me? Never punish Scott? You just buried it. Acted like he was still a perfect angel boy. And like *I* was the one who did something wrong. Do you know how that's made me feel?"

"Macy, I have *no* idea what you're talking about!" She sounded genuinely, utterly, completely insane with frustration.

She didn't know what I was talking about? Was she serious? Dad told her. He said he would. But . . . she really sounded like she didn't know.

Holy shit.

Wait. Hold everything.

Did Dad seriously never tell her? Was it even possible that all these years she never knew?

"Mom," I said. "You really don't know?"

"Macy, did he steal money from you? I need to know." Her face looked panicked.

I laughed at Mom's horror of a potentially thieving Scott, and then I ripped off the Band-Aid.

"No, he didn't steal money from me. Scott did sexual things with me. *To* me. For years."

I watched a million emotions cross her face. Disbelief, fear, panic, despair.

"What? What are you saying? How could that have—?" Her eyes teared up.

"I don't know. But it did."

"I don't understand—when? When did this happen?" She sounded slightly hysterical, her voice reaching a higher and higher pitch with each word. My heartbeat sped up, but I tried to stay calm.

"I was seven when it started. And the last time it happened, I was twelve. Remember when I almost drowned that day? That was the last time."

"Seven," she whispered. "Why didn't you tell me?" She sounded so confused; I felt kind of sorry for her.

"Dad said he would tell you."

Her eyes narrowed and flashed anger.

"Dad *knew* about this?" Rage replaced the confusion in her voice.

I nodded.

"I—oh god."

She started sobbing, and I was suddenly more exhausted than ever.

"Mom, I just want to go back to sleep now."

She nodded, grabbing a tissue from Rebecca's nightstand and wiped her nose. She pulled me to her and I let her hug me. I breathed in the familiar smell of her floral shampoo.

I pulled away and lay down.

"You just sleep, sweetheart." She rubbed my back and I fell asleep quickly.

When I woke, I could tell it was much later because the sun had shifted to the other side of the room. I stretched and turned over and nearly jumped ten feet when I saw Mom sitting on Rebecca's desk chair staring at me.

"Have you been sitting here this whole time?" I asked.

Mom came over to the bed and sat on the edge. She looked older suddenly—circles under her eyes, no makeup, her hair dull in the dimly lit room.

"It really happened, didn't it?" she asked quietly.

My heart pounded in my ears. "Are you saying you don't believe me?"

"Of course not. I want to not believe you. More than anything in the world. But I do. Of course I do."

She inched closer to me and put her hand on mine.

I shook my head and pushed her hand away.

"You've always just pretended everything was fine," I said. "As long as everything looks good, then everything *is* good, right?"

"I wasn't pretending, Macy. I didn't know about it."

"I thought you did," I said.

"But I didn't."

But Dad knew. What would it be like the next time I saw him? He'd lied to me. What could I even say to him now?

"Tell me what happened, Macy," Mom said.

I turned to face the wall.

"I need to know," she said.

Her tone was both commanding and understanding. She was right; she needed to know.

I cleared my throat.

"He came into my room when you were out," I said. "I was usually reading, so he'd ask me about my book, tell me I was smart and mature for my age. Then he'd ask if I wanted to hang out. That meant . . . you know, do stuff. He'd take off his pants and he taught me how to . . . um, use my hand until he . . . you know. Sometimes he would touch me too. Once he did oral . . ."

Mom sniffled. I kept my back to her, my nose nearly pressing against the wall. I felt my face burning—telling Mom this stuff—a mix of embarrassment, shame, anger.

"Did he have sex with you?" Her voice was shaky but I could hear the fury and the sadness underneath.

"He tried to once. I'd just gotten my training bra, so I guess I was eleven."

Mom gasped. We'd gotten in the biggest fight at Bloomingdale's over the training bra. I was so mortified that the old lady who worked in the bra department was feeling me up, but Mom insisted that she needed to measure me for the proper fit.

"Scott didn't say anything about the bra," I continued. "But he did say I had a couple of hairs down there, so we'd have to stop hanging out soon. He tried to have sex with me then anyway. When he started to do it, it hurt so much that I screamed, and he stopped."

Mom was quiet.

I turned back toward her. She was so still, just staring at the wall. Silent tears on her cheeks. She looked at me like she'd just woken from a dream—or a nightmare.

"I can see how much this changed you," she said. "I didn't see what you were going through. You must have been so confused."

"I didn't think I was at the time, but . . . now I know I was."

"I wish I'd been looking more carefully. I wish I could have stopped it." She took my hand and this time I let her. "I should have protected you. It was my only job really, and I failed."

I felt like I should hug her, but my body wouldn't move.

"You did your best, Mom."

She looked at me curiously, like she wasn't expecting me to say something that nice. Truthfully, I'd surprised myself.

There was a knock at the door, and Charlie peeked in.

"I'm sorry to bother you," he said. "Rebecca called and said you probably haven't eaten anything, so here." He moved quickly into the room and put a plate down on the side table. Then he backed out. "Sorry, sorry."

"Thanks," I called after him, grabbing the peanut butter and jelly sandwich and shoving it into my mouth. Nothing had ever tasted this good.

Mom pushed my dreads away from my face as I chewed. I let her.

"You have good friends," she said.

I nodded.

"I want you to come home. Let me take care of you now." She put her hand on my face and rubbed her thumb back and forth on my cheek. It made me feel like a little girl, but I liked it.

"Okay," I said. "I'll come home soon."

She leaned over and kissed my forehead.

CHAPTER TWENTY-EIGHT

I showered and borrowed clean shorts and a tank from Rebecca's dresser. Charlie's music blasted from behind his closed bedroom door so I was relieved to skip the awkward good-bye.

Mom must have heard my car pull into the garage because she was right there when I walked into the house. She pulled me into a hug and rubbed circles on my back.

She let go and looked into my eyes.

"Scott's coming here at five," she said.

I gasped. "You already talked to him?"

Mom shook her head. "I told him that I have the check he asked for—a loan. He's coming to pick it up. I'm not going to give it to him, of course, but I need to look him in the eye when I talk to him about this. If he tells the truth, maybe there's some hope for him. I just need to see who he really is. Because if he lies, then—" She cleared her throat, and continued. "It's your choice, but I think you should be here with me. I'm not asking you to forgive him, but I think you should tell him how you feel."

I didn't want to. But I knew from the way my heart was pounding that I probably had to.

"Why aren't you going to his apartment?"

"This is where it all happened. I have to fix my mistake, and it needs to be at our house."

I nodded. Mom was like a real person. A real mom.

At five ten, Mom paced the family room, her ponytail swinging back and forth. I sat on the couch. My phone buzzed.

GAVIN: Mom sent me away. U better tell me what's going on.

"You sent Gavin away?" I asked Mom.

"I told him that you and I needed privacy for a bit. He went to Eliza's."

I tried to picture telling Gavin what was going on. And then it hit me: Gavin was the same age Scott had been when it all started. I cringed when I thought about my sweet, skinny, awkward brother, who could never in a million years do what Scott had done.

Mom picked up the phone and dialed.

"Rob, call as soon as you land."

She hung up. "I don't even know where he was. Arizona, I think."

I felt sorry for her, that she had to do this without Dad.

Mom looked at her watch.

"Scott may not show," I said.

"I know."

I didn't want him to come. The idea of seeing him now, of having to confront him was making my stomach turn. I wanted him not to show up so Mom would just stop talking to him, and then it would be over. No more Scott. But

I knew that wasn't really possible. Even if he didn't show, Mom would keep trying.

My phone buzzed.

SEBASTIAN: I really need to talk to you. Please.

"Everything okay?" Mom asked, like that was even a possibility.

I shook my head. My heart hurt so much.

She sat on the arm of the couch and rubbed my back, which made it even harder not to cry.

The side door creaked open, and Scott walked in. I felt my face flush hot and red. I wanted to run to my room. He was his perfect pretty-boy self. I had a sudden pang that this had all been a big mistake. I never should have told anyone. It wasn't that big a deal. He was just a guy who did something he shouldn't have done a long time ago. Anger at Sebastian welled up. He'd put me in this situation, broken down my walls, and then left me to deal with the mess alone.

Scott smiled and looked as if he was about to give Mom a hug, but he stopped mid-stride and raised his eyebrows.

Then I saw Mom's face. When she looked at Scott, I saw her anger and disgust, and I knew that I wasn't alone. As much as my mother didn't protect me then, she would make up for it now.

"What's going on? What'd I do?" he asked, but he was smiling, like it was a big joke.

"I know what you did to Macy," Mom said.

Scott looked genuinely confused.

"What are you talking about?"

"You abused her, Scott. You sexually abused my daughter when she was just a little girl." Mom choked up on the last words. She cleared her throat.

"What the fuck?" Scott yelled and his face twisted up in anger. "Are you out of your mind? What the fuck, Macy? What is this ambush—I just came here to . . . what *the fuck*! This is insane. I'm leaving."

He started toward the door.

"Come back here and sit down," Mom said. "Now."

He turned around and glared at me.

"What is this, Macy? Are you jealous? You want attention? Is that what this is about?"

Mom opened her mouth, but I was the one who spoke.

"No!" I wanted to wring his neck.

Mom put her hand on my shoulder.

"Deb, she's always been jealous," he said, more calmly. It seemed like he remembered he could throw out some charming, logical words and get away with it, like he did with everything. "Jealous and judgmental and self-righteous. But she's taking this way too far, making up some hateful story to turn you against me."

I had words but they weren't making it to my mouth. I took a breath, tried to focus on what was important.

"I couldn't pretend anymore that we were a happy family," I finally said, my voice stronger than I'd expected. "I actually thought that what you did to me was normal. That I chose to do it too. But it wasn't normal, and I never had a choice. And I needed help."

It was the first time I'd given voice to this. *I needed help. I need help.*

Scott sat heavily in the leather armchair across from me and ran his fingers through his hair.

"Yes, I can see that," he said. "You do need help. You're making up stories for some reason when I've been nothing but nice to you. . . . I'm worried about you." He made a sad face like his heart was breaking for me. But it was all just a show for Mom.

"You're lying!" I yelled. I hated him right then. Every good feeling I'd had toward him over the years disappeared as he made me look like I was the one lying. Like I was crazy.

Mom sat on the couch next to me.

"Scott," she said calmly. "Just tell me what happened. Tell me the truth."

"Nothing happened, Deb," he said, his voice soft. "The only thing I can think where this could be coming from was that one day at the pool. I pulled down my bathing suit for a second. I flashed her. It was a joke. She freaked out. But that was it."

"You're lying, Scott," Mom said.

"I'd never do something like this. I'd never hurt her. I want to help her."

I felt my insides clench. He was convincing.

"You hurt her. You need to acknowledge it now."

He shook his head. "I didn't do it."

"Maybe you've blocked it out of your memory," Mom said. "Like False Memory Syndrome, when you really believe you're telling the truth. But you're not."

Scott raised his eyebrow at her.

"No, *she's* the one with False Memory Syndrome. Because this shit never happened."

"It happened, Scott," Mom said. "I need you to just say it."

No one spoke. No one moved. I didn't really care what his answer would be. Mom and I both knew the truth, and so did he.

"Scott?" Mom's voice shook.

"Fuck you," he hissed and stood. "Fuck all of you."

He stormed out, slamming the door. A second later, he was back in.

"So now what, Deb," he yelled. "You're just abandoning me like my mother? Huh?"

Mom was clearly prepared for this attack.

"It's no one's fault Judy left—she couldn't raise you and we could. And I've never invalidated your feelings of abandonment. But don't even think about using it as an excuse for what you did to Macy."

He shook his head.

"So, you still have nothing to say to me?" I asked him. I needed to be sure. To be sure he was as bad as I thought. Because a tiny piece of me got pulled along on the abandonment thing. I'd always felt sorry that Aunt Judy left him.

"I've got something. You're a fucking liar," he said.

"Scott," Mom said. "Being an adult means owning up to your mistakes, asking forgiveness when you've hurt someone. Maybe I haven't let you grow up. We've supported you long after we should have. But it stops here, right now. You have to accept the responsibilities of being an adult. When you're ready to tell the truth, let me know."

He looked at her once more with disbelief, and then he left.

I heard the car start up and the whirr, whirr of him reversing out of the driveway.

Mom got up and started making coffee.

"Mom," I said.

She held up one finger, a "hold on a minute." Then she whispered, "I just need a—I'll be right back."

She ran out of the kitchen. The sobbing started halfway up the stairs. Body-shaking, *my-son-has-just-died* sobs that only a mother can really feel. Finally I heard the door to her room close and the sobbing was muffled.

I sat for a few minutes staring straight ahead and then I pulled out my phone to answer Rebecca's insistent worried texts.

ME: Scott was here. Will fill u in latr.
REBECCA: Shit. Call when u can.

I took a travel mug of coffee to my car. I figured I should at least pick Gavin up since he'd been turned out like a dog. Just as I pulled into Eliza's driveway, my phone rang. Dad. I considered not answering it, but in the end, I guess I wanted to hear what he had to say.

"Hi, Dad," I said, letting all the bitterness come through in those two words.

I could hear muffled noise and airline announcements in the background.

"I'm so sorry, sweetheart. So, so sorry. You never—I mean, you didn't—I don't even know what to say. This had been going on since you were *seven*?" His voice cracked. "I had no idea. I—"

"Why didn't you ever tell Mom?" I asked.

"I didn't think she would be able to handle it."

"Bullshit," I said, tears stinging my eyes.

Dad sighed and it made a whooshing sound into the phone.

"That day after the pool," he said. "I was ready to skewer Scott. I wanted to kick him out of the house. But he said it was a one-time incident, that he was messing around and took it too far. And he seemed so remorseful."

"And you believed him?"

"I guess I did. He swore it would never happen again. I was protecting Mom by not telling her. I thought I could take care of the situation myself. As long as I made sure it didn't happen again, everything would be okay. I told Scott I'd tell Mom or even the police if he ever came near you again. I thought you'd tell me if you needed to talk; you and I were so close. But you've always been so strong, and then as time went on, I really thought you'd moved past it, so every time I considered bringing it up, I didn't want to reopen a wound for you."

"It wasn't just a 'one-time incident,'" I said, barely able to stomach the phrase.

"I know that now." I could hear all the regret, the defeat—everything he was feeling in his words. But I didn't *feel* them.

"Do you know that I've hated Mom ever since then?" I asked. "I assumed she was ashamed of me, of what I did."

"She has never been ashamed of you. I thought you were just a teenage girl being tough on her mom."

He didn't get me at all.

"I know sorry isn't good enough," he said. "I failed you. I should have done more. I was a coward. I'm so sorry, Macy."

He may have meant it, but his apology felt empty to me. Like a quick game of catch in the backyard to make up for all he'd missed.

"Okay, Dad," I said, mostly just because I wanted to get off the phone.

"I'll be home tonight," he said. "I love you, sweetie."

"Okay," I said again and hung up.

I turned the ignition off and got out of the car. As I started on the path to Eliza's front door, I saw a shadow of something in the backyard. I squinted and realized it was two figures, connected at the head. Gavin and Eliza sat on a bench, kissing with just their lips touching, nothing else. I saw the pure joy of this kiss and its innocent beauty, and I was relieved that it still existed in my world. I got back in the car and headed home.

I pulled into the garage, but I wasn't ready to go inside. I went around the house to my oak tree, which was always there for me—wide, solid, consistent. I put my hand on the rough bark and looked up at its bright green summer leaves. In a few months, the leaves would change—red, orange, yellow. And then they'd let go, fluttering, free.

My colors had changed. And now I wanted to let go.

Suddenly, I knew what to do. I kicked off my flip-flops and ran. When I got to the edge of the pool, I watched the evening sunlight make sparkles on the water's neon blue surface. I bent my knees, stretched out my arms, and dove. The force pushed me toward the bottom. I blew tiny bubbles out of my nose and felt the water swish around me. I touched the scratchy bottom and then kicked myself back up to the surface. I took a breath and swam the length of the pool. It had been five years, but I remembered how. With the help of muscle memory, I swam laps—freestyle, breast-stroke, backstroke—letting the cool water gurgle in my ears and flow through my fingers.

I stood in water up to my chest and twirled, leaning my head back, sweeping my hair along the water's surface. With outstretched arms, I swirled and spun.

And suddenly I was laughing and crying and smiling. In a way, I *had* drowned that day five years ago. Since then, I'd gone through the motions and hadn't felt much. But now, I felt everything I'd missed. I felt the years of innocence I'd lost, the pain of my broken family. I ached for Chris, my oldest friend in the world, and Dad, who wasn't really who I thought he was. I burst with love for Rebecca and for Mom, who'd taken care of me when I most needed them, and for Gavin, who'd just had his first kiss.

I felt everything. Now I was ready to start over, ready for the new leaves to grow.

"You're swimming."

His voice startled me. I rubbed the chlorine from my eyes. The sun was lower, but I still had to shade my eyes with my hand to see Sebastian standing at the edge of the pool.

"Yeah. I—" But I didn't know what to say.

"In your clothes?" He smiled.

I looked down. I was still wearing Rebecca's shorts and tank. I shrugged.

"What are you doing here?" I asked.

"I've been trying to reach you."

He crouched down so I didn't have to squint and crane my neck to see him. He looked so good, and his dark eyes were bright. But then I remembered the look on his face when he saw Jacqueline.

"I wasn't ready to talk," I said.

"I want to explain about Jacqueline," he said quietly. "Can I stay for a minute?"

I shrugged again, but it turned into a shiver. I was getting chilly standing still in the cool water with the sun going down. I swished my arms back and forth to warm up.

Sebastian sat at the edge of the pool and took off his shoes and socks. He put his feet in the water.

"I'm working through the steps," he said. "I asked her to meet me so I could apologize, make amends."

"Well, how did it go?" I asked, but my tone said I didn't care. His reason for meeting her didn't explain the look on his face when he saw her.

"I said what I needed to say. And then I had to be alone to process everything."

I nodded. I got that. As much as I thought I'd needed Sebastian to get through everything with Scott, with Mom, I'd needed to be alone to process everything too. At my oak tree. In the pool.

"But I should have told you that I needed time," he said. "I should've called you right away."

I stayed silent, waiting for the "friends" talk. I just wanted it to be over with.

"Can I come in?" he asked.

"If you want."

He pushed up on his arms and lowered himself into the water, then quickly dunked his whole body under before popping back up, the water streaming down his face. His wet shirt clung to his chest as he moved toward me.

"So, you're swimming? That's a big deal, right?" he asked, raising his eyebrows.

"Some major shit just went down."

He stood still, waiting for me to tell him. I realized that even if I'd lost him to his ex-girlfriend, even if we were going to be just friends, he was still the first person I'd ever told about Scott, and I wanted him to know everything that had happened since.

"My dad never told my mom what happened that day," I said. Sebastian's mouth opened but he didn't say anything. "So today, it all blew up. I told my mom, she freaked, but then she kind of turned into a real mom. Scott was here and he denied everything, and now he's gone. I don't know if he'll ever be back. And my dad called and said he's sorry, but I don't really care."

"Shit," he said. "Are you okay? How do you feel?"

I looked at my oak tree and then into Sebastian's eyes. "I feel," I said. "I feel everything."

He nodded.

"That's a good thing," he said. He understood.

He came closer, his body right in front of me so I had to tilt my head to look at him. He wrapped his arms around me. We stood leaning against each other in our soaking wet clothes, and his flat torso pressed against my chest. I laid my head against his neck and felt his pulse beating its fast rhythm.

A small, stubborn part of me didn't want to give up the fight so easily, but the rest of me just wanted to be close to him, even if I couldn't have him for good. I put my arms around him and held on tight.

"So you still love her," I said into his neck.

"No. I don't."

"It looked like maybe you did."

"I don't." He pulled away and looked at me. "You were right about how I'd never gotten closure. She left town and it never really ended for me, not really. Not until you. So when I saw her yesterday, I wasn't just making amends, I also needed to make a clean break, so I could be free."

I put my head back on his chest and smiled into his shirt.

"Did you really break up with Chris?" he asked.

"Yeah."

"I'm glad." I could hear the smile in his voice.

"You are?"

"Mmmhmmm," he said, possibly the sexiest two syllables I'd ever heard. "I want this. I want you."

"Me too." The words barely made it out past the swelling of my heart.

"When I couldn't reach you," he said. "When you wouldn't answer me, I was so tempted to just get high to deal with it. I thought about calling my old connection to score."

I pulled back and looked at him.

"I didn't. I won't," he said. "I have to do it the hard way now. Like coming here, even though you didn't want to see me. I won't run off and get high when things get tough anymore. I'll confront them, work through them. But I'm still scared."

"We can wait," I said. "I'll wait until you're ready."

"I don't want to wait," he said.

"Me neither."

He wove his fingers through my dreadlocks and looked at me, his brown eyes darker than ever. He bent his head closer, his breath warming my lips. We stayed like that—staring, breathing—making the moment last. He came closer, slowly, and his soft lips pressed against mine. Our first real kiss. Heat, electricity, love. Real love. I was me, really and truly me. And he was Sebastian. And, holy shit, were we in love. I grabbed the back of his head, breathing harder as our kiss deepened.

After what felt like forever, we stopped kissing and stared at each other.

Before that night at Rebecca's, I hadn't really realized that I'd been broken. But since then, I'd figured it out and then fit the jagged pieces back together. And, at the same time, Sebastian had done his own discovery and repair.

Now I put my arms around him and tried to combine with him.

"Don't let go," I said.

"I won't."

I imagined that glue was seeping into the tiny cracks between our reassembled pieces and we would just keep holding each other tight while the glue dried.

This moment—standing in the pool with my body pressed against Sebastian while the sun set—this moment was my choice. And all the moments that would come after—those would be my choice too.

RESOURCES FOR HELP

Sexual Abuse

RAINN (Rape, Abuse & Incest National Network)
www.RAINN.org

National Sexual Assault Hotline
800-656-HOPE (4673)

Pandora's Project
www.pandys.org

Depression/Mental Illness

National Alliance on Mental Illness (NAMI)
www.NAMI.org
800-950-NAMI (6264)

Substance Abuse

Narcotics Anonymous
www.NA.org

Alcoholics Anonymous
www.AA.org

SAMHSA (Substance Abuse and Mental Health Services
Administration)
www.SAMHSA.gov
800-662-HELP (4357)

Acknowledgments

I've always wanted to be an author, but I didn't realize how many people I'd need for the dream to become a reality. Thank you to all of these dream-makers:

Linda Epstein, my agent and friend—your honest advice, contagious laugh, and beautiful soul are more than anyone could ask for in a business partner.

Nicole Frail, my thoughtful, smart, hardworking editor who saw something special in Macy and wanted to share her story with readers.

Julie Matysik, Adrienne Szpyrka, Sarah Brody, Sara Winkelman, and the Sky Pony/Skyhorse team for turning my manuscript into a book that people can read and put on their shelves.

Jennifer Shulman, my go-to reader, receiver of emails both joyful and heartbreaking, and my trusted conference-attending partner. We've been through so much together already and there is so much more to go . . . onward.

Kendall Kulper, my brilliant and honest critique partner—your writing and even-keeled attitude inspire me to write better.

My insightful and encouraging beta readers: I. W. Gregorio, Laura Hughes, Kristin Brandt.

The GWKA writers group—especially Laura Hughes, Kristin Brandt, Karen Dowicz Haas, and Orla Collins—without our weekly brainstorming chats, I would have no plot and no pages.

My newer author friends including my Sky Pony pub-siblings, Fearless Fifteeners, Fall Fifteeners, Team Rogue YA, and YA Outside the Lines.

ML, DK, Dr. R, DM, CC, ME, AA for your inspiration and for answering my (often difficult) questions about sexual abuse, addiction, depression, and psychiatric hospitals. Regarding these issues, *The Fix* is one story, but it's not everyone's story. I hope I got it right. Or at least not terribly wrong.

Society of Children's Book Writers and Illustrators (SCBWI) for helping me find my tribe.

Every blogger and reader of young adult fiction—thank you for loving YA and making it a thing.

My go-to friends—your genuine interest and pride give me strength. In order of appearance: Claudia Kandel—friend who is family from four to forty-four and forever. Mara Bralove—compassionate, unstoppable, and every positive superlative that ever existed. Lucy Roberts—you know how much. Erin Sheehy and the rest of my Sidwell gang—you are as special to me now as you were in high school (and before). Nancy Lewand and Tifany Pedersen—my sister-friends with hearts of gold. Laura Hollenberg—your open and generous spirit. Amy Oringel—tg 4 u. every. single. day. And so many friends, old and new, who have enriched my life. (Yes, I mean you.)

My babysitting teammates over the years who have helped keep my boys happy and well.

My extended family—the Sinels, Cohens, Greens, Lewands, Pedersens, Winnicks, Hersches, Duchanos, Offenbergers, Pyners—and especially my parents-in-law, Norene and Laurence Green, and Suzanne and David Cohen. There are no words for the extent of my love and gratitude.

Ellen and Norman Sinel, my mom and dad, to whom this book is dedicated. Your influence and love are at the root of everything I do. Thank you.

Andy Cohen, my everyday companion for 150,000 hours and counting. You are everything that is good—my husband, partner, supporter, and the most magnificent father to our boys.

Finally, Nathan, Zachary, and Justin—my miraculous, unique snowflakes. Each of you takes my breath away with your kindness, warmth, and intelligence. I love you.

SOUL

STRUCK

NATASHA SINEL

ONE

Thunder is good, thunder is impressive;
but it is lightning that does the work.
—Mark Twain (writer)

My trusted local storm channels, sites, and blogs all lied. Even the big ones like weather.com, and Weather Underground. They all said overcast with a slight chance of showers, which is typical for early April on the Cape. Nothing about a storm.

But they were wrong. The sky suddenly turns dark gray, almost purple, and I can smell the moisture in the air, not just from the bay but also from the soaked heaviness of the thunderstorm on its way.

Even though I should know better now—that it won't change anything, that it's probably hopeless, that none of it makes sense anymore—my body feels the familiar rush anyway.

I try to ignore it by focusing on the sealed cardboard box I lugged out to the deck. I wipe a spider web off the label that reads FOR NAOMI FERGUSON'S EYES ONLY. Although I am not Naomi Ferguson, everyone tells me I have my mother's eyes, so I figure it's within my rights to open the box. On the other hand, according to mythical wisdom, nothing good ever comes from opening a box not meant for you. That's why I'm hesitating.

I sit on the edge of the lone lounge chair, its faded fabric worn and ripped down the center, and look out at the bay. In this light, the water is a soft gray with touches of white where the breeze makes a spray. A few cormorants swoop down to catch their late afternoon snack. A salty-sweet mist settles gently over my skin. Mom and I have been living in Wellfleet for almost three years already, but I'm still in awe every time I look outside—the wide yawn of the bay, smooth tan sand, clumps of tall green grasses swaying. The breeze blows the low-tide marshy stink over from the other side of the road, but even the smell feels new and promising. Like nature— mud and grass and life.

I assess the small side deck for anything that needs to be repaired. I'll have to pull the thorny vines that grow through the cracks of the planks and replace a few rusty nails that poke up but nothing major. The garage itself, though, is a dusty, smelly wreck; the concrete floor is an obstacle course of rusted garden equipment and mildewed boxes that have never been cleared out after my grandfather, whom I never met, died and left the beach house to Mom and me. It's going to take even longer than I thought to clean it out and make it into my bedroom. And the sliding door to the deck is off its track and warped so badly, I'll probably have to replace it entirely, and that will cost big bucks.

The separate entrance is one of the reasons I want to move into the garage. I can come home without having to talk to anyone. Day or night, I'm never sure who will be in the house at any given moment: no one, just Mom, or any number of the members from her lightning-strike survivors support group. Before we lived here, I used to love when it was time for meetings, when everyone would be at our place. We moved around so much, but the survivors came no matter where we were. When they were all with us, I'd imagine this was what it was like for normal kids who had families. I'd imagine the meetings were like other people's Thanksgivings—big gatherings with aunts and uncles, cousins and grandparents.

But now, the days when people are around seem to far outnumber the days it's just Mom and me. Since we live on the beach now, the survivors are willing to travel farther to get to us and stay longer.

"Oh, I decided to make it a vacation," they say. "I'll just find a hotel—oh, no, I don't want to impose. Really, I can't accept. Oh, well that's so sweet. Maybe just for a night or two." But it's never just a night or two.

Right now, though, the house is unusually quiet. Mom's at work and the others are wherever they are when they're not at our house.

I try gently lifting one of the flaps on the top of the box. If it comes up without the need for a knife or a pair of scissors to slice through the packing tape, then I will consider that to be a sign to look inside.

A sudden flash out of the corner of my eye makes me freeze.

I want so badly to resist, but the compulsion to go after it is still too powerful.

I grab the box, put it back in the corner of the garage where I found it, then go down the hall to my room. I knock over the pile of renovation books for dummies and idiots. FLASH. One-one thousand, two-one thousand, three-one thous—CRASH. Less than a mile. I'm breathing fast, panicking that I'll miss it. I pull a pair of steel-toed boots on over my bare feet and yellow and pink–flowered pajama bottoms and stomp around until I finally find the golf umbrella I'd shoved in the back of my closet. I haven't done this since before Reed came to town.

As I limp down the front steps, nearly tripping over the pointy toes of my boots, my mind is spinning, unable to land on a decision. Should I go to the tall pine on the MacPhersons' hill? Or should I go down to the bay? I remember that a few of the beach steps are missing after a couple of brutal high tides, and the last thing I need is to fall down another set of stairs. I run as fast as my sore legs will take me down the crushed-shell driveway, thankful that Mom's out. She'd want to lock me in my room if she knew I was leaving the house in a thunderstorm.

The rain hasn't started yet, but the sky is even darker than it was a few minutes earlier. Ominous and overbearing. Exhilarating. I run on the dirt road in my clunky boots to the Macphersons' side yard and then up the hill to the small grassy area with a lone tall pine tree. I've been in this exact spot so many times these past three years, sometimes I wonder if the tree recognizes me. Just as I get to it, I see another flash of light.

One-one thousand, two-one thousand—CRASH. I haven't been this close in so long. Before Reed came, the storms were infrequent and short-lived, and nothing ever seemed to come close enough for me to have a real chance. When I was with Reed, I didn't pay much attention to the weather. I thought I'd never need to again.

The rain starts. A few big fat drops first, and then all at once. Another flash. One-one thousand, two—CRASH. Yes! I open the umbrella and stand under the tree. Waiting. Now the rain comes down in sheets. The gutters at the house a few yards away spill over like a faucet. I stand still and close my eyes, trying to calm myself, to become the perfect conduit, to will it to me.

The healed wounds on the backs of my thighs itch and tingle as I wait, reminding me that I've been so stupid, so naive. I picture Reed's contrite expression just before I fell. I imagine the conversation he must have had with Mom while I was in the hospital, right before he left town more than a month ago.

"You should go," Mom would have said. *"You and Rachel aren't meant for each other."*

"Tell me who is *meant for me,"* Reed might have said.

And then maybe Mom did. Even though she swears she won't tell people who their soul mates are anymore, maybe she did just this once. Or maybe she told him who mine is—maybe someone, maybe no one, but not him. Definitely not him.

Mom can't help knowing what she knows about soul mates. But she says the information she carries is a double-edged sword. It has the power to ruin lives, and she never wants to be in a position to ruin my life. So, she's trained herself not to see who my soul mate is. I've never understood how she can do that. If the information appears to her, how can she control whether she sees it? I used to wonder if closing her eyes to it made her blind to other things about me, too.

A flash lights up the entire sky. A millisecond later, the crash of thunder, deafening, earth-shaking. I watch the afterglow of the lightning slice through the sky to the bay, spreading, stretching its fingers out to as many places as possible. As the thunder moves away, its rumblings a little quieter, farther apart, I drop the umbrella, collapse on the ground, and put my head between my knees. I chose the wrong spot.

I have no idea how long I've been sitting there when a car pulls up. It could've been a minute or an hour.

"Hey!" I barely hear the shout over the pounding rain.

ABOUT THE AUTHOR

© Alison Sheehy

Natasha Sinel is the author of the young adult novel, *The Fix*, which received the gold medal for YA Fiction in the 2016 Independent Publisher Book Awards (IPPYs). Her short story, "Moving the Body," appears in the adoption-themed anthology *Welcome Home*. She graduated from Yale University and University of Michigan's Ross School of Business and was a director of business development at Showtime Networks. Born and raised in Washington, DC, she now lives in Westchester, New York, with her husband and three sons.